TREASURE

Me

Aurora.
Always treasure life's many
moments!
Michelle
Louise

PS love all you write.'

MICHELLE LOUISE

Other Books by
Michelle Louise

<u>Pieces Series</u>
Loving You to Pieces (Novella)
Picking up the Pieces
Falling to Pieces

Disclaimer:
Due to strong language and adult situations, this book is
not suitable for young readers.

For the loves we've lost and the ones we treasure.

Daphne

1

"Decomber fifth?"

"Too cold," I grumble from underneath my pillow.

This is the third date he has rambled off in the last five minutes. Just when I thought I had him convinced I was still sleeping, he found another Saturday on the calendar. He can be so relentless.

"November twenty-first?"

Is he even looking at the calendar and the surrounding dates?

"Too close to Thanksgiving." Tossing the pillow to my feet, I sigh in frustration and slam my arms down to my sides. "Babe, do we really have to do this now? I literally haven't even opened my eyes yet."

I pull the sheet up to cover my face, hoping he takes the hint.

There are only two out of seven days in the week that I do not have to wake up at five in the morning to beat traffic on my way to work. Every other school in the district has a nine o'clock start time, but since we are a magnet school, we begin closer to eight in the morning. And that is the time the first bell rings, not what time I have to be there. Teachers are required to arrive no later than seven o'clock. Therefore, counting backwards with the hour commute and the hour to get ready, we reach my five o'clock alarm, five days a week. But not on Saturday. I have no alarm and fully expect to sleep until at least eight, but hoping for nine.

"Trust me. I would love to be able to lay right here with you for the rest of the morning. But, unfortunately, between my mother blowing up my text inbox and the influx of emails I have already received today, I don't get that luxury."

The sheet is ripped from my grip and my eyes pop open for the first time and immediately reveal his pleading grin. Blinking my eyes in an attempt to focus, my gaze bounces from his bright white smile to his blue-gray eyes and it didn't take long for them to wander further and observe his shirtless chest and bulging pecs.

The bicep that is helping hold up his upper half appears slightly swollen and alerts my attention to his abs, that are protruding from his midsection. His post workout physique is another level of sexy. There is a subtle glisten of sweat that coats his skin, giving extra definition to his finely sculpted body. It happens to be very similar to his post-sex body, a personal favorite of mine.

"Really? You already worked out? I don't even want to know how long you have been awake. And, why you feel the need to drag me down with you." I roll the rest of the way over toward him and curl up into his chest.

"You're being dramatic. And I'm being serious; we just need to pick a date. My mother is driving me insane. It's been almost and year and we haven't settled on – "

"I know, I know. Okay, fine. Today," I huff out.

"Today? You can't possibly think we can get married today?" His panicked reaction causes me to roll onto my back, releasing a fit of giggles.

"Relax, buddy. I meant today; I will make a decision today." Inhaling a deep breath, I release another heavy sigh. No reason to go back to sleep now.

"Okay, good. Just checking. There is no way I could squeeze a wedding into my schedule today. Even if it is to the most beautiful woman in the world." He leans down and kisses my forehead. "I'm taking a shower and going to the office for a bit. I have hours of research to do in preparation of my meeting on Monday, and I'd like to finish early so we can still go to the lake tomorrow and relax."

Nathan rolled out of the bed and my eyes followed his six-foot figure all the way into the bathroom. It's a view I have had the pleasure of admiring for the last three and a half years. He doesn't believe that you need to belong to a gym to stay in shape and be healthy. Rather, he prefers an at home method that he has been using for most of his adult life, a basic workout in the morning and the occasional jog around the park when the mood strikes.

I myself am more of a regular cardio junkie and also do not feel the need to belong to a gym to stay healthy. All I need is a path and pair of sneakers. My headphones help too, but if forgotten it's usually not a deal breaker. Listening to the city swirl around me is a song all it's own.

The sound of his vibrating phone on the nightstand jolts me back to my awake status. I hadn't realized I had been dozing back to sleep.

Leaning across the bed, I turn off the alarm and see the missed texts from his mother. She really has been badgering him this morning. I guess I should just do what I said and pick a date.

It has been almost a year and the excitement of our engagement has now started to fade, rather than grow. We originally decided to soak it in and take our time before settling on a date, but naturally time came and flew past us and here we are.

Nathan's proposal came as quite a shock to me at first. We have a great relationship, but it almost feels as though he asked because he felt it was 'that time'; the three-year mark that society seems to have set as a standard.

With both of us in our late twenties, we have managed to attend nearly ten weddings during the course of our relationship. As you watch your close friends vow their love to one another, the pressure begins. Not that we don't love each other and want to spend our lives together, but I want us to do this on our time, when my heart is ready.

TEN MONTHS EARLIER...

"Oh sweetie, glad you made it safely. Now tell me, what is this spontaneous trip really all about? You know I don't like

surprises," Grams called out to me as she stood from the porch swing.

I closed the trunk of my Nissan Altima and the white dust jumped from the black paint as it shut. She really should consider paving this driveway one day.

Nearing my grandma, I sat my bags down and threw my arms around her neck. It had been the longest span of time that I had gone without seeing her, but telling her this news over the phone was not an option.

"Grams, you look as beautiful as ever and I've missed you so very much." I held on a few seconds longer before pulling back.

As she grazed my arms down to my hands, she paused when she reached my left ring finger. Snapping her head down, her smile grew wide as she took her time admiring the two-karat, emerald cut diamond, perched on my shaking hand.

"My dear heavens, is this the surprise? My baby girl is getting married?" She pulled my arms back around her and embraced me in another long hug.

I giggled and simply nodded my confirmation, pulling back to meet her stare. Her wise emerald eyes read the story that mine were telling and she knew instantly that there would be more to discuss. She always did.

"Go on upstairs and put your things away. I'll start the teapot and you can meet me on the back porch when you're ready." She kissed my cheek and turned to head inside.

Releasing a deep breath I hadn't realized I had been holding, I felt my body relax. It has been an intense few days since Nathan proposed and this is exactly where I needed to be, here with Grams and Papa.

The aroma of the tea as I descended down the staircase would forever remind me of home. Grams always enjoyed making tea for us as children. My brother Derrick loved the tea, but hated the parties, complaining they were too girly. After a while, Grams came up with an adventure she could use as bribery to get him to play along so I wouldn't have to sit alone. She would make us treasure maps to follow that would always lead back to a private tea party with snacks and fake gold coins spread across the table. I would let Derrick hold the map and lead the way, something to make him feel manlier. Those tea parties will always be some of my favorite memories.

After a year or so, we began to grow out of the parties. Grams had grown so fond of our traditional daily tea, that she convinced Papa to let her open a local tea room downtown. A place where she could share her love for tea and the culture that it embodied. Grams put all her love and attention into building her dream and within a short amount of time, opened the doors to her second home, The Treasured Tea Cup.

And though, as much as I love to sit at the Tea Room and enjoy an afternoon high tea with Grams, nothing beats a warm cup shared with her on the back porch where it all began.

She already had most of the table set, so I grabbed our cups and sat down to wait for her to bring out the teapot. Traditionally, I used the same cup every time at home, a white Harebell Teacup with blue flowers and gold trim. The beautiful Coalport set was made in England and was given to me on my ninth birthday by Grams and Papa.

She, on the other hand, had too many favorites to count and would be satisfied with just about any in her collection. I reached for the matching Harebell with pink flowers and set it on the table.

"It's tea time!" she sang as she gracefully carried the teapot to the table and sat it on the warmer. "Nice choice, one of my favorites." She picked up the cup I chose for her and admired its charm.

"Mhmm. That smells like summer. Raspberry?" I ask, trying to pinpoint the aroma spilling from the spout.

"Yes, a new mix I came up with that should resemble a raspberry lemon zing. Perfect for a spring afternoon." She leaned the spout over my cup and filled it up.

After stirring in my cream with one of her homemade honey spoons, I brought the cup to my lips and enjoyed the first warm sip.

"Grams, this is amazing."

"Thanks dear, I'll send you home with some." She winked at me and slowly sipped from her cup.

We first talked about the proposal and how Nathan romantically asked me in front of our closest friends at our favorite restaurant. Grams listened intently to my words, and wore a smile that could light up the darkest of nights.

"You know, when Papa asked me to marry him we originally planned to wait for a year to have the wedding of our dreams. However, after only a few weeks, neither one of us wanted to wait any longer, so we eloped." Her eyes were misty as she peered behind me through the window, observing Papa as he fiddled with a broken clock in the living room.

"But, you have such beautiful wedding photos, I thought you had a big wedding with all the family there?" I asked.

"Well of course we did. But we were already married when the big day came. My mother would never allow me to skip having a traditional wedding ceremony and I wanted to give my father a chance to walk his only daughter down the aisle. They just didn't know that we had already vowed our love the way we wanted, between just us two. And Elvis of course."

"Please tell me you're kidding, Grams." No way did my grandmother get married by an Elvis impersonator.

She giggled and shook her head. "Only about the Elvis part. A kind woman named Jasmine married us at a chapel just outside of town."

"Was Grandma Jean mad after she found out?"

"Oh no, she never knew. I didn't want to break her heart. It was just something that we needed to do. Our love was intense and we didn't want to wait. And honestly, it made the rest of the planning a breeze. We were already technically married, so it was as simple as planning a party." She shrugged it off like it was no big deal, but it is honestly the most romantic thing I've ever heard.

They couldn't wait to marry each other and didn't need anyone there to see it. It was only about them and the love they had for each other. Grams and Papa were like no other. After fifty years of marriage, they still loved like they just met.

"Grams, you have ruined me."

"Ruined you? More like spoiled you," she teased.

"You know what I mean. Your relationship with Papa is straight out of a romance novel. It's what every girl dreams to find." I pause in thought, but take a sip of my tea without finishing.

Nathan is amazing, loves me completely, and would do anything for me. But I can feel in my heart that it's not the same kind of love like they have. Not that our love isn't real, I'm just not sure it's true.

Or maybe it's just that I am over thinking the whole thing.

But what if I make the wrong the choice and marry someone who I thought was the one, only to find that there is another one out there; someone that doesn't cause that tingling sensation in my stomach to ever go away, even after fifty years?

So many thoughts run wild through my head and Grams quickly takes notice.

"Daphne, I'm not going to tell you whether or not you should marry this man. You know that I adore Nathan and that you both love each other very much. Remember, you may have already said yes, but you do not need to get married tomorrow. If you love him, then he deserves for you to be certain and go into this marriage with one hundred percent of your heart. Sometimes it can take a person years to realize that the love they have for someone is real, and other times it can take merely moments. One way or another, there will come a crossroad in your relationship and you will just know. It may be something that tells your heart he is not your forever, but the other option is that there will be a moment when you know that he is. Follow your heart, and take your time. If he loves you, he will wait."

She read me like Sunday's paper. That is exactly how I felt. It's not that I didn't love Nathan; I just wasn't one hundred percent certain that he was my forever.

"Thanks Grams, you always say exactly what I need to hear. Did I tell you I loved you today?"

She smiled and lifted her cup. "I love you too, sugar. Here's to the moment. When you feel it, you will know and when you know, you will feel it. Love is infinite, but is not refined. That is our job.

We have to cherish it and find our own versions of it along the way."

"You are truly one of a kind, Grams. Cheers to that." I gave her cup a light tap and she laughed at the non-traditional gesture.

"Babe!" Nathan's voice rips me back awake. "You going to pick that up?"

He was standing in the bathroom doorway, naked, brushing his teeth. A spurt of desire spiraled through my body as I admired his chiseled frame. If he ever tires of his career in law, he should definitely consider modeling. Hell, I'd buy whatever toothpaste he was selling.

Hearing the phone vibrate on my nightstand, I roll over to the other side and swipe it open just a second too late.

Three missed calls from Papa.

A painful knot began to twist in my stomach as a rush of anxiety halted my breath in my throat.

Why would he be calling me this early on a Saturday? Something doesn't feel right.

I swipe my phone in an attempt to call him back, but his fourth call is already coming through. Accepting the call, I could hear his heavy breaths before putting the phone to my ear.

"Hi Papa, everything okay?"

"Hi Daffy." His fragile voice is shaky and I can sense his battle swallowing a lump in his throat to continue. "It's about Grams, honey. She's gone."

Finding my breath, a soft gasp escapes my throat as the knot in my stomach continues to twist and a heaviness builds in my chest.

"No, Papa." My broken voice is overtaken by my inability to breathe as the tears that were trembling on my eyelids fall to my cheeks.

Flowers of all colors painted the porch and filled any open space on the counters. The house was filled with friends and family, old and young. Stories poured from their lips, speaking the kindest words of the most amazing woman I have ever known.

She had been battling cancer for over a year, but never wanted us to know, and made Papa promise to keep it a secret. Although he knew her time was limited, it's evident that Papa was not prepared for her departure. None of us were, nor do I imagine we ever could be.

Feeling the heaviness return to my chest, I excuse myself from a conversation I had been half listening to and step onto the back porch for fresh air.

Closing the door behind me, I spot Papa on the swing and stroll over to take a seat next to him. Leaning my head against his shoulder, we continued to swing in silence, enjoying the breeze coming up from the lakeshore.

"How you holding up, darlin'?" he asked, wrapping his arm tightly around my shoulders.

Avoiding words that could possibly ignite the water works, I reply with a shoulder shrug.

11

"I know, baby girl. I miss her too." He takes a deep breath and continues in a softer voice. "Like I never imagined possible."

I nod to agree.

A few more moments pass and Papa taps me on the shoulder, gesturing for me to sit up. Unwrapping his arm from my shoulder, he reaches into his shirt pocket pulling out an envelope with a familiar handwriting on the front.

My eyes grow misty, as he hands me the cream colored envelope *with My Dearest Daphne* written on the front.

"She wanted me to give this to you and tell you to follow your heart, and take your time. You don't have to read it right now, just whenever you are ready." Kissing my forehead, he pats my hand before standing from the swing to head inside.

My trembling hands slowly lift the flap and slide the folded stationery from the envelope. Probably not the best time or place to be doing this, but I am desperate to hear her voice, even if only through ink.

Dear Daphne,

My sincerest apologies that I kept my illness a secret. Right now, though your heart is filled with grief and sadness, I want you to smile. Always remember that you are a strong woman with the largest of hearts. You are forever my sweetheart and I will be with you always.

Since the day you were born, your beauty and love have been a huge inspiration in my life. I would have never opened the doors to the Tea Room if you had not inspired me with treasure hunt tea parties. For that, I am forever grateful.

The Tea Room has been my biggest accomplishment and I have thoroughly enjoyed all the time we were able to spend there together.

It takes a big heart and a warm smile to keep the treasure alive and that is why I've chosen you, Daphne. The Tea Room is yours. It always has been; I've just been taking care of it for you.

I understand that you are engaged and may even be married by the time you read this, so this decision shall not be taken lightly. But no matter what, the choice is yours. The Treasured Tea Cup was signed over to you today, and is only awaiting your signature. What you do once it's yours is completely your choice. It would be a joy to see you carry on the tradition and keep the doors open, but I am aware of what a sacrifice that would be.

Take your time with the decision, Papa has things taken care of for now and you are in no rush.

I love you, Daphne. A grandmother's heart has never been more full of love. Take care of Papa, he will need you now more than ever.

A love to cherish, kept deep in the heart
A love far away, but never apart
Moments of laughter, moments of tears
Through all life's moments, throughout all years
Love holds no value, and cannot be measured
Like a fine cup of tea, it can only be treasured

Xoxo
Loving you Always,
Grams

Daphne

2

The knot that seems to be a permanent fixture among my organs twists and tightens as my eyes travel the length of the car. With my life packed inside, I slide into the driver's seat and inhale slowly. Closing the door, his face appears in my side mirror and the wetness of my eyes leaks at the corners. His simple wave and half smile pierce my heart as my breath quickens, yet I drive away leaving only his reflection growing smaller in the distance.

TWO WEEKS EARLIER...

"Please, read it." I handed Nathan the letter from Grams.

"Are you sure? Isn't this personal?" he asked, cautious of my fragile state.

My grieving consisted mostly of silence these past few weeks. I didn't have much to say and yet a million thoughts in my head. Grams gave me the greatest gift and I was feeling completely torn in two. How would I ask him to leave his life behind and start over in a new town? Nathan worked harder than anyone I knew and was so close to becoming a partner at his father's firm. How do you ask a man to leave it all so you can run a small town tea room?

I couldn't ask, so I'll just let him read.

"Please, just read it. It's fine." I pled, hoping it would help make this impossible situation a little easier.

He looked at the letter in his hands and raised his eyes to meet mine as a hint of a smile touched his lips. "Okay, I'll read it."

With my coffee cup in hand, I stood from the bed and went to sit in the living room.

A few minutes passed, which seemed longer than it should to read her words. I stood from the couch and peeked my head into the bedroom, where he sat with the letter still in his hands and eyes glued to it.

"Sorry, I'll let you finish," I whispered and turned to leave.

"No, its fine. This was the fourth time I've read it. I just needed to be sure I was understanding what she was saying." His struggling voice rang painfully in my ears.

I had no words. And apparently neither did he.

We sat in silence for what seemed like an eternity before he folded up the letter and handed it back to me.

"You know we can't go, right? Our life is here, Daphne." His voice was still soft, but a small amount of strength and control coated his tone.

"I am well aware of where my life is, Nathan. But it's not that easy."

"It is that easy, baby. Are you asking me to leave everything I have worked for and move to a town the size of a pea and try to make a living? My job is here and my future is here with the firm. What about our plans?" His voice was now slightly elevated.

I began to pace slowly across the room, while my heart was gathering courage.

"I haven't asked you anything yet. That's why I wanted you to read it yourself. I needed you to understand my sadness. I didn't ask you to leave because I already knew you wouldn't." The pools of tears were threatening to overflow my eyelids. "I just needed you to understand why I am leaving."

"You can't be serious, Daphne." He stood from the bed and stepped in front of me to stop my pacing steps. "Please, think about what you are saying. You don't have to make a decision right now, she told you not to rush."

He attempted to lift my chin and meet my gaze, but the moment I saw his tear filled, lighter than normal, gray eyes, I dropped my face as a chest deep sob escaped me. Wrapping his arms around me, he allowed me to release the pain that I had been holding onto for days.

With a deep inhale to calm my nerves, I lifted my head and returned my gaze to his. "I'm so sorry, Nathan. There was never a choice. Just like you could never leave your life and what you have built here, I could never close the doors and lose a piece of my heart; my home."

"Daphne, please. I understand what it means to you, but can't someone else take care of it and you stay here? You don't have to close the doors, but it will be fine without you. Let someone else take care of it." He rubbed his hands up and down my arms in an attempt to comfort me, but all I felt was patronized.

"Stop, please." I wriggled out of his grip and took a step back, probably more irritated than necessary. "You're making me feel like a child. If you understand what it means to me, how can you not see why I need to be there? The Treasured Tea Cup is home and it needs me."

"Truthfully, Daphne, it sounds more like you need it." He turned away and walked out of the room. A few seconds later I heard the front door slam.

My hand clutched to my chest and my head dropped to the floor. A single tear fell from my eye but was not followed by others. I was done crying and done feeling sorry for my decision.

Leaving Nathan would be the hardest thing I may ever do, yet in this moment the decision seemed so clear.

Grams was right, I had my moment with Nathan. The one that determined our future together, the one that let me know whether or not he was the one. If Nathan was the one, how could I ever leave him behind, or yet, how could he let me go?

The lone tear was joined with many others as I felt the wetness fall to my hand still clutched to my chest. I lifted my head toward the ceiling and embraced the moment, allowing a smile to reach my face, hoping Grams would be smiling back.

Poor planning on my part, I arrive in Truesdale after dark and pass my new street twice. Slowing down and turning on my brights, I can see my road up ahead.

"Meadow Lane. Finally." I switch off my high beams and turn on the street. A few feet later, I see the entrance to my new neighborhood, Village West. Driving through the rows of townhomes, I see number one-fourteen. Thankfully, the landlord had been kind enough to leave on the porch light.

Leaving all my belongings in the car, aside from my overnight bag, I walk up the well-manicured sidewalk and pause at my front door. I release a heavy sigh of relief and let myself inside.

Clean aromas swirl in the air, and every step echoes in the emptiness. Walking in to the kitchen, I notice a basket on the counter with a kind note from the landlord welcoming me to the neighborhood. What really catches my eye is the bottle of wine shining from behind a box of gourmet cookies.

Hallelujah.

Even more exciting, is the fact that it is a twist off cap and not a cork. At this point, I would have cracked the top of the bottle off on the counter just to have a sip.

With a few more important things to grab from the car, I make one more trip outside and begin to settle in for the night. Once the air mattress is full, I dress it with sheets and put away my bathroom items before taking a quick shower.

Recycling a disposable cup from my stop at the gas station, I rinse out the coffee residue and pour myself a generous cup of wine. As I sit on my temporary bed, I curl up my legs to my chest and sip my wine, thankful to finally be relaxing.

My eyes are growing heavy, so I tilt my head back and finish the last sip. Setting the cup on the hardwood floor next to the bed, I reach up and turn off the light. A quick flash has my stomach flipping in fright, before the vibration from my phone on the hardwood calms me back down. Just a text message, not a burglar.

Nathan: Hope you made it safely. Miss you.

Me: Here safely, thanks for checking :)

My eyes close tightly, fighting the lump forming in my throat. I did miss him but I can't say it. I don't want to give him the false hope that I'm coming back.

But, I miss him; his strong body wrapped around mine and his sweet kisses to say goodnight. I miss him already and it hasn't even been ten hours.

The darkness in the room returns as the phone screen goes black and the eerie silence causes my swimming thoughts to grow louder by the second.

Turning to my side and tucking my hands under my cheek, I finally drift to sleep as my tears create a stream to the pillow.

Rolling easily onto the floor, my mattress now resembles something more like a punctured lifeboat. I am awake before my alarm, which isn't an issue, however the lack of caffeine in this place is.

Changing into my workout clothes, I lock the door behind me and set off on a morning run, hoping my legs lead me straight to a store to find coffee.

After a few miles, I see the doors of heaven and pick up my pace, heading straight for the convenient store. Not my typical choice for a fresh cup of coffee, but at this time of morning, how bad can it be? Not to mention, I am desperate.

The surprising tasty liquid is like magic and wanting to finish my large cup and enjoy the morning, I slow my pace for a brisk walk back, rather than jogging.

Caffeinated, dressed and ready to leave, a tiny swirl starts in my stomach and the excitement puts a smile on my face. It's the first time since making my decision that I have allowed myself to feel excited about my choice.

Parking in the rear lot of the building, I wander around to the front porch to make my way inside. It has been quite some time since my last visit and this would be the first without the warm greeting of Grams on the front porch to welcome me. Instead, it is my dear friend Hilda, who has been the hostess at the Tea Room since the doors first opened. She has been a family friend for my entire life.

"Sweet Daphne, you look as dashing as ever. Hope your first night went well, it's so wonderful to see you," she spoke softly before kissing my cheek and wrapping me in a hug.

"Hi Hilda, I've missed you. First night went well, and I'm hoping my first day does as well."

"Oh honey, I'm sure it will. This place is in your heart and you'll be perfect. Let me know if I can help in any way, I'll be up front getting ready for the day's reservations. Welcome home, Daphne." Her warmth and genuine smile make me feel relieved.

Walking through the front door and taking a deep breath, I allow the aroma and familiarity to soak in as I take a look around. The hardwood floors are freshly mopped and the vintage desk is tidy and organized. My eyes travel the room, noticing all the fine décor. Grams made this place her home and her presence is apparent in every detail.

Returning my focus back to the front desk, my eyes meet Hilda's misty gaze and I decide it's best to get straight to work before letting my emotions absorb my thoughts.

"Thank you, Hilda. I'm going to head to the" – *BANG!* – "What the heck was that?" I all but shout as the loud noise makes me nearly pee myself.

"Oh sorry, I should have told you. Mr. Dean is here finishing up a few repairs that Kay had him working on. I believe he will be finishing up today," Hilda replies not even flinching at the loud noise, as she remains focused on her notebook.

Turning my head toward the direction of the noise I reply calmly, trying to lower my heart rate. "Okay, no worries. I'll go back and say hi. It's been quite some time since I've seem him."

Not responding right away, I look to Hilda, still scribbling in her book, before remembering that she is a little hard of hearing.

Raising my voice this time, I call to her again. "Thanks, Hilda. I'll see you in a bit."

Lifting her gaze, she gives me a smile and nods before returning her attention to her work. She has always been self sufficient and keeps the front of the house in perfect working order. It is a blessing having her here to help me transition into ownership. No one else knows this place better than her.

Walking through two rooms, noticing the clean tables set perfectly for the next guest, a smile grows from cheek to cheek. As always, even with Grams gone, the staff was keeping up and making sure every detail is perfect. Each table is set with a vintage teacup, saucer, and tea spoon, none of which typically match.

The folded napkins are being held down by a silver fork and knife, and each table is stocked with a variety of sweetener options, ranging from regular sugar to local honey. Along with the dishes, none of the furniture matched either. It is a unique combination of antique wooden tables and chairs. Some hold seating for four and some seat up to as many as eight. The Treasured Tea Cup exudes charm from every angle and has the ability to fill hearts with the traditional culture of tea time, making it truly magical.

Walking into the Doll House Quarters, which is one of the themed rooms here, I knock slightly against the doorframe to announce my entrance.

A gentleman stands from his crouching position on the floor and turns toward me, wiping a fallen hair back from his forehead.

Brown hair, not gray; young, sexy, luscious dark brown hair. Who the hell is this?

Mr. Dean is a local contractor and friend of my grandparents, who they hire to help out with maintenance and repairs here at the Tea Room and also around the house. However, unless he made a recent visit to the fountain of youth, this is not Mr. Dean.

The smile I walked in with slightly fades from my face and I feel the burrowing of my brow line. "Um, hi...sorry to

22

interrupt. Hilda said Mr. Dean was here and I was just coming in to say hello."

"Oh sorry about that, it happens all the time. I am Mr. Dean, just not Walter, who I am guessing you were expecting. I'm Curtis, Walter's son."

His chiseled jawline tightens as a grin reaches his lips. Taking a step toward me and removing his work glove, he stretches his hand out toward me.

Glancing down to notice his tanned, hardworking hand, I inhale a calming breath and return his friendly grin, before grasping it with mine.

"Very nice to meet you, Curtis. I'm Daphne Fields, Kay's granddaughter."

A single dimple appears on his left cheek as his lips stretch into a full, mega watt smile. His dashing features take me by surprise as my gaze meets his olive green eyes, involuntarily growing my smile to match his intensity.

He holds my grip a second longer, then releases his hand and turns his gaze toward the wall he was working on.

"I have a few more things to finish up in here, but should be done soon. Hopefully before any guests arrive." He lifts his wrist to examine his watch.

"Oh sure, no problem. Let me know if you need anything," I reply.

His flannel shirt is rolled up to three-quarter length and buttoned up to his chest, where a white undershirt peeks out. The dust from the drywall covers his jeans, but can't hide his perfectly toned backside that catches my eye.

He has a naturally toned, strong build, which I would imagine he developed through his work.

Removing his other glove, he runs his hand through his medium length hair and reaches into his back pocket to pull out his wallet.

"So, I'll be finishing up today, but you can call me if you need anything. Here is my card and my cell is the best way to reach me. I am available anytime." He hands me the card and stores his wallet back in his pocket.

"Thanks, Curtis. I appreciate it. I'll let you get back to it, then. Please let me know if there's anything you need."

He replies with a smile and nod and I make my way out of the room. Checking my reflection in the closest mirror, I hope my cheeks are not as flushed as they feel. The young Mr. Dean caught me completely off guard.

Curtis

3

"Hey, babe. Sorry I'm late, it was a busy day and I was a man short," I say, walking through the door, an hour later than planned.

Frank, one of my foremen, called out with the flu, which normally isn't an issue, however, this has been a week from hell. We have been running behind schedule with a few clients this week, so after leaving the Treasured Tea Cup, I went around to multiple jobsites helping the guys catch up. Now that this day is over, all I want to do is go home, eat dinner and pass the hell out.

However, I knew there was no way I could cancel my plans with Vera. At least not without catching major grief. I originally planned to call and explain how exhausted I am, but then received a text informing me she would be cooking dinner at her place and wanted me there by six. Vera cooking was a rarity and typically, if I hadn't made the meal myself, our dinners consisted mostly of take out.

"It's okay. Dinner is almost ready," she says, walking over and kissing me before returning to the kitchen. "Have a seat at the table and I will bring it out."

Taking a seat at her dining room table, I observe Vera as she moves about, preparing our plates. Something is definitely up. The fact that she cooked dinner should have been enough to tip me off, but if not that, her barely-there red dress, would have done it. Don't get me wrong, the way it hugged her slender body was sexy as hell, working exactly how she planned. Knowing that she didn't wear it to work today, this outfit was only for my viewing pleasure, and I was enjoying it.

Bringing our plates, mine piled high with spaghetti and garlic bread, and hers a salad, she places them down on the table. Before she can walk away, I reach out and grab her wrist, pulling her towards me. A carefree laugh escapes her, as she falls into my lap and I plant a sweet kiss to her flushed cheek. This is the Vera I want at all times. Only lately, it is extremely rare to see her this way.

"You look beautiful," I say, running my lips up and down her neck as my hand glides up her bare thigh.

She stops my advancement and pulls away from me, standing and moving to take her seat across from me.

"Thank you. Let's eat, before it gets cold." And just like that the moment is lost.

I brush off her sudden mood change, pick up my fork and dig into the spaghetti. One bite and I can tell she didn't exert herself making this meal. The noodles are not fully cooked and the sauce was simply poured straight from the jar. The best part of the whole meal is the garlic bread, even though the edges are a little blackened.

Not wanting to be rude, I eat the less than stellar spaghetti without complaint, as she picks at her salad. Sometimes, I swear she never eats, or when she does, it's only small amounts. She has a beautiful body, but it wouldn't hurt to have a little more meat on her bones.

After I finish my last bite, I set my fork down and stretch my arms above me, feeling the soreness run down my back. Today was rough and I know tomorrow will probably be just as bad. Looking at my watch, I see it is already past eight. I am exhausted and ready to crawl into my own bed.

"Curtis," she pauses, until I give her my full attention, "where do you see this relationship going?

"What do you mean?" I ask, the surprise evident in my voice. "We just got back together."

"It's been months. We've been at this for over a year now. Don't you think we should be ready to take it to the next level?"

I stare at her for a moment, in complete and utter shock. I am unsure where this is coming from, and I know I need to tread lightly with this. We had just spent a month apart after she decided that I work too much and never made time for her or our relationship. I knew that I had been spending more time working, but it was not unexpected. Vera was aware things would change when I took over the company.

My father built Dean Remodeling and Restoration from the ground up. He worked his ass off over the years to turn it into the successful company it is today. There is no way in hell would I ever do a half-ass job after everything he has put into it.

"Vera, we just got back on track two weeks ago, not months. Maybe we should spend more time working on us, and making sure this is what we want." The minute it leaves my mouth, I know I screwed up.

Her already dark eyes were turning black and her lips grew thin with anger. "I was merely suggesting we consider moving in together. Not like I am asking you to get married, but apparently you aren't even sure this is what you want. I guess I am just wasting my time."

"That's not what I am saying..." The ringing of my phone interrupts my thoughts. Not recognizing the number, I answer knowing its more than likely work related. "Dean R and R, this is Curtis, how may I help you?"

"Hi Curtis, this is Daphne Fields. Sorry for calling so late. Is this a bad time?"

You have no idea.

"You are seriously not...." Vera starts to say, but I raise my hand, silencing her.

The minute I hear Daphne's voice, my heated temper instantly calms. I had hoped she would use the number on my card when I gave it to her this morning, but didn't expect it to be so soon.

"No, ma'am. What can I do for you Miss Fields?" I ask, avoiding the use of her first name. I have a feeling keeping this conversation as professional as possible would be best as Vera's dark eyes continue to throw daggers my direction.

"Please, call me Daphne." She laughs.

I turn away from Vera, so she can't see the smile that is now plastered on my face after hearing Daphne's sweet laugh.

"I was doing a walk-through this afternoon and noticed a few weak boards in the stairway going down into the basement. If I am just walking down I can avoid them, but I worry about the times when I will be carrying boxes down after deliveries. Without paying attention I might hit one and end up falling down, breaking more than my butt I am sure." She rambles on with sincere concern but her tone keeps lightness in her words.

"Not a problem. I can be there first thing in the morning to take a look. How does eight sound?" When I scheduled work with her grandmother, this seemed to be the best time to start. Employees start arriving around ten, so it gives me about two hours to get the bulk of my work done.

"That would be perfect. Thank you so much."

I hear the clanking of pots and pans and know that Vera has moved into the kitchen to take her frustration out on the dishes.

"You're welcome. And Miss Fields?"

"Daphne." She corrects me again and I smile.

"The men who make those deliveries can also carry the boxes down to the basement. That's not something you should be doing."

"I will keep that in mind. Thank you again and I will see you in the morning, Mr. Dean."

I rub my hand over the facial hair around my mouth to suppress the laugh that wants to escape.

"Sounds good, take care."

Sliding my phone into my back pocket, I turn towards the kitchen only seeing Vera's back as she scrubs a pot.

"You are a busy man," she says, not bothering to turn around, but the distain is clear in her voice.

"Yes, well, owning a business means always being on call." Leaning against the counter, I cross my arms and wait for the lashing I am about to receive.

Rinsing the pot and placing it in the drainer to dry, she turns and mimics my stance.

"I remember, I just thought after our last conversation about it that you would have attempted to make some changes."

"What changes would you like me to make, Vera?"

"Why can't you put some of the other guys on call once in a while? Why do you always have to work late and be the one to receive calls well after closing hours?"

"Because this is now *my* company and is my full responsibility; no one else, which you knew when we got back together. It won't be changing, so maybe you should think about whether or not you can handle that." My voice is elevated with irritation, tired of having the same conversation with her.

"I get it. You don't have to yell. Sorry I even brought it up," she says, looking down at the ground, clearly upset.

Dropping my arms, I walk over to where she is leaning and pull her into a hug. "Look, I'm sorry I raised my voice. I've had a really long day and I am exhausted, so lets not talk about this anymore."

Bringing her gaze to mine, I instantly take notice of the wetness starting to pool in her eyes. She quickly drops her lashes to hide the hurt and I move my hand to the back of her neck and lightly kiss her lips.

"How about we relax on the sofa and watch a movie?" Kissing her lips softly one last time, I pull away and watch her nod her head.

"That sounds nice," she all but whispers.

With my hand in hers, I guide her to the living room. We both take a seat on the couch and reaching my arm around her shoulders, I pull her into my side.

As the movie plays out on the television, my mind can't help but wander back to our argument; the same argument we had the last time we broke up.

Growing up, my biggest dream was taking over my father's company. A year ago, he finally decided it was time to retire, but it took six months before he actually stopped working. I was beginning to think Ma would have to tie him down to his recliner to keep him from showing up every day.

It wasn't that he didn't trust me taking over, but more so that he wasn't ready to quit working. He doesn't know how to sit still and relax. Even after retirement he has found multiple projects around the house to keep busy. I know it drives Ma crazy, but it keeps him happy.

The majority of our clients have been long-term customers, most of which, I have been doing jobs for since I was in high school. Daphne's grandparents, Mitch and Kay Ellis, have always been one of my favorites. Especially, Kay, with her amazing lunch and desserts she would prepare for me. She always knew the way to a man's heart was straight through his stomach. And her food was always the best, there is nothing like it.

Doing odd jobs for her over the years, I had noticed her granddaughter long before meeting her today. Daphne Fields was not a woman that could be easily overlooked, even as a teenager. Her beauty was innocent and natural.

Kay always talked about her grandkids when we would sit together during my lunch break. I knew that Daphne had been recently engaged, and it was also obvious at the funeral that the guy in the expensive suit, holding and consoling Daphne, was her fiancé.

It was great to be finally be formally introduced and I could sense the same charm of Kay in her granddaughter. Her honey blonde hair had been pulled back, away from her face and a light blush stained her cheeks. She seemed a little nervous at first, which set me on edge, but once she smiled and I felt her tiny hand in mine, I was instantly put at ease. Her frame is small, but not frail and her curves hug her body in the most beautiful way.

As we talked, all I could focus on was her full lips, and I am hoping she didn't realize it and think I am a creep. I also couldn't help but notice the missing diamond that once rested on her left ring finger and can only assume that the fiancé is no more, and that selfishly makes me smile.

Not that it should, since I am with Vera, even if I don't have the slightest idea as to what is going on with us. She always makes me feel like she is so unhappy, yet when we break up, she comes crying about how miserable she is. This time it only took two weeks before she started her usual games. I honestly don't see this working out in the future and feel the end is inevitable.

When the ending credits roll, I pick up sleeping Vera and carry her to the bed. After tucking her in, I kiss her cheek and leave.

The second I make it home, I strip down to boxers and fall into bed. Anticipation of tomorrow morning keeps me from the instant sleep I was hoping for, and tonight as I lie here, it's blonde hair and green eyes that fill my mind.

Arriving at the Tea Room just before eight, I am greeted at the door by Daphne. Her hair is pulled back again, with a few wispy pieces falling down around her face. My hand twitches, wanting to reach out and tuck them behind her ears. Thinking better of it, I grip my clipboard tighter.

"Good morning, Mr. Dean," Daphne says, the smile beaming on her face, reminding me of our phone conversation last night.

"Morning, Daphne. And, we already discussed that Mr. Dean is my father." I watch as her lips widen even more with her smile. "Shall we get started?"

"Yes. Come on in."

Daphne leads me to the basement, telling me about a few other issues she has come across that she would like for me to take a look at before I leave. I don't catch everything she is saying because I am briefly distracted by the pastel yellow capri pants that are cupping her perfectly toned ass. I pull my eyes away, just as we get to the basement door, hoping she didn't catch my stare.

"Okay, it's the third step down and then the second from the bottom," she says with a sweet grin and I swear it seems this beautiful girl is always smiling. She has one of those beaming contagious smiles that you can't help but return. When I do, the light blush from yesterday returns to her cheeks.

Getting back to the task at hand, I glance down the stairs and can already see a few of the boards are worn.

"These stairs haven't been touched in years and I can tell some more will need to be replaced. I'll take a closer look at them and see how many will need worked on."

"Okay, I will let you get to it then. If you need anything, I will be in the kitchen."

After further examination, I determine that six of the steps will need to be replaced, for now. Eventually, due to age and wear, the entire staircase will need to be rebuilt. At least for now, I can make it so they are safe to use.

I make a quick note of the measurements in my clipboard before finding Daphne in the kitchen. Placing a batch of scones in the oven, she is laughing with one of the other girls and seems right at home.

I clear my throat not wanting to startle anyone and to keep myself from looking like a creep, just staring from the doorway.

Wiping her hands on the yellow and gray frilly apron that is wrapped around her waist, she walks towards me.

"Was it worse than I thought?" she asks, reaching for a glass and filling it with iced tea.

"Well, after further inspection, it looks like we will need to replace six steps. You may want to consider having the entire staircase rebuilt a little further down the road, but this will hold you over for a while."

"Okay, I didn't realize they were that bad. Here's some iced tea, its vanilla-pomegranate."

I accept the glass she is holding and take a sip of the cold, sweet drink.

"Thank you. It's delicious." She smiles at my compliment and I take another drink to hide my grin. "Do you want to go over the other concerns you have and then we can schedule the work?"

"Sure, that sounds great. Lacey, I will be back in just a few minutes." Turning to address the young girl, who just waves her off, Daphne removes her apron and leads me around the old house, pointing out her concerns.

We complete a thorough walkthrough and I have an extensive list of jobs that need to be done.

"Alright, I will write up an estimate and I can email it to you by tomorrow." Pulling out my phone, I open the calendar app to confirm that my morning is free tomorrow. "Looks like I can be back here in the morning, same time if that works for you?"

"That would be great. Here, let me write down my email for you." Reaching into the drawer of the hostess desk, she produces a pen and piece of paper. After jotting down her information and stuffing the pen back into the drawer, she hands me the paper. "Here is my email and I also included my cell number, in case you have any questions or need to reach me."

My inner teenage boy is high-fiving himself right now for getting her number. But, I tone down my excitement when I remind myself that I have a girlfriend.

"Okay, I will get that email to you and will see you in the morning. Have a good day, Daphne."

"You too, Curtis."

I reach my hand out for hers and feel a jolt when she grazes my palm. What is it about Daphne that keeps me twisted up in knots?

Daphne

4

"Don't you have somewhere to be?" Hilda's voice cuts through the air and startles me, sitting in the next room over from the lobby.

I hadn't realized she even knew I was in here. At this time in the afternoon, there were only a few customers remaining and the staff would be finishing up and cleaning for the next day. This room was usually the first one empty and cleaned up, allowing me to enjoy the serene silence while trying to complete my last task for the afternoon.

My food order normally only took about fifteen minutes to write out, however, I have been sitting here with the pen and paper for nearly half an hour. It isn't that I don't know what I am doing, but more so that I am severely distracted.

The tingle in my palm from when our hands grazed against one another has yet to fade. It's ridiculous; I don't even know this man. Not too long ago I was engaged to a sexy lawyer who I imagined spending the rest of my life with. Today, I am daydreaming about ripping the flannel shirt off the hot construction worker that I literally just met.

"Daphne, those delivery drivers don't like to wait." This time, her voice didn't have to cut through too much air since she is now standing in the doorway. "Darling, do you have a fever, your cheeks are flushed."

"Uh, no. I'm fine, it's just warm in here." Quickly, I avoid any more thoughts of Curtis, hoping the color in my face will return to its natural pallor. I pick up my paperwork and head into the lobby. "Thanks, Hilda. I totally forgot."

Pulling my bag from behind the counter and stuffing the paperwork in the front pocket, I grab my keys and push my sunglasses up my nose.

"Thanks for closing up for me. I owe you big time. For lots of things. I'm going to finish the food order and email it later tonight when the furniture people leave."

"Not to worry, dear. We've got things under control. Good luck, see you tomorrow." She waves me off while heading toward the kitchen.

I have been looking forward to this since I arrived and have no clue how I let it slip my mind.

Since my appointment with the furniture company is scheduled as an hour window of time, they may or may not already be at my house. I really don't want any extra fees for making them wait on me.

Pulling into my neighborhood, I see the moving truck and start to panic. Rushing out of the car with my apologies at tongues edge, I notice they are just getting out the truck and looking to make sure they have the right house number. I was right on time.

"Hi there! You are in the right place. I'm Daphne." We shake hands and the fun begins. Well, at least for them anyways. I am not moving an inch. Just going to supervise and make sure everything I ordered arrived in one piece.

"Ahhh." The instant my rear-end hits the cushion, I feel like a million bucks. This couch is worth every penny and will be with me for many years to come.

My house is finally starting to come together. I now have furniture, some groceries, cable and Internet. With just a touch of decoration and a little personalization, I could definitely consider this home.

For all their efforts and for my avoidance of a mess tonight, I ordered a pizza and shared the pie with the movers. They were more than appreciative and I was just happy not to have to wash any dishes.

Finally relaxing, I pull a throw over my legs and reach next to me for my laptop. It is crucial to get this food order in tonight; otherwise we may run out of a few house specialties. This tends to get the customers upset and I try my very best to keep up with the inventory so it does not happen often.

In record time, I finish the order and open my email to send it out. Waiting in the inbox, with the boldest of fonts, is a new email from Dean R & R. My relaxation fades as a familiar knot twists inside my stomach. My eyes lift from the screen and search the room as if I am going to find him standing here with his clipboard in hand.

TO: dfields@treasuredteacup.com
FROM: curtis@deanr&r.com

<Attachment: DeanR&R-estimate.pdf>

Hi Daphne,

Attached is the estimate for the work we discussed today. Please look it over and let me know if you have any questions.

Thank you,
Curtis Dean

I open the attachment and review the prices and timelines for each item we discussed earlier. As I read them over, my mind runs a play-by-play of the afternoon as we walked through the Tea Room discussing each one and his ideas for updating or fixing them. He is extremely knowledgeable and had answers for everything.

It is easy to say that Curtis intrigues me. How can his slight touch from earlier manage to stay with me most of the day? It doesn't make any sense. I have met a million men in my life that were sexy and sweet and everything a woman would want. Yet, none that leaves me reeling this way after only a simple touch.

Once upon a time, it was Nathan that could have a similar effect on me, but it wasn't this quick. It took months for me to warm up to him and he had to work hard for my attention. Once I finally gave him my time, I was hooked. He had all the right words and made me feel the tingle with his touch. This lasted for a good portion of our relationship, but as usual, the puppy love faded and our friendship grew into a new kind of love.

Watching Grams and Papa's love throughout my life set a high bar for my expectations. I always thought that I would get that tingle even after ten years in a relationship with the same person. That a man could look in my eyes and hold a gaze no matter what chaos surrounded us. And that with any bad day or troubled time, a simple thought of that man would make me smile and lighten my mood even if only for a moment.

I think Gram would be happy that I followed my heart and found the moment that answered my question. The question I had not even realized I was asking myself. Was Nathan the one? And though it seems I may have made my decision, I still feel unsure it was the right one.

Nathan is a good man and would take care of me forever. But he also knows how important this move is for me and how dear the Tea Room is to my heart. It was never a choice for me, but it was an option for him. He made no attempt to compromise with the move and decided our fate the minute he read the words in the letter. If love is forever, we all have to make sacrifices in order to make it last.

Nathan consumes my thoughts on a daily basis and I miss him with every breath. It seems only natural that after being with someone for multiple years that it would be a hard habit to break. It is a struggle to wake up every morning and look to my side, only to find there is no one there. Not to mention cooking for one. Who knew how difficult a single person recipe could be.

But with all things, time is the best medicine. It seems my mornings are getting easier and I will figure out the cooking thing soon enough. What also seems soon, are the feelings that I am experiencing for another man. Though my heart still belongs to Nathan for the time, it's been fluttering and flirting with another man. My head swims with negative thoughts about why it is wrong to feel this way, while my heart sings an entirely different tune, like it could care less what my head thinks.

A loud marimba beat escalades from my purse and I jump off the couch to answer my phone.

"Hey, Dad! How are you?" I answer.

"Hi Daph. Things are good. We miss you like crazy." His voice full of sincerity.

"I know, I miss you too. Been busy at work?"

"Yeah, seems like the summer brings out all the criminals. Our case load is full and Nathan has really been stepping up lately. He should be close to partnership here vey soon. Speaking of Nathan, you know he hasn't been himself lately. The guy really misses you. We all do."

Here he goes again.

"Dad, do we really have to have this conversation again? I made the right choice, the only choice. This is where I belong and trust me, I miss Nathan too. I'm just sorry there wasn't a better compromise." I stop there, not feeling the need to go further into explanation for the millionth time with someone else.

I am sure they all think I am crazy for up and leaving my life behind. And yet for me, it seems like crazy is more normal than expected. I am adjusting to my new pace of life and really starting to feel at home.

"I know, sorry to bring it up. I just feel bad for the guy. Anyways, have I ever told you how much you sound just like your mother on the phone?"

I chuckle, knowing he is trying to lighten the mood. "Almost every other time we talk, Dad."

There is a brief silence between us, as I am sure he is thinking the same thing I am; how much we miss her.

"You know it's almost been twenty-years?" he asks and his voice is a little shaky.

"Wow, that sounds so much longer than it feels. I'm glad she has Grams up there to be with her now."

"Me too, honey."

Another brief moment of silence covers the air.

"Alright, Daph, I'll let you go. Just wanted to call and say hi. Have you talked to your brother lately? He hasn't called me back in a few days. Not that I am worried about him since we know how much he loves to talk on the phone." My dad laughs and a smile fills my face.

"Ain't that the truth. No, I haven't spoken to him recently so I will call him tonight to see if I get an answer."

"Okay, honey. Have a good night and call me soon. Love you."

"I will. Love you too. Night."

"Goodnight."

Dad hangs up and I clear the call and scroll through my favorites list.

The phone rings several times before going to my brother's voicemail.

"Hey Derrick, it's your sister, your only sister and I haven't heard from you in a while. Hope your doing okay. Dad misses you, so please call him. And call me back too. Love you, D, goodnight."

I knew he would more than likely not answer, but if I leave enough messages he will eventually call me back. Derrick was never one to talk on the phone, he is more of a texting guy and even that is hit or miss.

Derrick lives a few hours a way and although we are twins, he acts like he is five years younger than me. He still lives in his own world making bad decisions and its hard to guess when he might actually decide to grow up. He bounces from job to job and has yet to find something that really makes him happy. But for whatever reason, it works for him. He pays his bills and stays healthy and really, that's all I could ask for.

Setting my phone down and returning my attention to the email on my screen, I open a reply message to send to Curtis. Knowing his prices are fair and that he will do good work, I type my acceptance and ask when he thinks he can start the work. With a thank you and my signature block, I hit send.

As if he were waiting for the email, his response came nearly instantaneously.

TO: dfields@treasuredteacup.com
FROM: curtis@deanr&r.com

Hi Daphne,

We should be able to start in a couple weeks. I will email you a schedule by Monday and I will see you tomorrow morning to take care of those stairs.

Have a good night.
Thank you,
Curtis Dean

His simple words fill me with more than one emotion. In one hand is a bittersweet excitement that I get to see him tomorrow but in the other is a yearning that I will have to wait a couple of weeks before seeing him again.

Curtis

5

"Hey boss man, what time will you be over to the jobsite today?" Rick, one of my foremen, asks, his voice coming through my speakerphone.

We have another busy day with Frank still out sick. My presence at the various job sites is more essential, especially since the new guys lack the work ethic I am accustomed to. Without a supervisor constantly observing their work, nothing gets done right, or even at all.

Both Frank and Rick are my two most reliable employees. Hell, they started working for my dad back when I was just a kid. I had been apprehensive about taking over the business at first, wondering how some of the guys would take me becoming their boss, especially the ones who had been with the company for so long. I was pleasantly surprised by the respect I received and the faith that the men had in me. It is what inspires me to be the best leader I can be.

"It will be sometime after lunch. I have a job I need to take care of this morning but will swing by soon after."

While most of the work at The Treasured Tea Cup can wait a couple weeks, I refuse to go another day without fixing the stairs. I can't stomach the thought of Daphne falling down and injuring herself.

"Roger that. I have the material list for the remodel at the Jones' place that we are starting next week. I just need you to sign off on it while you are here and I can put the order through."

I have told Rick countless times that he can order any materials he needs for the job, but he refuses to place any orders without my signature. Instead of bringing up the topic again, I tell him I will take care of it when I see him later on, ending our phone call just as I am pulling into the parking lot for the Tea Room. It's still early, so there is only one other car, which I assume to be Daphne's, who isn't waiting to greet me on the front porch today. I try to ignore the disappointment that comes with the discovery.

The bell over the door dings as I enter and Daphne comes around the corner, wiping her hands on the floral apron tied around her tiny waist. The white residue left behind is evidence she must be in the middle of baking.

"Hey, good morning Curtis. You're just in time. I am working on a new scone recipe and am in need of a taste tester." Her radiant and genuine smile lights up the room.

"Of course. I would be happy to help." I return her smile and she briefly looks down at her feet before meeting my gaze again. A move I might have missed, had I not been studying every feature of her beautiful face.

"Thank you," she says, a light blush spreading throughout her cheeks. I am beginning to think this is my favorite color on her. Blush. "I have been wanting to incorporate new things around here to make it more of my own, while still leaving Gram's touches. This is the first recipe I am trying that didn't come from her cookbook."

"Look at you, already going rogue."

A small giggle escapes her, bringing my attention to her full lips.

Damn it, keep this professional, Curtis.

"Not quite. I am only making one batch and planned on asking one of the girls to try them, but now I think you would be a more suitable candidate."

"Is it that obvious how much I love food?" I ask, laughing as I my hand moves up and down my shirt, rubbing my stomach. It wasn't a lie I love food; especially Ma's home cooking because nothing beats that.

Back in my twenties, when I had more free time, I spent a lot of it on strenuous workouts to keep up my build. Sometime after thirty hit, I misplaced my once defined six-pack. Not saying that I am, by any means, out of shape. I get a workout in whenever I can, but at thirty-four, it just isn't as much of a priority as it used to be. Thankfully, working in the labor industry, my daily tasks provide as much of a workout as I need to keep fit. This allows me to enjoy as much food as I want without gaining weight.

I catch Daphne as her eyes do an appraising sweep of my body, which only causes her cheeks to darken even more. I want to tell her to keep looking, because the pleasure I get from knowing I affect her the same way she does me is indescribable.

With a gentle shake of her head, as if to clear her thoughts, she returns to our conversation. "The girls are way too sweet and might not give an honest answer. Plus, I prefer to have a larger sample group to keep the opinions equally unbiased."

"You make a good point."

"Okay, so I will go start baking them. I promise I am actually a good cook and won't try to poison you."

"I'm sure they will be delicious. I will get to work on the stairs. Do you mind if I pull around back? I figure it would be easier to use the back door, rather than dragging everything through the front entrance."

"Absolutely. I will go unlock the door for you. If you need anything, please don't hesitate to ask."

There are several things I would like to ask Daphne, but not one has anything to with this job. I don't know what is wrong with me, but there is something about Daphne that is captivating. When I am around her my relationship with Vera completely slips my mind. This is not good. I need to get a grip and gain some self-control.

After moving my truck around the back of the house, I set up my tools and get to work on repairing the stairs. Concentrating on the work in front of me should keep my mind off of what Daphne might be doing a floor above me.

Last night I was able to avoid going over to Vera's, because she was going out with a couple of her friends from the Day Spa, where she works. She insisted that I joined them, but I convinced her that I would just be a buzz kill and really needed the sleep.

I still had work to do once I got home, writing up estimates and emailing them out to clients. Top of my list was The Treasured Tea Cup. I had been in the middle of working on an estimate for another client when the notification popped up for her reply. I stopped what I was doing and opened her email, sending my response back immediately.

It was a little after eleven when I finally made my way to bed and fell asleep. Three hours later, the endless ringing of my phone abruptly woke me up. I hit the ignore button a couple times before finally answering Vera. She was drunk and looking to start a fight about how I am never there for her and how she could do much better than me. She informed me of all the guys who throw themselves at her and how she has to turn them down, because she is committed to me. I kept falling asleep through her rants, which only pissed her off more. Eventually, she had enough and hung up, allowing me to return to my slumber and I have yet to hear from her this morning. She doesn't work today, so I would imagine she is sleeping off a nasty hangover.

A sweet aroma invades my senses causing me to look up, my eyes landing on Daphne standing at the top of the stairs, holding a tray in her hands. She looks down at the open spaces where I have ripped up boards needing to be replaced. Before she can attempt to make her way down, I drop my measuring tape and pencil and walk over.

"Wait. Let me come to you."

She nods and backs away from the entrance, sitting the tray down on a nearby table. I carefully make my way up the stairs, cautiously avoiding the holes. It's not a difficult task and I make it up without causing any more damage or hurting myself in the process.

"They smell amazing," I tell her.

Daphne smiles while placing a scone on a napkin before handing it to me. "Let's just hope they taste amazing as well. Here you go, my cinnamon-apple scone."

I bring the treat straight to my mouth and bite into it. The flavors hit my taste buds instantly and I wouldn't be surprised if a moan escaped. Still warm from the oven, the scone practically melts in my mouth and the tiny apple chunks explode even more.

Daphne watches me intently, waiting to hear my opinion. "Wow, Daphne. This is really good."

"Really?" she asks, handing me an iced tea and then biting into a scone herself. She slowly chews, her eyes directed at the ceiling, deep in thought. Suddenly, she gets a sour look on her face before setting down the remainder of the scone. "Oh no. This is terrible. I used way to much cinnamon."

I stare at her in shock. Did she even eat the same things as I did?

"You're crazy. There is nothing wrong with these scones. Your Grams would be proud." I regret saying the last part when I see the sadness flash in her eyes. But it's true. I know

Miss Kay would be proud of everything Daphne has done since her passing.

Her lips pull up in a small smile. "Thank you. Curtis. That's sweet. But I know that I can make them better. I'll try another batch in the morning."

"I think they are perfectly fine, however, you are the expert."

"Well, I am not so sure about that. How about I box up the rest of these for you?" she asks, picking up the tray.

I rub my hand up and down my stomach, same as I did earlier. "I would gladly accept them."

This earns me a soft laugh from Daphne, which is music to my ears.

"Okay, I will let you get back to work." She turns and I watch the sway of her hips as she retreats. She looks back as she turns the corner, catching me in the act. For a long moment our gazes are locked together and I know I need to look away, but I just physically am unable. Daphne makes the first move when she redirects her eyes and continues walking away.

I spend the next couple hours finishing up my work on the stairs, stopping to take a call from my sister, Jill. We were always close growing up, being only a couple of years apart. After college, she landed an impressive job at a lucrative financial firm outside of town. It was there that she met her husband, Alex, who was her boss at the time.

When she first brought him around to meet the family, I wasn't his biggest fan and really didn't see a solid future for them. Growing up I was extremely protective over Jill, and I guess I still am. No guy was ever good enough for my sister. This made dating in high school a nightmare for her. Especially if any of my friends showed too much interest.

So, when she showed up that night with a guy who was at least seven years older than her, I was a little thrown off to say the least. It wasn't that he was a bad guy, but I just never pictured him being my sister's type. They have now been married five years and blessed me with the cutest little niece on Earth.

Hannah stole my heart the first time I held her little bundled body in my arms. What is it about a baby that can bring a grown man to his knees? Here we are, four years later, and she still has me tightly wrapped around her finger.

A year ago, Alex received a promotion, which transferred him to the company's North Carolina firm. Watching my baby sister pack up and move five hundred miles away was a sad day for our family and I know Ma's heart broke knowing her girls were leaving. Of course, we are in constant contact and Hannah is always wanting to FaceTime so she can show off her latest moves she learned in dance class. With her birthday approaching, we have all been planning a surprise party down here for when they come to visit.

With the job complete, I clean up my mess and load my tools back into my truck. I always make sure to leave my jobsites clean and returned to their original state before leaving. Last thing you want to do is leave a disaster that your customer has to go behind you and clean.

I walk up the staircase, frowning at the way the boards are now mismatched between the color of the old ones and ones replaced today. I need to make a note to bring a wood stain with me next time to even it out.

Feeling a little awkward over our intense stare down earlier, I decided to leave out the back door where my truck is parked without bothering Daphne.

The diesel engine roars to life and I take a brief moment to talk myself out of going back inside to tell her bye. It is the professional thing to do, and is something I do with every other customer I have. I greet them when I arrive and touch base before I leave.

Shifting my truck in reverse, I look ahead just as Daphne comes out the back door, carrying a white box and waving her other hand in the air. I roll down my window after putting the truck back into park as she rushes over.

"Hey, you almost forgot your scones," she says casually, as though nothing out of the ordinary happened earlier. Maybe to her it was nothing and I am just blowing things way out of proportion over a little crush.

"Thank you. Sorry about that, one of the guys called and I have to get to another job. The stairs are finished and safe for your using. I will contact you Monday about setting up the days for the rest of the work we talked about."

She looked up at me, confusion written all over her face, but then she blinked and it was gone before I could even question it.

"Thank you, again. I need to get back in there, so have a good day." Without even so much as a smile, Daphne turns around and walks back inside, leaving me to wonder what just happened.

I let out a heavy breath pulling in my driveway, irritated that Vera was sitting in her car waiting for me. After not hearing from her all day, I was hoping I could get a peaceful night sleep. I am not currently inclined to deal with her but I also know I shouldn't put it off any longer.

We both exit our vehicles and make our way into my house without a word. I walk straight to the kitchen and grab a bottle of water out of the fridge, unscrewing the lid and gulping down half.

"I haven't heard from you all day," she says, causing me to turn and face her. She stands just three feet away, with her hands on her hips and her lips puckered in annoyance. Dressed in yoga pants and a tank, with her hair in a tight bun on top of her head, she must have just come from the gym. Not one to be seen any less than perfect, I know she showered before leaving, erasing any proof of sweat and changed into clean clothes. She put more effort into her appearance than any woman should.

Leaning back against the counter, I cross my arms over my chest, broadcasting my irritation. "I had a busy day. Besides, I figure enough was said last night."

"What are you talking about?" she asks, curtly.

I shake my head. "That's rich, Vera. You go out, get drunk, and call me, only to inform me of what a piece of shit I am."

"Huh? No I did not."

A sarcastic laugh leaves my mouth before I can stop it. "How convenient. You don't remember, so it must not have happened. Just like all the other times in the past, right?"

"So, I had a few too many cosmos with the girls. I was upset you weren't there and missed you. Anything negative I might have said, wasn't me speaking, it was the liquor. You know how vodka sometimes brings out the worst in me."

Boy did I ever. Nights we went out together drinking usually resulted in a fight over me not paying attention to her and questioning my relationship with other girls. For such a beautiful girl, Vera lacks confidence and is jealous beyond belief.

"You know what they say Vera? Drunk words reveal what sober thoughts conceal."

"What do you want me to say, Curtis?" She throws her hand out in question.

This is it, no backing out now.

"I want you to tell me why you are still with me, if you are so unhappy?"

"I am not unhappy." Her tone softens and I see a slight fear in her dark eyes.

"Really? You could have fooled me. Do you even remember the last time we were truly happy? I mean, how many fights have we had just in the last weeks since we got back together?"

"Those were just petty fights that ended in amazing make up sex that I never heard you complain about."

"Why are we together?" I ask the question that should have the simplest answer.

"What do you mean? What kind of question is that?" Vera's voice has started to get shaky and I think it is starting to sink it where this evening is headed. There will be no make up sex at the end of the night.

"Just answer the question. Shouldn't be too hard."

She pauses in thought and glances around the kitchen surrounding us.

"We're together because we fit. It's not like we are getting any younger and we were lucky to find each other when we did. This town isn't overflowing with desirable suitors. We are together because we are the same, you and I." An expression of satisfaction shone in her eyes, as she looked impressed with her response.

"You are wrong. We are not the same." I shake my head and meet her gaze. "For me, the reason I am with someone who I see a future with isn't because I am just settling for the best option." Her confidence deflates at my statement. "Don't worry, I knew that would be your answer. It's just not the right one."

"And that is?"

"Love. We should be together because we love each other. Because there isn't a day that goes by that we don't want to be near one another. The last time we broke up I should have missed you more. But the fact is, I enjoyed being able to come home after a long day of work and just relax on the couch. Not worrying about the latest argument or what I need to do in order to avoid setting you off. We aren't happy and I refuse to stay in a relationship for anything less than love. That is why it is best that we go our separate ways."

I watch as an array of emotions wash over Vera's face, tears filling her eyes as she fights hard to keep them at bay. It's the same show I have seen time and again with every break up. Only this time it will be permanent; no going back to the past with us.

"Come on, Curtis. Let's not get drastic here. This is just a silly fight."

"No, it's not. This is over, Vera. I am done."

"You're just upset, but you know I love you, baby. That's why I didn't say it before. I thought I was just obvious that we loved each other." She brings herself to stand directly in front of me, sliding her hands under my shirt and grazing my skin.

Grabbing her wrist, I remove her hands from my body and put space between us. "Don't start throwing around love now, because if we did love each other this wouldn't be so easy for me."

Vera's features harden and her black eyes convey the fury within. "Why is this so easy for you? Is there someone else? Of course there is. Who is she? How long has this been going on?" The questions continue to come at me as Vera rushes through the emotional stages of the break up – denial, bargaining, and straight to anger.

"There is no one else. This relationship is bringing us both down and it will be better in the end, you will see." I keep my voice calm, not letting my frustration get the best of me, which will only set Vera off even more.

"You are a liar. I will find out who this bitch is and I will destroy her. She messed with the wrong girl. Thinking she could take my man. You will regret this decision, I promise you that."

Giving me one last cold look, Vera stomps out the house, slamming the door on her way out. She didn't even attempt to take any of her belongings that have collected here over time, leading me to believe that I haven't seen or heard the last of Vera Malone.

I finish the last of my water and toss the bottle in the trash, before locking the house up. I spend twenty minutes in the shower just standing under the hot water as it pelts down on me. With a huge weight lifted off my shoulders I relax in my bed and hope for a good night's sleep. I try to place the thoughts of what I can expect from Vera and what lengths she is willing to go with the reminder that Jill and Hannah would be back home soon.

Before I know it, my mind wanders to blonde hair and hazel eyes, thinking of the girl with a beautiful smile and heavenly laugh. I am thankful for the distance from Daphne in the next week or so. The last thing I need is for Vera to speculate there is something going on and bring her drama to Daphne. I don't know what Vera is capable of, but I would rather not take any chances.

Daphne

6

Increasing my pace as my favorite song radiates through my headphones, I turn the corner to my street and sprint towards my neighborhood. My morning jogs have become less of a hassle now that I am finally getting back into shape.

After the breakup, I took a brief hiatus from running in an attempt to stay out of my own head. It used to be that running was the only way for me to clear my thoughts and release stress, but after Grams passing and leaving Nathan, I found that the solitude left too much room for my maze of thoughts to run wild. It wasn't until a few weeks ago, when I moved here, that I attempted my morning runs again.

Now, they usually just stir around while I lay my head down at night. But, with a little wine and a good book, I am able to push the thoughts aside. Time is passing and with each new day, my heart and mind are finding a better line of communication.

The Tea Room has been flourishing and it is a relief things are going well and I have yet to tarnish Grams' name. In fact, Hilda made a comment that she hadn't seen quite a summer rush in many years. Summertime in Truesdale is typically quiet, as most folks take their families on vacations. This summer, however, we are experiencing a high number of out of town guests who are very interested in experiencing local staples, such as The Treasured Tea Cup.

When Grams passed, they featured the Tea Room in a newspaper article that spoke about her kindness and impact on the community and they also mentioned her passing on the legacy to me. It was a sweet and heartwarming piece that is most likely contributing to the influx of guests.

Anticipating the slower pace of a typical summer, I was excited to get the minor renovations in progress so that we would be ready for fall, our busiest time of year. But, the people keep coming and it's been a little difficult to have workers banging and clanging in what is supposed to be a relaxing and serene environment.

With much hesitation, I called Curtis last week and postponed the renovations until today. It was not an easy decision and one that I regretted the minute I hung up the phone. It was easy to say that I was excited to get the renovations done, but there is also a gaping part of me that was really looking forward to seeing him again. The buzz of his touch has finally worn off, but he still manages to consume my thoughts. My body is craving his touch and my head is curious to see if the electricity will return.

Turning into my neighborhood, the smile that resides on my face quickly fades as the next song on my playlists triggers another thought, or rather, another face. This song was practically written for Nathan and I. The words describe our uphill climb to our relationship and lead right into the crashing end of it.

I slow my pace in an attempt to cool down for the remainder of my walk home. With my mood a little heavier than the previous few minutes, I hang my head and focus on the pavement ahead while letting the melody ring loudly in my ear.

"Ah! What the-" Screeching and ripping my ear bud from my left ear, I turn quickly and am greeted by a friendly chocolate lab who had just been sniffing my backside.

"Oh my gosh! Gus! I am so very sorry. He ran out of the house before I could put his leash on. Some mornings he is just too quick for my pre-caffeinated self to handle."

The young woman, barely over five feet reached down and clipped the leash to the puppy's collar, quickly planting herself into the ground to keep from being pulled away. With a small but athletic build, she made it seem easy to control the large puppy, who was half her size.

"Hi, I'm Daphne. I just moved here a few weeks ago." I held out my hand and she met my grip while still keeping Gus at bay.

"So, you already met Gus, and I'm Katie. I live right over there around the corner." She pointed back behind her and then quickly put her second hand back on the leash to pull Gus back from jolting after another neighborhood jogger. "Gus! Relax. I am dog sitting for my neighbor."

"It's nice to meet you both. I live down Second Lane over that way."

"Oh, those are nice over there. So, you're new to town? How do you like it so far?" she asked.

"Well, technically, I'm not super new. I was born here, but left when I was eight. My grandparents have lived here forever, so I have visited many times. But, I do love it here. I inherited my grandmother's tea room and moved back to take care of it."

"The Treasured Tea Cup! Duh, I should have known. With a name like Daphne, there can't be too many of you around. Some of the ladies at the school were planning an afternoon tea and mentioned the article from the paper. So sorry about your loss." Her smile filled eyes, were instantly saddened but it was something I was getting used to around here.

"Thank you. It was very hard at first, leaving everything behind, but I am really starting to think this could be home for good. So, are you a teacher?"

"Yes, I teach fourth grade at Truesdale Elementary and just finished with my summer in-services. Only a few more weeks and it's back to the grind."

"Oh, I used to love my summers off. I taught third grade when I lived in Garrison. I'm really going to miss it."

"Really, that's awesome. And, you can substitute for me anytime you feel like it." She let out a giggle and a smile filled my face.

Katie was a genuine soul and I can sense an instant friendship. She has the potential to be my first good friend here in town and lucky for me, she only lives a few blocks away.

"Katie, it was so very nice to meet you. I got to run, but would love to hang out sometime, maybe dinner or coffee?"

"Sounds good to me. Here, give me your phone and I'll add my number. I've lived here my whole life, so if you have any questions or need any help just give me a shout. Like I said, it's the summer, so I am free as a bird for a few more weeks. Let me know if you want to grab dinner sometime." She quickly types her number and hands me back my phone.

"Will do, take it easy. Bye Gus, keep that nose clean buddy." We both laugh and wave goodbye as I place the ear bud back into my ear and head home.

With the hours I have been putting in at the Tea Room, I haven't really had time to make any new friends. Katie seems sweet and I look forward to getting to know her. Every girl needs a best friend, or at least someone to talk to. Hilda is great, but not the wine drinking, trash talking kind of best gal pal I am looking for.

Noticing the time on my phone as I close my music application, flurries of butterflies begin to swim in my belly. Curtis is going to meet me at eight-thirty to get a head start on the work for the day so he can be at a good stopping point by eleven when the Tea Room opens.

This only leaves me thirty minutes to get ready and I will need every second of it today. The nerves of a teenager on the first day of high school pang though my body as I run the curling iron through my long blonde hair.

With the last curl complete, I flip my head over, spray a light mist of hairspray and flip it back to tussle the curls with my fingers. With a loose hair band, I pull it to a side pony draping the curls into place over my left shoulder and finish my make up.

Picking up my lavender and melon sundress from the end of my bed, I slip it over my head and tighten the ribbon around my waist. With a final look in the mirror, I grab my coffee and head out the door.

Traffic is mild and with only a moment to spare I arrive just before Curtis, in enough time to give one last touch up in the mirror.

This also gives me a chance to look myself in the eyes and realize how ridiculous I am behaving. He is here to work, not pick up a date. Plus, he probably has a girlfriend and who is to say I am even ready to date in the first place?

Pesky, annoying, overbearing thoughts.

Pulling myself together, I stroll calmly to the front door and begin to unlock it. A clean masculine smell invades my senses just as his footsteps sound on the wooden deck. Struggling briefly with the lock, slightly distracted, it finally twists right and the creaking of the door is the only noise that could cover the beating in my chest.

"Good morning, Curtis," I quietly utter as I turn to welcome him inside.

"Good morning, Daphne." His gruff morning voice resonates in my chest and sends a chill to my toes. "I just need to take a few measurements and then I'll set my stuff up out back."

"Sure thing. I will go ahead and unlock the back door and you can head in when you are ready. Would you like some tea?" I ask, with my voice sounding much calmer than my nerves.

"That sounds great. Thank you."

"Any particular flavor?" I ask.

"Nah, you can surprise me. I trust you." He smiles and heads into the Fountain of Youth Room.

This is one of our many themed rooms and has a large fountain in the corner that was built into the wall by my grandfather. Over the years, Papa normally took care of the upkeep, but with Grams being sick and with his age increasing, it has been slightly neglected. Unfortunately, without the running fountain, the room has lost its charm.

Curtis has plans to re-plaster the surrounding wall, seal the edges and apply a fresh coat of paint. His draft of the final appearance is breathtaking and I can see why his father would be proud to pass him the business. The detail of his work is impeccable and I have no doubt this fountain will look the best it has in years.

Sweeping around the kitchen, I pop a fresh batch of scones into the oven and steep a teapot with one of my favorite blends, chai vanilla spice. And if my senses are correct, this should go perfectly with the cinnamon-apple scones I have finally perfected.

Preparing a few other items for the day's menu, I continue my work on the kitchen while the tea finishes steeping. Grabbing a regular glass from the cupboard, I pour in the tea and walk it across the hall.

"Here you go. Chai vanilla spice. I thought I should just bring it in a regular cup since I didn't image you would like to sip from a vintage tea cup while hammering away at this old thing."

The smile that reaches his cheeks could melt the glaciers.

"This is true, probably not a good look for me. Thank you, I'm sure it's delicious." He lifts his cup to his lips as I blurt out my warning a second too late.

"Wait! It's-"

"Hot! Yep, should have guessed." Curtis wipes his mouth as a drop of tea slides down his chin.

I sure wouldn't mind licking that off his scruffy face.

"I'm so sorry. I should have told you sooner. Let me get a napkin."

"I'm fine, really. No worries. See, all clean." He wipes his mouth one more time and lifts his head proudly with a wide smile.

I am pretty sure Florida is now covered in water and I found the real reason for global warming.

Afraid he could read my thoughts, I turn my face toward the fountain to calm my nerves.

"Okay, so it looks like you have your work cut out for you. Please let me know if you need anything at all. I will be in the kitchen for a bit and then in the lobby setting up a new display." With a quick glance his way, I nod my head and turn to leave the room.

Well, I tried to leave the room.

Stepping back to pivot and turn, my foot lands on something and my balance is lost, as I nearly plummet to my death by embarrassment. A rough hand grips my wrist as another sweeps behind my back and pulls me back onto two feet.

"Whoa, you okay?" Curtis just saved my butt, literally, and all I can think about is the electric current coursing through my body.

"Uh, yes. I'm fine. Thank you for catching me. Probably should watch where I step while in a construction zone." Trying to make light of the situation, I search his face wondering if he feels it too.

"So sorry about that. I'll, uh, try to be more careful about leaving things lying around." His smile is lessened but the light in his eyes was brighter. "I'll let you know if I need anything. Thanks again."

I simply return his words with a nod and carefully head back to the kitchen, ready to distract myself with some baked goods. The last shock I felt from Curtis lasted for days, and it was only a simple hand graze. This one, however, I'm not sure will ever go away.

I could really use a best friend right now. All this nonsense, electric feel, palpating heart stuff needs advice. Pulling out my phone, I browse for Katie's name but quickly lock the screen thinking it may be too soon. I would hate to scare her off right away. I mean, we did just meet this morning.

Sipping my tea, I take a few deep breaths and calm myself down. I am nearly thirty years old and should be able to handle a simple crush. Lord knows I have had my fair share over the years.

With the first few batches of scones ready, and the soup simmering, I finalize the menu board and head into the lobby to set it up. It's been almost two hours and Curtis has been hard at work and I have been trying to stay out of his way and not bother him. My anxiety about the fountain is getting the best of me, so I decide to casually stop in with a scone and check out the progress.

Walking into the room, disappointment fills my heart as I notice the big tarp that is covering the corner and the fountain is out of view. Along with Curtis.

"Curtis? You in here?" I tip toe over, hoping to sneak a peek.

"Hey there, no looking. I don't want you to see until it's all finished." Walking in from outside, I turn to see his smirk filled face and my eyes drift to his chest.

The white t-shirt is clinging tighter than it was this morning and a light mist of sweat glistens on his skin. His hair is messy but seems perfectly in place and my fingers tighten into a fist to avoid reaching to run through it. My words are lost for a moment before I realize he spoke again.

"Trust me. It will be worth it." His voice is coated with flirtation and I decide to try my hand and play along.

"Really? Not even just a little look?"

"Not a chance. Bribery?" He points at the scone in my hand and his smile widens.

"Will it work?" I fake a cheesy smile and he lets out a deep laugh.

"Depends on how good it tastes." The desire is now apparent in his darkened eyes.

"Trust me. It will be worth it." Repeating his words, I raise a smirk on my lips.

"I'm sure it will be. But I really can't let you look, you might get nervous and I want you to be surprised. So, as good as I am sure it is, I do not except your bribe. So sorry." He shakes his head in regret, but the corners of his mouth upturn slightly.

"Oh geez. Fine. Have it anyway. It wasn't actually a bribe to begin with, I just wanted you to taste my perfected recipe." I hand him the scone on a napkin.

He lifts it to his nose and inhales deeply.

"Cinnamon-apple, right?"

"Yes, sir."

He takes a generous bite and chews twice before his eyes grow large and he starts nodding his head in approval.

"You were right. The first attempt was not perfect, but these, wow. " His sincerity is apparent.

"Yay! I worked so hard on this recipe and it is finally perfect!"

"Delicious, really. Might be my new favorite."

"Thank you. Now, back to work. I got more to make and you got a fountain to wow me with."

"Yes, ma'am."

Leaving the room, I feel the smile plastered to my face and try to tone it down before entering the lobby. The door just creaked open and it would most likely be Hilda arriving for her shift. I would hate for her to start asking questions about Curtis and I. I'm not sure I would even know where to start.

The rest of the morning goes by quickly and I am nearly finished with the new display of teapots that came in for the fall collection. Hilda wisps around humming to herself and stops over to view my work.

"Well, what do you think?" I ask.

"It's stunning dear. The lighting in this corner is perfect for the display and will really showcase the collection. I say, you really do have a knack for this, don't you?" She wraps her arms around my shoulders and embraces me for a quick hug.

"Thanks, Hilda. I couldn't do it without you."

She smiles and releases me, heading back to her desk area.

"Oh yeah, I almost forgot, this package came for you earlier." She lifts a box from behind the counter and sets it up top for me.

Walking over to admire the large box, the contents of what it could be slip my mind.

"Lights, Camera, Action? What on Earth did I order?"

"Hmm. You probably should cut back on the wine while shopping online." She giggles at her own rhyme.

"Oh wait! I remember, it's the lamp for my side table."

"I don't know why you like that online shopping stuff anyways. I prefer to hold it in my hands and see it in real life before I buy."

"But, you just can't always find the same deals in the store. The prices can be super low online. Now if only my entertainment center were in the right place, I could finish the artwork for the walls and have one completed room."

"Still haven't moved that thing yet?"

"With what army? The moving guys had a hard enough time with it, how would I even move that thing alone?"

My new entertainment center is a beast. The movers got it in and in the place I suggested, however, I had not realized that the cords are in the wrong place and it needs to be moved by about two feet to the left. You would think I could just push it myself, but trust me this thing is going nowhere fast. The TV is able to be plugged in, but my other electronics just don't reach. I really could use a good chick flick, but my DVD player is one of those items.

"Ahem. Hey there, sorry to interrupt. Daphne, I'm all set for today."

"Oh hey. Okay. Sounds good. You coming back tomorrow?"

"Yes ma'am. Same time?"

"Sounds good. Here, let me walk you out back, I saved you a few scones for your hard work today."

Curtis smiles and nods toward Hilda.

"Have a good afternoon, Miss Hilda."

"Take care, Mr. Dean."

Following me towards the back door, Curtis talks in a lowered voice. "You don't have to give me scones. I would be glad to pay for them."

"Not a chance. You work your butt off for me and I appreciate you coming in early to accommodate the Tea Room hours."

"It's no problem." He pauses for a moment as we reach the back door, then continues, "The fountain is still covered, so I am trusting you not to peek. I'll be back in the morning and you should have a finished fountain by tomorrow afternoon."

"It's a deal. And I promise I won't peek. I kind of like surprises." Holding out the box of scones, he reaches for them and is careful not to touch my hand.

"Oh yeah, and one more thing. I wasn't eavesdropping but I did happen to over hear that you may need some help moving something at your place."

"Oh lord. The beast. I mean my entertainment center. It only needs to be moved a few feet, but it's not a huge deal."

"Well, if you would like some help, I would be more than happy to come take care of that for you."

My initial thought, is hell no. I have a hard enough time being around him in a professional manner, much less in my home on a personal level. But, lack of communication heart to mind made a different choice.

"Really? That would be amazing, I mean, if you don't mind. I just don't know anyone else and would greatly appreciate it. I would pay you of course."

What have I done? Was this a good idea?

"Yeah, I would be glad to help. How about Thursday evening? I can come by around seven. And really, no need to pay me. This one I can do as your friend. Plus, you pay me enough in scones." He lifts the box and winks.

"Seven sounds great. Thank you, Curtis, I really appreciate it."

"Yes ma'am. See you tomorrow morning."

"Take care."

Closing the door and locking it behind me, I would love nothing more than to slide down it and melt to the floor.

Curtis

7

"So you still haven't heard from Vera?" Ma asks, sitting on the couch across from me in their living room.

Most Wednesday nights you will find me at my folks' house for family dinner. It is our one guaranteed day to catch up with one another and I get blessed with Ma's home cooking.

"No, which is surprising knowing her. Hopefully she has realized that we aren't going to work out." As I glance around the living room in my childhood home, I take note at how not much has changed over the years. You can still find school pictures of Jill and me decorating the walls.

"You know, I never did see you two together. There always seemed to be something . . . off."

I return my gaze towards Ma and let out a laugh. "Why didn't you ever mention anything?"

Ma was never anything but kind and welcoming whenever Vera was around. We never spoke much about any of my relationships, but it still comes as a shock to hear this opinion from her.

"That's not something a man needs his mother to point out. I knew you would figure it out yourself, eventually. Although, I didn't think it would take you this long." Narrowing her eyes, she gives me what we always call the 'mom look'. "So, what was it that sealed the deal for you this time?"

The first thought that crossed my mind is Daphne. Memories of our encounter earlier today and the anticipation of going by her house tomorrow have kept her close. I felt no guilt when I shamelessly flirted with her at the Tea Room or when I offered up my services to help move her furniture. But as much as Daphne has been in my thoughts since our first meeting, she is not the reason for the ending of my relationship with Vera.

"I stopped missing her," I explain. "Since we had gotten back together this last time, something changed within me. I kept waiting for the feelings I once had to return, but they never did."

There was a time when I couldn't wait for the workday to be over so I could rush home to see Vera. She was constantly on my mind when we were apart. Lately, working late nights became a saving grace because it enabled me to avoid spending time with her. It wasn't fair to either one of us to stay together when I didn't feel the same about her.

"You have to do what is best for you, Curtis," Ma says with understanding etched visibly on her face. "I just want my kids to be happy."

"I know, Ma."

"And more grandbabies wouldn't hurt either."

I shift uncomfortably in the chair and let out a nervous laugh. "You need to talk to Jilly about that." My sister gave Ma and Pop the greatest gift when she made them grandparents, and since then they have been itching for more.

"Speaking of, did she mention anything going on with her the last time you spoke?" I watch as she slides her pendant back and forth across her gold chain, something I have observed her doing over the years when she is nervous or worried.

"No, we just talked about their upcoming visit and Hannah's birthday. I almost have her dollhouse complete and all that is left now is painting." I came up with the idea of building Hannah her very own custom dollhouse. When I approached Jill about it, I swear I heard tears in her voice.

"Why, is something going on?" I ask, now worried that I may have missed something in our conversation.

"No, no. You know me, always worrying about my babies. She sounded a little off when she called last night, but I am sure it was nothing." I can tell by the look on Ma's face that she is still worried about Jill.

"She was probably just stressing over getting everything ready for the party. I imagine it's not easy planning a party so far away. You know she would tell us if something was wrong," I reassure Ma, but make a note in my mind to pay better attention next time we speak to see if I notice anything.

The sound of the back door closing echoes through the house before I hear the water running in the kitchen, signaling that Pop must have come inside.

"You're right. I don't think I will ever adjust to not having her right here. The thought of something happening to them and knowing I would have a good eight hour drive ahead of me before I could reach them... well it just kills me," she says, the pain evident in her tone.

"Ma . . ." I start.

"I didn't realize you were already here, son. How is business?" Pop asks, taking a seat next to Ma on the couch.

"Same as it was when I spoke with you yesterday." Almost daily he will call me and ask the same question over and over again and my answer rarely ever changes.

"Right, right. Listen, I know you mentioned how busy the crews have been, so why don't you let me come help out."

"Pop, you are retired. You do know the meaning of retirement, right?" I ask, as Ma glares at Pop as though he has lost his mind.

"Of course I do. You don't need to pay me. I just need to get out of this house. I am going stir crazy. I knew I retired too early." Pop doesn't have the last word out of his mouth before Ma smacks him upside the head. "Ouch! What the hell, woman? What was that for?"

"You will do no such thing, Walter. We finally got your blood pressure regulated. You want something to do? Help me tend to the garden or build something in your shed. Heck, get a couple guys together and go fishing. I don't care what you do, but you will *not* be going back to work."

"Yes ma'am," Pop responds with his head lowered.

A chuckle escapes me and Ma turns her hard glare to me.

"And so help me, Curtis Walter Dean, if I hear you allowed your father back on a job, I will tan your hide. Do you understand me?"

I lower my head, much like Pop had. "Yes, ma'am."

"Good. Now that we have that cleared up, let's go eat supper." Standing from the couch, Ma walks to the kitchen and Pop and I jump to follow.

"All of these vegetables came from your garden?" I ask, after finishing the last bite on my plate, one step away from licking it clean.

"Yes, this has been a good season. I have an abundance of cucumbers and squash this summer."

"Way more than we could ever consume," Pop says. "And your mother wants to expand the garden after this season."

"Why don't you go up to the farmers market and set up a table to sell them?" With the size of vegetables that her garden is producing she could make a killing in one weekend alone.

"I'm not interested in selling them. Gardening is just a hobby that I have always loved and this year we have been blessed. I was actually thinking about reaching out to local restaurants and donating our extras. I hate to see any of these vegetables go to waste."

"That's a good idea. In fact, I bet Daphne would love some."

And I would be happy to deliver them for you.

"Daphne, as in Mitch and Kay's granddaughter?" Ma asks and I nod. "That would be perfect. Kay used to always tell me that my squash made the best soup. Are you and Daphne close? How is she settling in?"

"We met her first day here while I was finishing up work at the Tea Room that I had started for Miss Kay. Since then, I have scheduled a few other repairs for her to update the place. She seems to be settling in well, as far as I can tell. If you would like, I could ask her when I see her next if she would be interested in the veggies."

I finished the work on the fountain earlier today and the look of amazement on her face made my day. Tomorrow night, I could bring it up while I am at her house, since I won't doing any work at the Tea Room. I don't mention to Ma that I am going to help her, knowing she would read way too far into the situation and make too much out of it.

"That would be great. I have been meaning to get down there and check on her. It has been a few years since I have seen her, besides the funeral services. Kay was always bragging about her grandkids and sweet Daphne has grown to look so much like her mother." Ma takes a moment to reflect on something in her head before a smile appears, lighting her face up. "You know, I heard from Sally down at the beauty salon that Daphne is single. She is such a pretty girl, I imagine it won't be long before some lucky guy swoops her up."

Pop laughs, reaching over and placing his hand over Ma's on the table. "Why do you think our son refuses to let anyone else complete the work at the Tea Room?"

"That's not why, Pop," I say, taking a sip of my sweet tea. "It was the same with Miss Kay. I always worked those jobs myself."

Miss Kay always knew that no matter the size of the problem, she was to call me first. I would go out and inspect the issue and the majority of the time was able to fix it myself. Some of the smaller issues, like when her bathroom sink was leaking and it took me all of five minutes to tighten the valve, I would even refuse to bill her. Those were the times when I accepted food as payment. I have done plenty of work over the years from Mitch as well, which I did on my own.

"So have you asked her out yet?" Ma asks, practically bouncing with excitement.

Standing from my chair, I scoot it under the table and place my napkin on my empty plate. "Dinner was delicious as usual. I love you and will talk to you both later."

"Love you too," Ma tells me as Pop laughs his ass off at my discomfort.

Once she gets an idea in her head she becomes relentless and I could see her wheels turning at the thought of me having an interest in Daphne Fields. The last thing I need is my mother trying to play Cupid. She did that once when I was in high school and set me up with the daughter of a lady in her book club. It is semi-cute when you are sixteen, but completely out of line when you are a grown ass man.

The day has flown by unexpectedly today. All of the jobs are running smoothly and I wasn't needed on any other sites, which gave me time to get some much-needed paperwork done. This is the part of ownership that gets tedious and Pop refused to ever hire a secretary or bookkeeper. Nights when I worked late were typically because I was stuck finishing up the day's paperwork.

Daphne sent a short text about midday to confirm that I was still able to swing by tonight at seven to help her. I have been looking forward to closing time all day, so I could run home and shower before heading to Daphne's. The address she sent me was in a neighborhood I was familiar with and should only take me a few minutes to drive there.

After a quick shower I throw on jeans and a dark gray t-shirt, but when I look at my reflection in the mirror I almost feel too casual, so pulling a button up shirt from my closet, I roll the sleeves up to my elbow. Inspecting myself one last time in the mirror, I exit my house before changing my mind.

Walking up to the door, I feel an instant nervousness that I remember experiencing when I picked up my date for prom seventeen years ago. Giving myself a quick pep talk, I keep repeating in my head that I am only here to move an entertainment center. It shouldn't matter what I am wearing or that I sprayed my favorite cologne before leaving. It shouldn't take all of my strength to reach up and press the button for her doorbell, and my palm sure as hell shouldn't be sweating.

The door opens and Daphne stands in tight ripped jeans that fit her like a second layer of skin and a purple shirt with a deep V-neck, showing just a tease of cleavage. Her hair was down for the first time and fell in loose golden waves past her shoulders. My eyes swept up and down her body, watching as a blush spread to her cheeks and down her chest.

This is new. I think to myself. Or maybe it's the fact that this is the first time her chest has been visible.

"Hi. Thank you for coming," Daphne says, opening the door wider, allowing me to enter.

As I scan the open living room area, my eyes fall upon the entertainment center. It's no wonder she couldn't move it alone. I feel sorry for the guys who we in charge of putting it together.

"This must be the beast?" I ask pointing towards the monstrosity.

"That would be it. I didn't account for cords needing to reach the plug before telling to guys where to set it up. It is only off by a couple feet but the carpet makes it a little resistant to sliding."

"I can imagine. It must way a ton." I laugh. Even with the shelving bare, just the solid wood alone is heavy enough.

"I bought these slider things from the store the other day, but I couldn't lift the side up by myself to insert them underneath."

"You shouldn't have been trying to lift this alone anyways. You could have seriously hurt yourself. Next time call someone." My tone is harder than I intended, but my mind is playing all the things that could have gone wrong.

"I didn't have anyone to call," Daphne says, her eyes cast down. "Papa is too old to be lifting and moving something like this and I would never call my landlord over something so minor."

Stepping closer, bringing my body mere inches from hers, I press my thumb under her chin and lift until our eyes meet. For a moment I am lost noting the different colors mixed in her hazel eyes: browns, greens, grays, and yellows.

"Next time, you call me. For anything."

Daphne nods her head softly, never breaking the contact we share. My breaths deepen and my eyes move down to her parted lips. Stopping myself from moving for the kiss I crave, I step away and take the sliders from her hands.

With my back to Daphne, I walk to the entertainment center, running a hand through my hair. In that moment I could have sworn she wanted me to kiss her just as much as I wanted to. But something deep in my brain told me she wasn't ready and I stopped myself.

"I'm going to lift the sides up and I will need you to slide these under the corners. Can you do that?" I ask, glancing back where Daphne stood frozen in place.

With an abrupt nod of her head, she looks up as if just noticing I moved across the room.

"Yeah, I can do that. No problem."

When she gets to where I am standing by the beast, I pass the sliders back to her and she drops to her knees at the first corner. Now I am the one frozen in place. Staring down at Daphne on her knees while she looks up at me with her eyes wide in expectation, I feel myself harden in my jeans.

Daphne's gaze drops to below my waist, as if she is about to read my thoughts and then drops her eyes to the floor. I need to get this moved and go home to take a cold shower.

Finding the best sections to hold onto, I lift the side up first, allowing enough room for Daphne to place the rectangular slider underneath. Without a word to one another, we continue the process until all the sliders are placed in all the corners.

"What do you need me to do now?" she asks, standing from the floor.

Ignoring the loaded question, I answer the simplest way. "I am going to push it down, I just need you tell me when to stop."

"Okay."

Once we have the entertainment center where Daphne wants it, we work the same routine to remove the sliders. I keep my mind on the task at hand to avoid trailing off into forbidden territory.

Now the couch is off center from where the television sits, so I offer to help rearrange the rest of the living area. I know if I don't get it done tonight she will attempt to do it herself and possibly end up with an injury.

The coffee table is the last piece we move and like every other piece in the room its solid wood and heavy. We set it down in front of the couch and as Daphne steps back to admire the new locations, she trips over her feet and falls to the ground.

"Are you okay?" I ask, rushing to her aid.

She holds a hand to her stomach, the fall causing her top to rise up, exposing tanned skin. I am unable to tell for sure whether the noise coming from her is a laugh or cry. It looked like it could have been a hard fall.

When I reach Daphne, I squat down and pull the hand away that's covering her red face. Her smile and laugh washes away the worry and I laugh with her. At least I know she isn't seriously injured.

"Leave it to me to trip over my own feet," she says between breaths.

"You definitely made the fall look more graceful than I ever could have. You all right?" I ask again.

"Yeah, just a little embarrassed."

As I look down at her, out of breath and flush, I lose all control. Standing up, I reach my hand out and Daphne places hers inside mine. With a tight grip I pull her up and into my arms, her hands resting on my chest. My left arm is wrapped around her waist as I bring my right hand up to cradle her jaw. My gaze falls to her chest, admiring the rise and fall, as my need for her becomes unbearable.

I lower my face, pressing my lips against her soft mouth. She parts her full lips and I trace my tongue against her bottom one before claiming her mouth with my own. Daphne's hands glide over my shoulders and into my hair, tugging lightly. She returns the kiss with just as much reckless abandon and I know that it will change everything.

Daphne

8

T he masculine aroma of his aftershave invades my senses and reaches my core, causing me to deepen the unexpected connection of our mouths. Then there is the return of this crazy electric current and it starts to course through me as his soft lips and smooth, recently shaven face brushes against mine.

For a brief moment all thoughts have left my head, but that is short lived as my guilty conscience gains momentum, causing me to pull my arms from around his neck and break the contact of our lips.

Out of breath and drunk off his touch, I stumble backwards a few steps, crossing my arms over my chest and reach my right hand up to feel my swollen lips.

"I'm sorry, it's just…" I pause, searching for the words to explain that it's not his fault and that I still feel a connection to my ex. Who by the way, has only been my ex for a month.

Sensing my guilt and confusion, Curtis speaks in a low husky voice. "Don't apologize, I shouldn't have done that.

I'm sorry, I just..." he too pauses in the same place and struggles to continue his explanation. Running his hands through his hair, he looks to the ground for an answer and subtly shakes his head.

Returning his gaze to mine, a little smirk touches his lips as he continues, "I'm not sure what to say. I'm really sorry. I should go."

Curtis widens his smile, which reads that he is not upset with me and I am thankful. Unsure how to interpret the million thoughts and electric currents racing through my head, I simply nod and walk towards the front door.

He nods his head and I finally find the words that I need to say.

"Thank you, Curtis. You didn't have to come over and help me, but I really appreciate it." My gratitude is aimed towards his help with the furniture, but a part of me feels my heart may be aiming the words in an underlying direction towards the kiss.

"It was my pleasure. Again, sorry about, uh..." he clears his throat and continues, "I'll see you at work next week and will email you about the other projects on Sunday. Have a good night, Daphne."

He offers a warm smile and a handshake and I gladly accept them hoping we can get past this and be able to maintain our professional relationship. His work is impeccable and I would hate for him to feel uncomfortable at the Tea Room.

"Goodnight," I say.

As he turns to leave, I slowly close the door behind him and head straight to the kitchen.

Pouring a glass of wine, I replay the kiss in my head and swear I can feel his strong hand on the small of my back as he pulled me from the ground into his chest. My heavy hand lets the liquid nearly fill the tall glass before replacing the cork and bringing the bottle with me to the living room.

Turning on the TV, finally able to watch cable, I flip through the channels and stop on one of my favorite chic flicks, *Never Been Kissed*. With the glass to my lips and a long sip, a smile reaches my cheeks. What they really should call this movie, starring me, is *Never Been Kissed – Like That*.

Seriously. Never.

I try to recall a time in my past when a kiss made my toes curl up, or swirl that much desire coursing through every vein in my body. Surely, with Nathan, I would have had this at one point.

I think.

Sipping my wine, my mind jogs through thousands of memories trying to make sense of this kiss. While thinking of my relationship with Nathan, I begin to realize how fresh it sits in my heart. A little more than a month ago, I was planning to marry him and here I am making out with a stranger in my new living room and drinking wine like its water.

I refill my glass and refocus my attention on the television. Picking up my phone, I slowly scroll through my contacts wishing I had a girlfriend I could call and talk about this damn kiss with. Most all of my close friends are also close with Nathan, which there in turn leaves the option to call them completely out of the question.

Back to the glass it is.

Flipping onto my back, the blood rushes quickly to my head as I see the culprit on my nightstand. One empty bottle of wine and a lipstick stained glass sit shamelessly next to my alarm clock.

"Shit!"

It is nearly eight o'clock and I need to be at work in half an hour. Attempting to get out of bed, I roll off the edge and stand up straight. The blood is pounding against my skull and I head to the kitchen for much needed water and aspirin.

With hesitation and shame, I send a text to Hilda letting her know I am running late. It is not my style to be late and I hate every second of it. With a quick shower and light coat of make-up, I settle on an easy day dress and Mary Jane's. My coffee is almost finished brewing and if I'm lucky, I can still arrive before nine.

The drive is quiet during this hour of the day, however the thoughts in my head are as loud as they were last night. At a long stoplight, I pull out my phone and start a text to Curtis.

Me: Hey there. Again. So sorry about last night. I just got out of a seri-

The vibration in my hand sends me into panic mode as Nathan's name appears boldly on the screen, causing me to drop my phone down into the gap between the seat and the console.

"Just friggin' wonderful," I mutter to myself as I reach my slender arm down into the world's tiniest crevice to save my phone. The light turns green as my hand is still wedged in the seat and I decide to leave it be and not cause an accident this morning.

After parking in my spot, I am finally able to maneuver my hand to grasp my phone and pull it out. There is one missed call and a new text message from Nathan.

Nathan: Hey, just thinking about you. Hope all is well. Miss you.

Here's this nice guy, missing his ex and here I am kissing the next. What am I doing and why does it have to feel so good? The memory of Curtis' lips across mine as our tongues slow danced, causes me to squeeze my thighs and shiver, as a chill races over my body. It is a passion I can't deny and I am not sure I want to.

Opening my message inbox, I see the draft I started to send Curtis and decide it best to just delete it. Then, I look at Nathan's text message again and close out of it quickly. I will call him back this weekend and see how he is doing.

Finally making my way inside, I am apologetic to Hilda who seems to care less that I am half an hour late. I stay busy for most of the morning and manage to keep my thoughts clear of the two men who haunt me. Cleaning up in the lobby and seeing that it is a slower day than normal, I untie my apron and decide I am going to head home.

"Hey, Hilda. I think I am going to go. I have a bit of a headache and would like to get some rest. Hope you don't mind."

"Not at all, my dear. Things are slow and steady and I can have Carolyn lock up this afternoon. Go take care of yourself, you have been working your tush off."

"Thanks Hilda. I'll see you tomorrow."

I refill my travel mug with today's lemon blueberry iced tea, grab a scone and head home.

After a long nap and two bottles of water, I start to think I might be up for a jog to clear my head. Only about five minutes into the run, I decide what a terrible idea this was and slow my pace to a walk. I continue forward and keep to a brisk walk up the street about a mile.

On my way back home, I count my steps in an attempt to keep my thoughts free of flannel shirts and suits. With my head down, I see a familiar furry animal approach and I drop down to say hi to Gus.

"Hey buddy! On the loose again?" I look up and see Katie, my new neighborhood friend quickly approaching.

"Jesus, Gus. Get it together, will ya?" She re-attaches his leash and looks up to me. "Hey Daphne, so sorry about that! He is too damn quick sometimes."

Today she is dressed to work out and I imagine they were on their way out since she is not even slightly glistening with sweat.

"Oh, it's not a problem. It's nice to see you. How's your week been?" I ask, hoping she does not sense the

"Yeah, sounds great. What should I bring?" I try not to
MICHELLE LOUISE

desperation in my voice. I really could use small talk with a
woman my own age.

"Ugh. What a week. I had two bad dates, so I figure it's
probably a good time to stop picking up guys at the bar. It's
just so hard to find a good man in this town. Oh, maybe I
will try Internet dating. How about you, any lucky fish on
the hook?" she asks, and looks way too interested in my
dating life. It appears she maybe as desperate as me to find
a good friend in this town.

"Um, well, I just got out of a pretty serious relationship,
so I'm not really looking."

But, I did just kiss a sexy man in my living room last
night and want nothing more than to call him back over and
see where it was going before I stopped it.

That's what I want to say, but can't.

"Oh, I see. Yeah, that's tough, but you'll bounce back."
Her words are sincere and a genuine smile spreads to her
cheeks.

I return her smile and feel Gus brush aggressively past
my leg.

"Oh boy, I better get going before he rips out of this
leash. Hey, why don't you come over tomorrow and we can
have dinner and wine?" she asks casually as Gus pulls at
her arms.

"Yeah, sounds great. What should I bring?" I try not to
sound too excited, but I am really looking forward to some
girl time.

Gus jolts forwards and she calls back over her shoulder
as she walks away. "My house at seven, bring a bottle of

your favorite wine. I'll provide dinner, hope you like alfredo! Later, Daphne!"

"Sounds perfect, see you tomorrow!" I shout back and turn to walk home with a smile plastered to my face.

Locking up the door, I wave goodbye to Joshua, our afternoon prep cook, as we both head to our cars. Today was a seemingly smooth day at the Tea Room and I am thankful it is Friday. I do not plan to work the rest of the weekend, which will be a first for me since I arrived. Tomorrow I have plans to stop by to see Papa and need to get some chores and grocery shopping done. Then, I plan to do nothing. Just sit on my behind and catch up on some R&R.

I drift off in my thoughts of Curtis. Dean R&R now ringing a whole new picture in my head, a hammock on the beach, wrapped in Curtis' arms, enjoying his pure Dean Rest and Relaxation methods.

A honk from behind brings me back to the driver's seat and I turn onto my street.

After a quick shower, I slip into a summer maxi dress and grab a bottle of wine from the fridge. With such a small distance between our houses, I decide it is best not to drive and enjoy the summer night air as the sun settles behind the clouds.

With a dog like Gus around, there is really no need to even knock. Katie already has the door swinging open before I can switch hands to ring the bell.

"Yay! Glad you could make it. Here, let me get that for you." Her green eyes are illuminating with excitement.

"Oh, thanks. Me too. I could really use a good friend here in town. Wait, does that sound desperate?" I joke, knowing that she must understand.

"I totally get it. But not to worry, we are already neighbors and can just as well be good friends. Especially if you keep bringing me wine."

"I'm good with that. You cook and I'll pour. Got a corkscrew?"

"Why of course." She reaches into a drawer and hands me the corkscrew, then opens the cupboard and pulls down two glasses.

As she sweeps around the kitchen preparing dinner, I pour our glasses and place the bottle in the fridge.

Glancing around, I can see that her floor plan is almost exactly the same as mine. Her décor is slightly different as we have our own personal tastes, but for the most part, they are very similar.

We maintain a light conversation and ask each other the basic questions about family, work, and so forth. It is an easy flowing conversation and we have a lot in common. She has one brother who is a little older than she is and they grew up here in Truesdale. She doesn't talk much about her parents and I decide not to dredge it up.

"Paul is my best friend. He can be an idiot a lot of times, but he would do anything for me." She speaks of him highly and I can tell they are a lot like Derrick and me.

"Girl, you are preaching to the choir. My brother Derrick, my twin, can be so dumb sometimes, yet there is nothing that I wouldn't do for him and vice versa. He just needs to do a little growing up. He is super smart, but just doesn't know how to apply it." I shake my head in frustration, thinking about my brother. I need to make sure to call him this weekend.

"Oh, how cute. You guys are twins! How awesome is that? I always wanted to be a twin." She thinks about it for a moment then retracts her statement. "Then again, I am not too good with sharing and that would more than certainly cause an issue I presume."

"Yeah, you get really good at the whole sharing and matching thing. I'm just glad my parents didn't do the real matchy name thing like Carey and Mary, or Tyler and Skyler. Daphne and Derrick have the same letter, but are different and not too confusing."

She laughs at my matching names and raises her glass for a toast.

"Here's to a set of good names and a set of good brothers. We are very lucky ladies."

"Cheers to that. I look forward to meeting Paul and for you to meet Derrick." I tap her glass and we both finish the last sips of our wine.

The buzzer on the oven goes off and Katie pops up from her barstool and heads into the kitchen. Not two seconds later, the doorbell rings and then a knock wraps on the door.

"Need me to get it?" I ask, trying to be helpful.

"Do you mind? It's probably just Paul, he said he might be dropping by," she hollers from the kitchen.

"Sure thing," I reply and walk towards the entryway.

Opening the door, my gaze lands on a familiar pattern of flannel, but then follow it up the rest of his tall frame meeting his intense green eyes. His brow wrinkles and he reaches up to scratch at his scruffy chin.

"Hi, come in. Sorry, Katie is in the kitchen and asked me to get the door. I'm Daphne." I reach out my hand, waiting for him to clear the confusion from his face.

He drops his hand from his face and places it in mine. "It's a pleasure to meet you. I'm sorry, I just wasn't expecting such a beautiful woman to be answering my sister's door. She didn't mention she would be having company." His confusion melts into a pleased smile and I can sense he was turning on his charm.

I drop his hand and turn to walk back towards my barstool. He follows behind and turns into the kitchen on the other side of the bar.

"Katie, I'm a little disappointed I wasn't invited. You know I love alfredo."

"Sorry pal, it's a girls' night. But I'll save you some." She gives him a quick hug before punching him in the arm. "Which by the way, you still have my Tupperware from the last two times. You better bring those back or I won't cook for you anymore."

"Ouch, crazy. Okay, I'll bring them by tomorrow," he says, rubbing his arm for a second and grabs a beer from the fridge. He opens it up and takes a long sip before reaching into his pocket and pulling out a set of car keys. "Here you go, good as new."

"You're the best. I'm surprised there was any oil left in it to change. Thank you."

"No problem, just don't wait so long next time. It's dangerous and not good for the engine."

"I know, I know. I'm sorry. Really. It's just been a crazy summer," she replies.

"Alright, well you two enjoy your delicious dinner. I'm going to enjoy some hot wings and beer at the pub. It's guys' night." He throws up air quotes and I let out a little giggle along with Katie.

"Well, have fun with that. I'll call you tomorrow. Be safe and don't drink too much." She winks at him and turns to walk him out.

"It was nice to meet you," I say to him as Katie is practically pushing him out the door.

"You too. Have a good night. Don't let crazy here tell you anything bad about me." He turns his head in time to catch my smile and his widens in reaction. Then he winks, attempting to turn the charm up a notch.

I shake my head to myself, waiting for Katie to return. She never mentioned how strikingly handsome her brother is. Although, it makes sense seeing as how beautiful she is. They have a natural tan olive skin tone and both rock gorgeous green eyes. His eyelashes are dark and long and I am sure she is envious of them. Hers are nice too, but his will melt a snowman in winter. With looks like that, he really doesn't need all that charm.

I walk into the kitchen and grab the bottle of wine as Katie is returning. She starts plating our food as I refill our glasses and we sit down at the dining table.

The rest of our dinner is filled with laughter and stories of our silly brothers and their antics on getting women, particularly the ones where they find it okay to hit on all of our friends. The wine is flowing quickly and our cheeks are beginning to flush pink with a buzz.

Curtis

9

or the first time in a while, I had a slower day at work, allowing me time to focus on getting paperwork done in the office. Typically, I would be grateful for the change of pace, but today, without the distraction of work, all it did was give me time to obsess over my night with Daphne. Not only being in her house and touching her, but more importantly, kissing her. I can't even come up with the correct words to describe how kissing Daphne made me feel. I swear I can still taste her sweetness on my lips. Reliving that moment is the best part of my day, until I recall the look on her face after she pulled away – guilt and regret.

I very well could have ruined everything with that stupid stunt. What was I thinking? As much as I want to regret making that move, I don't. Plus, she kissed me back and that has to count for something. I attempted numerous times to shoot her a text today apologizing once again, for my behavior, but can't seem to hit the send button.

After spending the entire day with Daphne consuming my thoughts, I wanted a night off. Yet, here I am sitting at the bar with half a pitcher of beer gone and her still on my mind.

"Hey man," Paul says, from behind as he slaps my shoulder, "What's the score?" Grabbing the pitcher, he fills the empty mug that's been waiting for him.

"No one has scored yet. Took you long enough. Did you get lost?"

Taking a long pull from his beer he sets the mug down. "I had to swing by Katie's to drop her car off and pick up my truck."

"How is Katie?"

Paul and I went to school together and with Jill only being a couple years younger, she was often found running around with us. Katie, on the other hand, was seven years younger. For the longest time she was just this little girl with dark hair and bright green eyes, who followed us around. We spent so many years acting as the overprotective brothers, that even now, we forget she is a grown adult.

"She's good. I met a new friend of hers tonight, actually. A cute little blonde and I was tempted to bail on you and crash their girls' night."

Knowing Paul I do not doubt that he would have, but knowing his sister, I ask, "What happened? Did Katie kick you out?"

He laughs, taking another swig and motioning to the bartender for another pitcher. "Something like that. You know how she is about me when it comes to her friends. I am to stay clear, but we all know what happens when something is forbidden."

"With the way you go through women, it is no wonder Katie doesn't want you near her friends. You would kill any friendship she has."

Paul has left a nasty trail of heartbroken women throughout the years. Katie has every right to enforce the no-friends rule with Paul. After he hooked up with her dorm-mate when she was in college, Katie spent the rest of the semester listening to the girl pine and cry over him.

"Whoever this poor girl is, you better stay away."

"I know that up here," he says, tapping on his head, "but this guy," he gestures his hand towards his zipper, "has a mind of his own. And I am telling you, this girl is beautiful. She has that whole sweet and innocent thing going for her and a tight little body to boot."

It never takes much to grab Paul's attention and I couldn't even tell you that he has a specific type. He just loves women in general.

"Did you catch her name or were you too busy drooling?"

"Of course I got her name," he says, in offense.

I stare at him for a beat, waiting for the name. "And?"

He lifts his hand and rubs his jaw for a moment, "Uhh, it started with a D. Daisy? No, that doesn't sound right."

I start to laugh but stop short when a sobering thought hits me. "It wasn't Daphne, was it?"

"Yes! That's it!" Paul exclaims, slapping his hand down on the bar. "You know her?"

Of course, it had to be Daphne. She has been on my mind so much lately that I should have just automatically known it was her that Paul met. She is new in town and lives in the same development as Katie.

"She took over at The Treasured Tea Cup and I have been doing some work over there for her."

"Son of a bitch," Paul mutters, shaking his head.

"What?"

"You like her?"

"What are you talking about?" I ask while refilling my mug.

"I could tell by the look on your face while you were talking about her. You had this little twinkle in your eyes." Paul wipes a non-existent tear from his cheek.

"What the . . ."

Laughing, Paul slaps my back. "I'm just screwing with you. But I did hear from Rick that you have been spending quite some time over there."

"Yeah, working."

"Hey, no need to get defensive. Don't worry I will back off, but only because I hope she can keep your dumbass from getting back with Vera. Are you finally done with that crazy bitch?"

I ask the bartender for a round of shots before filling Paul in on the latest Vera drama. He was there the first time I met her and has seen the change in her over the years.

When Vera and I started to fight a lot, he began to question why I stayed with her. I suppose I thought one day the vibrant bubbly girl I met would return.

"I don't fully understand why she was so adamant about continuing on with our relationship when all she did was complain about how unhappy she was. I told her this time I was done. And I am serious about it."

"Yeah, right. I have heard that one before." Paul laughs, referring to all the times we have broken up and I claimed to be done.

"I told her I didn't love her."

Paul's eyes snap to up mine and he responds once he sees there is no trace of humor in my statement.

"Ouch. Damn man, that's harsh."

"I know, but what else was I supposed to do? She wasn't grasping anything I was saying and sometimes you just have to give it to them straight, I guess." Taking a long sip, I wonder if I had been too hard on Vera that night, but there was no going back now. "It's permanent this time around. Once she picks up her things from my house I will be officially wiping my hands clean of her."

"Oh shit. She still has stuff at your house?" Paul asks and laughs as I give him a quick nod. "She is not done with you then, so good luck with that."

Noticing the stress taking over my face, Paul flags the bartender down and orders another round of shots. Tomorrow, I need to pack up all of her belongings and drop them off somewhere neutral, like maybe her job.

"Enough of that, let's discuss what is going on with you and Daphne."

Picking up the glass of amber liquid, I nod my head and toss it back, welcoming the burn that follows.

Before I can respond, Paul's phone starts blaring sounds of an obnoxious hyena laugh. The ringtone he uses for his sister.

Swiping the screen to answer, Paul presses the icon for speakerphone and holds it up between us.

"Hey, favorite brother of mine." Katie's overly sweet tone comes through the speaker.

"You know that's a terrible way to suck up when I have no other competition. What do you want, little girl?"

Paul and Katie have always had a close bond. From a very young age Paul has basically raised her himself. They didn't grow up in a loving home like Jill and I, but they never allowed it hold them back from anything.

Katie giggles and the sound is followed by a laugh that I could never forget, which means they are still together.

"We are out of wine and were hoping you would be the extremely loving brother that I know you are and bring us some more."

"I don't know. I remember a few hours ago being told I was not allowed to be there due to a certain girls' night." Paul smiles, always enjoying teasing his sister.

Katie moans and the line goes quiet for a moment before a sweet voice flows through the speaker and hits me directly.

106

"Paul, Katie didn't mean that earlier. We are in desperate need of more wine and are unable to drive. Please?"

I don't hear Paul's response, as I am too busy waving the bartender over so I can get two bottles of Katie's favorite wine and a bottle of whiskey for Paul and me.

After signing the receipt and properly tipping for the great, fast services, I shove the credit card back in my wallet and finish off the last of my beer. Turning to Paul, he is barely controlling his laughter.

"Someone a little anxious?" he asks.

"The girls need wine."

"Yes, and they called *me* to bring to them."

"Right," I agree. "But there is no way in hell you are going over there right now without me."

"What are you saying? You don't trust your best friend?" Paul asks, acting more hurt than he is.

"Absolutely. Now come on, let's go." Picking up the heavy paper bags off the bar, I cradle them with my arm and walk to the exit. Behind me Paul's laughter rings out and I smile, knowing he is following behind me and within a few minutes I will be face to face with Daphne Fields.

Daphne

10

"**S**uckers," Katie yells, reaching across the table with her hand awaiting my high five. "Seriously, that was too easy. I might have to keep you around after all. I mean, my brother rarely says no to me, but it usually takes more bribing."

"Maybe it's just the combo of both of us, 'cause I have the same effect on my brother. And, if I were to put you on the phone in the same situation he would be a glutton for punishment. Our brothers are very much alike." I shake my head at the thought.

"True. But, I guess it could have been the combo of guys on the other end too. I'm pretty sure I heard my brother's friend Curtis already ordering the wine before my brother agreed. He must be bored with Paul and itching to meet the new girl." She wiggles her eyebrows.

"Wait, who?" I ask, because although my ears aren't drunk, I am pretty sure I heard her say Curtis.

"His best friend, Curtis. They grew up together. He is super nice and really handsome. I'm sure you'll like him."

My nervous giggle is all I can stifle at the moment. And the look of panic on my face must be more evident than I had planned.

"What's wrong, you look totally freaked out." She starts to laugh, and it makes me feel at ease.

As I start to explain, it's obvious the alcohol is going to allow more words than I care to share slip between my lips.

"Curtis Dean. Dean R&R. He handles all the construction and handy man work I need around the Tea Room. And he is gorgeous, like, really friggin' sexy. I moved here wanting time to get over my last relationship and focus on me, then in walks a flannel shirt with a hammer and I'm a mess." My words keep coming and her eyes grow wide, but not as wide as her open mouthed smile. "Then, to top it off, he makes the nice gesture to come over and help me move some furniture, and we kissed! Now I have to see him for the first time since then, and we are supposed to be professionals. Oh, lord help me."

I lift my glass and drink the last few sips in one fast gulp. Katie still hasn't said a word, but passes me her half empty glass. Quickly finishing the wine, I wipe my mouth with the back of my hand, and sigh deeply.

"Well, I'm sure you must have something to say, no?" I ask, sarcastically.

"Oh, honey. I have plenty I want to say. But, I will say only this. You go girl! What a catch! Curtis is one of my favorite people and I am glad you met him. He needs a nice girl like you. So what else happened, you know, like after the kiss?" She lifts off her butt and pulls her knees underneath as if sitting higher will get her closer to the story.

"Nothing. I pulled away and then he left. It was super awkward and we haven't talked since."

"Ouch. Not even a text?"

"Well, I wanted to. But then my ex called me the next morning and it got even weirder in my head. I feel guilty, even though I shouldn't."

Standing from the table, my legs wobble slightly, but I catch myself without too much damage.

"Yikes. I'm buzzed." I laugh and Katie joins in as we head to the kitchen for a glass of water.

The loud knock on the door sends a shock to my heart and I look at Katie in horror.

"Relax. I'll get it. And really, you look great, and have nothing to worry about. Curtis is easy going and I promise it won't be awkward. Just relax." She winks at me and turns the corner toward the front door.

Fixing my shirt and smoothing my hair, I paste a smile to my cheeks, just as they round the corner to the kitchen.

"Hey Daphne, long time no see." Paul is being an obvious flirt as he pulls me into an overly friendly hug.

But I play along. "Oh, hey pal. Good to see you," I reply.

His goofy demeanor puts me at ease and I am thankful he said hi first, giving me the courage to approach Curtis next.

"Hi Curtis. How are you?" I ask, not moving closer, unsure if he expects a hug, or handshake, or anything.

"I'm doing well, Daphne. And yourself?" His smile is genuine and beautiful, and I can tell he doesn't have any ill feelings toward me, or the incident from the night before.

"Doing good, as well. It's nice to see you." I give a little nod and notice the two bottles of wine that he sat down on the counter. "And thank you for the wine. I have cash in my bag, how much do I owe you?"

"No need. It's on me this time."

"No way, let me pay you," I insist and attempt to reach for my bag, which is situated slightly behind him.

"Not a chance. Really." He lightly grabs my arm to stop my advance. "Maybe you can buy me a beer sometime."

His touch on my skin sends a chill to my spine and a heat to my thighs. I better just say thank you for now and let him win this one.

"Well, thank you. And I will definitely take you up on that."

"Okay, let's get these open." Katie breaks through the tension and begins uncorking the wine bottle.

The two boys get their glasses of Jack on ice and head into the living room. From the open kitchen, I can hear their hushed voices but am unable to make out what they are saying. I swear, boys are worse than girls. They can't go two seconds without gossiping. I wouldn't always just assume I am being talked about, but Mr. Obvious Paul, keeps looking over at me and smiling. He is such an easy read.

Katie pours our glasses and opens the last drawer on her way out of the kitchen, grabbing a deck of cards and heading to the table.

In her wild Katie way, she slaps the deck down and shouts, "Time to get Shitty!"

We all laugh, and join her at the table taking our seats in typical boy girl fashion.

Shitty is a drinking card game involving simple odds of guessing right or wrong. There is no real skill involved, just luck. If you guess right, you give drinks away to people, and if you guess wrong, you have to take them yourself. It can get real shitty, really quickly.

After just one game, it's clear that we are all pretty drunk and decide to order a pizza. Katie is further gone than the rest of us, and Paul is a very close second. I'm having a hard time deciding if Curtis holds his liquor well, or if he is a master of disguise. Of course, I don't think I am that drunk, but after standing to use the bathroom, it's apparent that I am struggling and causes me to laugh out loud.

"Sorry, I'm just really drunk and didn't realize it until just now."

"Yeah girl, me too. Need some help?" Katie starts laughing and it makes me laugh even harder.

"Um. I think I'm good. Thanks anyway, friend."

"Good. I really don't think I am moving anytime soon," she replies as she slips deeper into the couch.

I briefly glance towards Curtis and catch his gaze as his smile spreads wide across his face and he lets out a low chuckle.

Leaving the bathroom, I can smell the pizza as soon as the door is open. Katie has found her strength and is sitting cross-legged on the floor with two large slices and a breadstick, flipping through the TV channels. Paul is devouring a slice in the kitchen and Curtis is politely eating his at the table. I grab a slice and a breadstick and decide to join him.

"Seriously. How are you not drunk?" I finally ask what I have been thinking for an hour now.

"Me? I am definitely drunk," he replies and then smiles. It's right then, that I find his tell. His eyes. His normal stare is warm yet intense and tonight it is more carefree and light.

"Really? Other than your eyes, I can hardly tell."

"My eyes? Are they bloodshot or something?" he asks as he opens them wider, expecting me to see something different.

Now I am able to hear it in his voice as well. He has been quiet most of the night, though being around Katie and Paul together I am not sure how anyone gets a word in. His voice is deeper and a little raspy and I hear a slight drawl linger on his words as well.

"No, not red at all. Just different; lighter." I smile, reassuring him that it is not a bad thing and he just smiles back.

We finish our pizza and he nods his head toward the couch. Turning around, I nearly fall out of my chair at the sight of Katie passed out, with a slice still in her hand. We silently laugh, trying not to wake her and notice that Paul is barely keeping his eyes open as well.

We look back at each other and smile, both sitting in silence for a moment.

"It's getting late, I should probably head home," I say.

"Yeah, me too. Can I walk you home? It will give me a chance to sober up and I don't think you should be walking alone this late." His voice is smooth and protective and my eyes watch every word leave his lips.

"Sure. That would be great."

We stand from the table and clean up as much of the mess as we can without making too much noise. Paul waves goodbye and makes his way into the guest room, after covering Katie in a blanket.

Locking the door behind us, we head toward my house.

"So, do you go around kissing all your clients?" I laugh, hoping it isn't actually true.

"Shit, I knew you would think that." He lets out a laugh and tilts his head toward the stars.

"I'm kidding. It's not a big deal. We can pretend like it never happened," I reply.

He shakes his head, but doesn't say anything.

"What? You already forgot, didn't you? See, it was easy, now we can move on being friends." I smile, knowing it will not be that easy.

"No, Daphne. I did not forget and it would be pretty hard to." His voice trails off at the last words and I decide not to reply, though I agree.

"I am sorry though. I know I caught you off guard and didn't mean to offend you." His apology is sweet, but completely unnecessary.

"Curtis, it's really not like that. You don't have to be sorry. Honestly, I just panicked." It was now or never and drunk always signals now. "Before I moved here, I was engaged. When you kissed me, it was amazing, but then I got in my head and felt guilty." Not sure what else to say, I simply shrug my shoulders.

"Well, then I am sorry. Not for kissing you, but for whatever you went through. It must be hard starting over in a new city alone after being recently engaged. I'm glad you met Katie though, she is really great and you guys seem to get along pretty well."

"Funny, she said the same thing about you."

"Oh yeah? That is nice of her. Though, she probably would be happy with anyone I met that isn't Vera." He goes silent after saying her name and I can tell he wasn't ready to bring her up. Once again, the alcohol wins.

"Is that your ex?" I ask, hoping he doesn't correct me with 'current' girlfriend.

"Yeah. We have been on and off for the last few years, but this recent break-up is final. It just isn't the same between us and we both need to move on." He doesn't seem overly torn up about it, but the tone of his voice says he took his relationship seriously.

"Sorry to hear that."

After a few quiet steps, I can see my front door up ahead.

"Want to race?" I ask, suddenly feeling energetic and charged up with mixed emotions from this night.

"Seriously?" he asks, but before I can reply I just take off.

Quickly catching up, I hear his footsteps grow louder but he doesn't pass me. Instead, he runs up next to me and we both start laughing. Out of breath, we reach the front door and I let us inside.

"Water?" I offer.

"Hell yeah. I mean, yes please," he says between breaths.

"Sorry, I love to run and it just felt right for the moment."

"I noticed, but it was fun. Helped me get some energy back."

"Speaking of energy, I'm still kind of hungry." I look around the kitchen for a moment and see my spatula from this morning. "Oh! Pancakes, my other love. Can I make you some?"

"Sounds great. I love pancakes too." The desire in his smile could melt a snowman, but it heads straight south to melt me instead.

Honestly, I'm not sure I am actually that hungry, but more so looking for any reason to keep Curtis around longer. His presence is intoxicating and addictive, and I may have just set myself up for a long night.

Curtis

11

I am mesmerized watching Daphne move around her kitchen, grabbing various items from her cabinets and drawers. To make matters worse, when we arrived to her house she wanted to change into something more comfortable. While short shorts and a tank top may be more comfortable for her, it doesn't leave much to the imagination and is pure torture for me. The shorts make her tan legs appear to go on for miles and the tank molds to her body tightly, bringing my attention to her chest.

It's amazing how easy it is to be with Daphne. We hardly know each other, yet, at the same time, it feels as if we have been friends for years. It's been fun seeing such a different side of her. Most of our encounters have taken place during work, aside for the night I came over here and we kissed. I have been worried that I may have screwed up big time, and the kiss would complicate things between us, but now, I feel better after our conversation.

"Chocolate chips?" Daphne asks, bringing me out of my daze.

"Definitely." I watch as she turns to the pantry and reaches up for the bag of chocolate, causing her top to rise and reveal a sliver of skin. "Have you always been an amazing cook?"

Opening the bag of chips, she dumps a generous amount into the bowl of batter and I watch a hint of blush color her cheeks before she responds.

"Amazing might be a bit of a stretch. Growing up, I spent a lot of time in the kitchen with Grams. When Derrick and I would return from our summers down here with Grams and Papa, Dad was always excited to see what new recipes I had learned." She pauses for a moment, lost in thought, then looks up and smiles. "I guess I have always loved to cook."

"You and your Grams were close?"

"Oh, yes," she beams. "Being their only grandkids, we were quite spoiled, but only in the good ways. Then after we lost our mom, we seemed to grow even closer. I cherish every moment I spent with Gram's. She always had a way of keeping my mom's memory alive and I think that's why I jumped at the opportunity to take over The Treasured Tea Cup. I may have lost some things in the process, but in my heart, I know this is where I am supposed to be."

"It's great that you have this legacy to carry on and a way to keep your Grams' memory alive."

"I can only hope that I do right and make her proud, you know?" Daphne stops stirring the batter and sets the whisk down as a forlorn expression takes over her beautiful face.

I reach across the counter and place my hand over hers, meeting her hazel eyes. "Hey, you are doing great. I know she is proud of you. Numerous times, while I was doing work at the Tea Room, we would have lunch together and Kay would tell me all about her grandkids. You couldn't miss the love and pride in her eyes as she spoke about you and your brother."

"Well, Grams always was a bragger." Daphne winks and pats the top of my hand with her other. "Thank you. Enough serious talk though, I am going to cook these up real quick. How about you go find something on TV for us to watch?"

Pancakes will never taste the same again. I typically enjoy the box mix where you just add water and stir, but Daphne's homemade recipe beats out anything I have ever tasted. I don't know how she makes something so simple come out so delicious, but she has ruined me.

We start out with the TV as background noise while we eat and spend more time getting to know each other. She tells me about the career in teaching that she gave up before moving here, and I can tell she misses it. The way she talks about the students, it's apparent she really had a love for it. I would bet anything that Daphne is an amazing teacher.

Filling me in a bit about her ex, Nathan, I learn he is an attorney from her father's firm, whom she has known most of her life. They have a lot of history to compete with. My question is, what kind of man lets someone like Daphne Fields just walk away? How did he not fight for her, or better yet, come with her? Just one moment spent with Daphne and I am left wanting more.

I share stories of my friendship with Paul and the trouble we got into as kids, but decide against diving further into my past with Vera. I could spend the rest of the night talking with Daphne, but I see her eyes growing heavy. We focus on the TV for a few minutes and as I glance over to ask her a question, I notice the sleeping beauty.

Not wanting to wake her, I slide my arms under her legs and back, gently lifting her. Wrapping her arms around my neck, she nuzzles her head against my shoulder. Luckily, she has the same layout as Katie's and I have a good idea where her bedroom is.

"I can walk, you know," Daphne says in a sleepy voice with her eyes still shut.

"But then I wouldn't get to hold you."

Bringing her nose to my shirt, she inhales deeply. "You smell good."

"Thanks." I laugh and carefully lie her down in bed. "I will be right back."

I grab a bottle of water from her refrigerator and take it back to the room, setting it on her nightstand. She is still lying above the covers, but her eyes are now open.

"Thank you for the wonderful pancakes, Miss Fields. I hope you sleep well."

Daphne smiles up at me and opens her arms wide, inviting me in for a hug. With one knee bent on the bed, I lean down to embrace her.

Pressing her lips to my cheek, she kisses me before whispering, "Thank you for tonight."

I pull back to tell her how much I enjoyed the evening, but lose my train of thought once my gaze meets hers. Her golden locks fan across the pillow and a flush pink graces her skin. Daphne lifts up from the bed and with one hand on my neck, she pulls me close until our mouths meet. I feel the same electric shock I get every time we touch, but this time it pulses throughout my entire body. The kiss starts slow but soon turns hard, yet unhurried. I move fully on the bed and situate myself between her legs, bracing my weight with one hand pressed to the bed, and the other resting on her hip.

Sucking on her bottom lip, I pull away from her mouth and press a kiss to her jaw. I tilt her head to gain better access and pepper her neck with kisses, stopping to suck and nibble at all the right spots.

A small whimper leaves Daphne's lips and I move my hand down her thigh, wrapping her leg tighter around me as I thrust forward. Her hands slide underneath my shirt, rubbing up and down my back, gripping harder when I bite down and grind into her.

I tear my mouth from her neck and peer down at her. If her smile wasn't enough, the blush across her cheeks and lust in her eyes is my downfall. Dropping my eyes to her mouth, I lean back down and devour her, our tongues sliding against each other frantically. My hand moves up her body and soon finds her breast, squeezing lightly. My mouth catches the next moan that escapes her lips, before I kiss a trail from her jaw to her chest.

With a light touch, I trace the line from her neck to the start of her cleavage, watching as her chest rises and falls with each deep breath. Running my finger across the peaks,

I slowly pull down the tank until her full breasts are bare. My breath catches in my throat as I look down at her perfect body. I trace around her nipples and moan when they pucker under my touch, causing me to only grow painfully harder under my jeans. Lowering my head, my mouth closes around one nipple while my hand grasps the other.

"Oh, God," Daphne whimpers, her hands squeezing my ass and pulling me closer toward her heat.

She is squirming beneath me as my mouth moves to the other side. I could spend an entire day devouring every part of Daphne's body and can only imagine how sweet and addicting her taste would be. Just this small sample and I will never be the same.

Kissing my way back up her chest and neck, I meet her lips with a brutal kiss that has our hips grinding in sync. Daphne's hand lowers down my back and I jump the moment she rubs it against the front of my jeans. I know I should stop this now, but damn it feels so good.

Moments from losing it all together, I pull my mouth from hers and grab her hand before she can unbutton my jeans. Linking our fingers together, I rest them on the pillow next to her head and rest my forehead against hers. We are both panting heavily, attempting to catch our breath.

Her hand squeezes mine and I lift up to get a full look at her face. She smiles up at me and I lower my mouth back down, planting soft kisses on her lips while I pull her top back up.

"I should probably get going," I say, sitting up on my knees, using strength I wasn't sure I possessed, pulling myself away from Daphne's body.

"You could stay," she suggest in a sweet whisper.

Her offer only makes this harder. Spending the night with Daphne is tempting, but there is no way I could resist burying myself deep inside her.

"I would love nothing more," I pause when she rises to a sitting position, bringing her body closer to mine and distracting me, "but I know what that would lead to, and I don't think we are ready for that."

"My, my. Curtis Dean, are you being all chivalrous?" Daphne teases, her hand running up and down my denim clad thigh.

"Something like that." My hand rests against her jaw with my thumb softly grazing her cheek. Daphne's eyes close as she leans into my touch. "Sleep well, Daphne."

"Goodnight, Curtis."

Bringing her mouth to mine, I fuse our lips together in a searing goodnight kiss. Pulling away, I press a kiss to her forehead and stand from the bed. With one last look at the sexy temptress, I turn and leave the bedroom.

I make sure to lock her door and stepping outside, it hits me that my truck is still at Katie's. I spend the walk back thinking about everything that transpired tonight and mentally note this as one of the best nights I've had in quite a while.

Daphne

12

Rolling to my side, I stretch out my arm in search of warmth. The cold sheets are a quick reminder that I am alone in my bed as the pounding against my skull reminds me that I drank too much wine last night.

I quickly roll to my other side and see the water bottle that Prince Charming so generously brought to my rescue. Unscrewing the cap with as much strength as I can muster, I tilt the bottle and consume every drop. The sunlight barely breaking through the window is enough reason for me to pull the covers over my head and try to get a little more shuteye.

A buzzing on my side table pulls me from the delicious dream I was having about pancakes. I rip the cover down and crawl to the edge of the bed, heading straight to the bathroom before my bladder explodes. Walking around the corner, I notice the mess in the kitchen and slap my own wrist for not cleaning it up last night.

Ugh, I am really not a good cook when I'm drunk. My standard method of cleaning while you cook went straight out the window. Batter is everywhere; the floor, the wall, the sink. It's completely dried up and is going to be bitch to clean.

The scream from my kettle is a sweet sound and puts me one step closer to a hot cup of coffee from my French press. Though the mess is overwhelming, my level of stress is at an all-time low this morning. I am relaxed and ready to enjoy my Sunday.

Well, once my kitchen is clean that is.

With caffeine now flowing, I whisk about the kitchen scrubbing up the memories of last night. A smile touches my cheeks, as I replay the sweet moments of having my lips on his. Curtis's strength and warmth compares to none. His touch makes me feel safe and his breath on my neck makes my heart beat differently. The ease of our conversation was refreshing and I didn't feel like I had to pretend to be anything other than myself.

It's an alluring feeling that tickles my soul. It has been years, if not forever that I have felt this way, and as much as I would have loved to feel him inside of me, he was right to stop. It is too soon, and I am not sure I am ready to move that fast.

Just like that, the kitchen is clean and the full relaxation of this Sunday afternoon can commence. I have nothing to do, and plan to keep it that way. It will just be me and the TV today, catching up on someone else's drama for a change.

Grabbing another water bottle and bowl of fruit, I sit down and prop up my feet. A faint buzzing noise from the bedroom reminds me that I never checked my phone earlier. With a somber grunt, I lift from the couch to retrieve it.

Curtis: Good morning Chef. Had a great time getting to know you. ;) Hope you have a nice Sunday.

Katie: Dang, we drank some wine! Bottles everywhere! Thanks for a fun night, hope you're not too hung over. Talk to you soon! Xoxoxo

Derrick: Got your message. Things are good. Miss you. I'll call you soon to discuss our birthday. Love you, sis.

Typical Derrick. Short, to the point, but always sweet. I miss him so much and can't wait to see him later this month. We always celebrate our birthday together no matter where we are, and this year is his turn to come to me. It's going to be great to have him here to see what I have done so far with The Treasured Tea Cup. Hopefully, he will have some good advice to offer up, as well.

Derrick is a business major and has been helping Grams over the years make decisions on advertising and marketing. Thanks to Derrick, Grams was one of the first local owners to get involved with *Groupon*. Her discount through the popular website brought people here from miles around.

Along the way, his input helped keep the business current and spread the word about its charm. With the passing of Grams and the newness of my ownership, now is a crucial time to maintain the momentum.

Me: I'm good too. Miss you always. Don't forget to call xoxo love you too

I never ask too many questions. Derrick has a one to two text maximum. He is easy-going, yet always busy. In fact, it reminds me a lot of Katie. She doesn't seem to ever slow down; always on the go, finding something to keep her busy. It's endearing to have her around. They would probably get along great.

Thoughts of Curtis creep into my mind as I re-read his text. Things could have gotten way out of hand last night, but thankfully he is a gentleman and kept drunken Daphne at bay.

Me: This Chef had quite a mess to clean up this morning :) But also had a fun night getting to know you. Thanks for being a gentleman.

It's easy to see what a great guy Curtis is. Everyone I meet that knows him only speaks highly of him. Some men were just brought up right.

Katie and Paul also share a special charm and I am glad to have met them both. There is something special about their relationship as siblings and their need to take care of each other. Derrick and I have always felt that way, since Mom passed, and makes me wonder where their similar bond stems from.

Me: Morning Sunshine. Hangover not so bad, really looking forward to relaxing all day with reality TV to keep me company.

Katie: Oh heyyy! Glad you're up and alive. Hope you enjoy your Sunday. I hear there is a Project Runway marathon this afternoon!! Call me soon!

Katie: Oh and don't think I'm not going to ask about your walk home either ;)

Me: I figured lol Talk to you soon.

I am not sure how much detail I will go into with Katie. I will have to test the water of our new relationship with a little at a time. I am not one to kiss and tell, but I would definitely like to see what else she could spill about Curtis. Therefore, I may have to give a little to get a little.

Flipping through the channels, I see Heidi and stop surfing. This marathon is exactly what I need for today. No thought process needed, just good ole' fashion – no pun intended – reality drama.

Biting into the most delicious piece of cantaloupe, my phone alerts a new message and I would be lying if I didn't hope it was from Curtis.

Curtis: Sorry, wish I could have stayed to clean up. Hope it wasn't too   much.

Me: Nah. It wasn't so bad, plus ... it wasn't your fault. I'm the crazy one who wanted to make midnight pancakes lol

Curtis: Well, next time you cook for me, I'll be sure to take care of the cleaning.

Next time?

Instant images of me cooking while he sits on the barstool and watches run wildly through my head, and the subtle flutter in my belly begins to increase.

Me: That sounds nice.

Curtis: So, you busy this week? You don't have to cook for me, but I'd like to take you out to dinner.

My heart is pounding and my smile could not get any wider.

Crap! This is my late week, where I stay each night working in the office dealing with the business side of the

Tea Room. The only night I have off, I already made plans to eat dinner with Papa.

Me: Unfortunately, yes. This is my week to stay late at work, and I don't have any nights open. Maybe this weekend?

Curtis: How about lunch? Tomorrow when I finish up, we can grab a bite. What do you think?

Me: I think I can make that happen :)

Curtis: Great, I'll see you tomorrow.

Me: Bright and early :)

Curtis has more work scheduled for this week at the Tea Room, and will be there first thing tomorrow morning. I'm glad we didn't let things get too far; it could have made for a really awkward Monday morning.

Curtis

13

T he remainder of my weekend consisted of thoughts of Daphne and Saturday night. She thanked me in a text for being a gentleman, but if she knew half the images that have been replaying in my head, she may think otherwise. The way her body responded to my touch was like we were built for each other. Her skin tasted just as sweet as I imagined it would, leaving me to wonder how sweet she is everywhere else.

Arriving at the Tea Room earlier this morning, I wasn't allowed much time to speak with Daphne. There was a last minute booking for a big lunch party, causing everyone to rush around in order to prepare all the extra food needed for the day. After a brief hello, I set off on my own and started on the work planned for the day. I have a very special lunch date and want to make sure I complete the majority of my work beforehand.

Checking my watch, I note that it has been a couple hours now and stop for a water break. I am currently working on a small nook in the front of the house, with only a few final touches to go. It had previously been open, wasted space, but after building out a bench around the windows, has become extra seating for customers waiting to be taken to their tables. Once I finish up today, Hilda is taking measurements and creating the pillow cushions for the top. With a little extra care and added trim work around the bench I was able to match the original crown molding in the house.

"Wow, this is looking really great."

Lowering the water bottle, I turn my attention to the beautiful blonde behind me. I don't know how she does it, but Daphne looks great every time I see her. Whether it's first thing in the morning when I arrive at the Tea Room, after several bottles of wine with Katie, or now, her hair falling loose from its braid and flour splattered on her apron, she always looks amazing.

Daphne glances away briefly as crimson touches her cheeks, and I realize that I have been staring at her like a fool with no response.

"Yeah. It was a good idea on your part to better utilize this space. I am just about finished; will you still be able to sneak away for lunch?" I ask, hoping this last minute reservation hasn't ruined my chances of taking her out.

"That's what I was coming to ask. Do you think we would be able to have an early lunch? We basically have everything prepared since they ordered ahead for the whole party, but I need to be here when they arrive as an extra set of hands." She smiles shyly.

An early lunch works out great for me, because once I finish securing these final boards, my work at the Tea Room will be complete

"No problem, I can be ready in twenty. Would that work for you?" I ask.

"That would be perfect. Just come get me when you are ready." Turning on her heels, Daphne walks back towards the kitchen and I watch as she disappears.

Quickly and efficiently, I screw in the final panel and clean the area, before loading up my equipment. I check the cab of the truck and make sure there is no trash. Once it's straightened up, I pull my shirt over my head and toss it into my duffle bag. Reaching behind the seat, I grab the plaid shirt that's hanging up and put it on. It is rather warm out today, so I roll the sleeves up my forearms.

Pushing the last button through its opening, I turn around and find Daphne standing frozen with her lips parted. Unable to miss her obvious examination and approval, I stand straight and wink.

"If you keep looking at me like that, we won't be making it to lunch, sweetheart."

"Sorry, I was coming to tell you I was ready, and then you were half naked, and I wasn't ready for that... I mean I wasn't expecting it. But, umm, yeah, so I am ready to go." She stumbles through her words and it only brings me joy, knowing that I affect her in such a way.

"How do you feel about East Street Diner?"

"It happens to be one of my favorite places. They have the best grilled cheese."

I stare at her for a moment after she has climbed into the passenger seat of my truck. "Grilled cheese? It's bread and cheese, how great can that be?"

"You would be surprised. They use only homemade bread and it isn't like they are just slapping American cheese singles on there. I believe they combine four different cheeses and it is cooked perfectly and practically melts in your mouth."

Never in my life, did I think someone could describe a grilled cheese to the point where it sounded sexy, but that is what Daphne just did. Or maybe it was that slight moan that she followed up with.

"I might have to try this sandwich one day. Sounds like a big deal."

"Oh, it is," she states, seriously.

I laugh and close the door, making my way to the driver's side.

The drive to the diner is fleeting and doesn't allow much time for conversation; however, once we sit our conversation flows just as easy as Saturday night.

True to her word, Daphne orders the grilled cheese with a bowl of tomato soup, and I stick to my usual, ordering a bacon cheeseburger. She offers me a bite, which I accept and gladly admit it's amazing.

Laughing over a story about her brother using an Australian accent to pick up a girl at the bar, my cell vibrates on the table.

Vera.

I reject the call, sending her to voicemail, and give my full attention back to Daphne.

"Do you need to get that? I don't mind," she asks, using the last bite of her grilled cheese to scrape the remaining soup from the side of the bowl.

"No, it's not important." There is no telling what Vera wants, but I can guarantee it won't be anything good. I refuse to allow her to cast a shadow on this date, and immediately get back to our conversation. "So, Daphne, do you have any tales of picking up guys?"

She tilts her head in thought for a moment, smiling widely before answering. "Not really. I just invite them over to help me move furniture and then throw myself at them. Or trip over my own feet."

"Well, that sounds like a good plan." I laugh.

"What about you, Mr. Dean? Any hidden tricks?" she asks, crossing her arms in front, bringing my attention to her bust.

"Nah. I just wait for a beautiful woman to mistake me for my father."

Daphne laughs, her chests bouncing, and I force my gaze to stay locked on hers. "It was an honest mistake. Once I got a good look, it was obvious that you weren't him."

Just then the server drops the check and I pull out my wallet, laying down enough cash to cover it and a generous tip.

"I guess our time is up. I better get back before the party shows up."

The ride back seems to fly by quicker and before I can blink, I am parked in front of the old house.

We both sit in silence a moment before Daphne speaks up. "Thank you for lunch, Curtis. I had fun."

"Me too, and I would still like to take you to dinner some time."

"I think we can arrange that." She smiles and unfastens her seatbelt. "Talk to you soon."

I reach out, grabbing her wrist and pull her across the leather, never more thankful for the bench seat. She gasps in surprise, and as I press my mouth to hers, she threads her fingers through my thick hair. This kiss starts out as a soft caress, but quickly becomes more demanding. My hand claims her hip and pulls her body tighter against mine. Feeling the change in urgency, Daphne rises to her knees in the seat and is on the verge of straddling me when the ringing through my truck speakers breaks our trance. We pull away, our foreheads resting against each other, catching our breath.

"I need to get back in there. And you should get that." Daphne starts to pull away, but I stop her, and bring her lips back to mine.

Not ready for our moment to end, I shower her mouth in tender kisses before nibbling her bottom lip. I could kiss her every second of the day. How is it possible to feel this kind of connection with someone I just met?

"Have a good rest of your day." It's still a struggle to separate our bodies from one another, but Daphne eventually slides back over and opens the door. "Talk to you soon," I say, and with a smile and wave, she shuts the door and walks away.

I spend several minutes sitting in the cab of my truck wondering why I couldn't have met Daphne sooner. She is an incredible woman with a great energy and I think we complement each other very well.

The ding of my phone signals that I have a new text message and reminds me that I am currently daydreaming about Daphne in front of her business. Looking down at the phone, all happy thoughts are lost at the sight of Vera's name.

Vera: I am going to swing by tonight around eight to pick up my belongings. If this doesn't work for you, let me know.

Trying to keep up the positive attitude Daphne left me with, I send Vera a message back letting her know that tonight works for me. The sooner we get this over with, the better. I have been enjoying my time spent with Daphne and I want to make sure that nothing stands in the way of that.

The afternoon flies by and with all of our other jobs running on schedule and I even manage to catch up on backlog paperwork. With that said, today is also a little bittersweet. By finishing the work at the Tea Room, I no longer have a reason to spend so much time around her, but I'm hoping that we can continue to see each other outside of our professional relationship.

When I finally get home after work, I only have an hour to spare before Vera plans to stop by and pick up her things. There isn't much left behind, so it was easy to gather and is waiting on the dining room table in a box. Hopefully this will be as painless as possible.

Upon entering my bedroom, my text alert beeps and I smile, sliding the screen to read the message.

Daphne: Thank you again for lunch. I had a great time.

Me: Me too. I swear I can still taste your kiss on my lips. I want to see you again.

I instantly regret it the moment I hit send, but can't undo it. I stare at my phone waiting for her response and my heartbeat increases as the three little dots pop up, letting my know she is typing.

Daphne: I want that too.

Four simple words ease my anxiety. She ends the text using an emoji with blushing cheeks and I can picture her in my head the same way.

Tossing my phone on the bed, I head into my bathroom to take a shower.

The heat from the water streaming down helps in relaxing my muscles from my day of work. As per usual, my thoughts quickly turn to Daphne and it doesn't take long before I am hard as steel. Squeezing body wash into my hand I rub it along my length, needing the release. My mind filters through thoughts and images of our intimate moments. Then I imagine what it will feel like when I finally get the chance to slide deep inside her. I have no doubt it will be incredible.

With my left arm extended in front me, bracing myself against the wall, I increase the speed and pressure of my other hand. Feeling myself tighten and knowing the release

I desire is on its way, the picture in my head of Daphne with her full lips wrapped around me is ripped away when I hear a clatter from my bedroom.

Shit!

Shutting off the running water, I listen for a moment, hoping I was hearing things. Surrounded by silence I reach for my towel and wrap it around my waist, after a mental promise to finish what I started.

I am taken by surprise when I walk out of the bathroom and find Vera sitting on my bed with her back to me.

"What are you doing in here, Vera?" I ask, hoping she didn't see anything while I was in the shower.

"I'm here to pick up my things. Did you forget already?" She still isn't looking my way, but I can hear the bitterness in her voice.

"No, I didn't forget. What I meant was, what are you doing here, in my bedroom? You can't just let yourself into my house anymore."

Standing abruptly, she turns towards me, shooting a cold look in my direction.

"Why? Worried I might catch you and your new girlfriend?" With her hand raised, I notice that she is holding my phone.

"What the –, you went through my phone? Are you serious, Vera?" I take a step closer, with the bed being the only thing to separate us.

"So, you aren't even going to deny it? Then again, after what I just read, there would be no point. What was it you said, you could still taste her kiss on your lips?" She tosses the phone on the mattress and crosses her arms.

"I owe you no explanation. We broke up. You had no right to go through my phone. What is wrong with you?"

"How long has this been going on?"

"It doesn't matter," I answer, tightening the towel around my waist. The last thing I need right now is for it to drop.

Shock and anger light up her eyes. "It most certainly does if you have been screwing someone behind my back."

"I never cheated on you," I fire back, clenching my jaw tightly. "Look, I need to put some clothes on. Wait for me in the kitchen."

"Nothing I haven't seen before." She smiles and my teeth grind together in annoyance. "Right." Turning on her heels, she exits the room.

After I throw on a pair of gym shorts and a t-shirt, I quickly check my phone for new messages from Daphne and luckily there are none. When I move to the kitchen, Vera is waiting with a glass of red wine and I can tell this is not going to end well.

"All those late nights working and constant phone calls, was that *her*?" The distain is evident in her voice.

"No, that was work. Again, I never cheated on you, Vera. I am not that guy."

"You have really hurt me, Curtis." Her bottom lip trembles and I can tell that she is fighting to hold in her emotions. "You break up with me out of nowhere and here we are now and you have already moved on. What am I supposed to think?"

"We have had issues for a while now and our break up was a long time coming—not just out of the blue. Give it some time and you will realize that it never would have worked between us."

She stands there for a moment glaring at me and raises the glass of wine, draining its contents in one gulp. "Sorry that I can't just turn off my feelings by a flip of a switch like you. I will just grab my things and be out of your way."

When I hear the front door slam shut, I let out a frustrated breath and reach into my cabinet to pull out my bottle of Gentleman Jack. After pouring a generous amount in a glass, I take a steep swig in celebration of the bullet I just dodged.

Daphne

14

S lowing down to stop at the red light, I flip down my visor and examine my lips in the mirror. It has been over twenty-four hours and I still feel like they are swollen from his kiss. I'm sure it is all in my head, but there is definitely a tingle that courses through them when I let my mind drift back to the cab of his truck.

Our lips seemed to melt together as we matched each other breath for breath. Almost too intense to wrap my thoughts around. Traveling down my torso, there is now a lower tingle as I replay my personal short film, *Shirtless Curtis*.

The moment my eyes swept across his labor-toned back, the slow motion film began, allowing me to enjoy every single second of him stretching the clean shirt over his sexy body and turning to catch my gaze. His confidence was evident in his award-winning smile.

Squeezing my thighs together in attempt to calm the throbbing, I flip the visor back up and continue driving.

Papa and I made plans for dinner and I am really looking forward to spending time with him.

Papa has always been self-sufficient and quite content spending time alone, and also not one to talk much over the phone. After Grams passed, I think some of that faded. We talk on the phone a few times a week and it's apparent that he enjoys our quick conversations. Being busy with the Tea Room has kept me from seeing him as much as I would like, but I hope to make more of an effort once I get into the swing of things.

Making my way down the lengthy driveway, small flutters of sadness fill my heart. This is usually my favorite part of the visit, getting to drive up and see Grams on the porch waiting for me. Although now, it breaks my heart to pull up and see there is an empty swing that only sways with the breeze.

Stepping out of my car, I clear the sad thoughts and paste a smile on my face for Papa. He needs my strength as much as I need his. We share the loss of two very special women and our bond is a match for none. I am Papa's only girl left and I plan to take care of him until he is hand in hand with Grams again.

"Papa, I'm here," I holler as I make my way inside.

"Out here, sweetheart." He returns my shout through the screen door at the back of the house.

The aroma of the grill hits my senses as I near the porch door. He is making his famous cheeseburgers and I brought the potato salad.

"Mmm, that smells good. I am starving."

"Good to hear, burgers should be ready in about five minutes." He closes the lid of the grill and joins me on the porch swing. "So, what's new?"

"Well, let's see. Since I talked to you last there really isn't much new. Though, I am excited for you to come by and see what Curtis has done at the Tea Room. He really does amazing work," I brag.

"Yes, he does. That boy is hardworking and talented, just like his father."

I could say so much more about Curtis, but think it best to skip that conversation for the night. "So, what have you been up to?" I ask.

"Well, let's see." He looks around the backyard and then gets a smile across his face. "See that tree over there?" he asks, pointing to a large oak. I nod in response as he continues, "Well, I am working on a little project that I think you will really love. It's not ready yet, but when it is, you will be the first to see it."

"Well, you going to tell me what it is?" I ask, nudging his arm.

"Let's just say it will give you butterflies." He smiles and winks at me, as both of our eyes grow misty.

My Papa used to call my mother his little butterfly. I imagine he is working on a butterfly garden with all of Grams' favorite flowers that will attract hundreds of them. He has the biggest heart that has somehow been able to withstand a lifetime worth of breaks.

"Can't wait. I am sure it will be amazing." I lean into his shoulder and look out over the water.

MICHELLE LOUISE

One of the few memories I have of my mother is sitting in this exact spot, swinging slowly, gazing out across the lake. I remember looking up at her and thinking how beautiful she was.

"Hm." Papa chuckles and keeps the smile cast across his face.

"What?"

"You look just like your mother. I swear I looked up and saw her sitting here beside me."

I smiled back, but did not have the right words for the moment. My heart was still fragile and needed to take caution in order to avoid the tears.

Papa stands from the swing and checks the burgers before covering them each with cheese and closing the lid back.

"Will Derrick be coming to town this weekend?" he asks with his back turned to me.

"Um, not sure, did you talk to him?"

Papa chuckles out loud. "Yeah, right. I just figured he would be here to celebrate your birthday together as usual. It's kind of a big one, no?"

My eyes widen as I recall today's date. Derrick's and my birthday is this weekend and we will be turning thirty. We have never missed one together and I don't plan to start now. How on Earth did I let this slip my mind?

"Oh lord, I totally forgot my own birthday."

"Yeah, that happens with age." Papa has quick wit, which puts a smile on my face.

"Ha, very funny old timer. I will make sure to call Derrick tonight. We will probably come by on Saturday for lunch or dinner if that is okay."

"Of course. I would love that. Plus, I got some things I want to discuss with him and considering how often we get to see him, I better take advantage."

Papa removes the burgers from the grill and we head inside to eat. We finish the night at the dinner table, enjoying a few beers and laughing at old memories. With a kiss to his cheek, we say goodnight and I head home.

Plopping onto the couch, I grab my phone and start to scroll through my favorites. A photo of Derrick sporting his goofy smile stretches across my screen as his call rings through.

"Derrick!" I exclaim with more excitement than realistically necessary.

"Hey, ugly. What are you up to?" he asks.

"We are twins, so really that makes you ugly too."

"Oh stop, you know I am kidding. But, I'm still the prettier one." Always the over confident one.

"Yeah, yeah. Anyways, I'm glad you called. Our birthday is this weekend and I really hope you are still planning to come stay with me. Papa really wants to see you and I don't think I can handle thirty alone."

"Just like you couldn't handle twenty-nine alone either, right?"

"Exactly." I smile at our banter and remember how much I miss my brother.

"Well, you are in luck. I have the weekend off and will be arriving sometime Saturday morning."

"Yay! I can't wait. We can have lunch with Papa and then I'll have some of my friends meet up with us at the bar later for drinks."

"Sounds good. Do any of those friends happen to be single?" He asks his usual question and I wish he could see how far back my eyes are able to roll after the years of practice.

"You are ridiculous. Just get here safely and we can worry about finding you a *nice* girl later."

"Alright, sounds like a plan. I will see you soon."

"Yep. Love you, night."

"You too, night."

Hanging up the phone, I see the one minute, thirty-one second timer flash the screen and realize that may have been the longest phone conversation we have had in months. My brother is such a special person and can be quite the handful, but I wouldn't trade him for anything.

With the weekend only a few days away, I text the few friends I have and try to throw together a quick plan for Saturday night. Katie is more than excited and a little mad I didn't tell her sooner. I got a few other responses and should have a pretty solid turnout.

After sending out all my texts, there is only one pending response that keeps me checking my phone like a teenager. Slightly saddened, I put the phone down and realize it is after ten and he is most likely sleeping. Relaxing into the couch, I catch up on my missed shows for the week and try not to think too much into it. I am sure I will hear from him in the morning.

Curtis

15

I have been looking forward to the opportunity to sleep in all week. Although for me, sleeping in is making it to seven before leaving the bed. This morning, I was awake by six-thirty. So much for extra rest.

I spend the better part of the morning getting work done on a few renovation projects I started around the house. When I purchased this place five years ago, it was a foreclosure in need of major work. It had a strong and sturdy foundation, but my father and I have basically gutted the interior over the years. The inside is brand new and everything is done exactly how I want. I can't help but feel a sense of pride as I walk through the house and admire all the hard work I have put into it.

Whenever there is something on my mind or bothering me, it is extremely easy to get swept up in the work and forget everything going on around me. It's kind of my way of relaxing and I enjoy the feeling of accomplishment afterwards.

This morning while working on my landscaping in the backyard; pulling weeds and planting new shrubbery, Ma called and asked me to come by. She has been working in her garden and has more cucumbers than she knows what to do with. After our last conversation she wanted to offer the vegetables to Daphne and would like me to run them over to the Tea Room.

Hot and sweaty from the yard work, I quickly jump in the shower and take a little extra time as I'm getting ready. I haven't been able to see Daphne since the day we had lunch and I am looking forward to seeing her today. I sent her a message after Vera left the other night, but never heard back from her. I have been trying to play it cool and keep my distance, not wanting to push her too much. I feel as though I made my desires clear last time we were together and I want to make sure she doesn't rush into anything she may regret later on down the road.

When I pick up the cucumbers from Ma, she gives me a knowing smile and kisses my cheek, to thank me. I feel like I should be the one thanking her for giving me this excuse to see Daphne, but instead I leave and hurry on my way.

The parking lot is fairly empty when I arrive, but I recognize Daphne's car on the side of the house.

The door jingles when I walk in and Hilda welcomes me. "Well, hello, Curtis. How are you doing today?"

"I am well, Hilda. How are you?"

"I woke up this morning, so that means I am great." She laughs and I shake my head. "Are you here for lunch?"

"No, ma'am. Ma wanted to see if Daphne would be interested in some cucumbers from her garden," I say, holding up the box in my hands.

"Oh, how lovely. I am sure she would love it. Let me go find her for you. Have a seat." She motions towards the window seats I recently finished. The new cushions are on and they look great.

Preferring to stand, I set the box on the desk and walk around the front, browsing the selection of tins containing various teas for customers to purchase. Next to them is also a case displaying teapot sets.

My attention is pulled from the tins and teapots when I hear the sound of glass breaking. Turning around, my eyes fall to the body bent down picking up pieces of what looks to be a teacup. Hilda rushes over with a broom and they are far enough away that I can't make out what is being said. The girls is wearing a monstrous pink hat with white long feathers running around the brim. I don't know what would possess someone to wear such a thing, its hideous.

The girl stands and brings my attention to her backside as she straightens her dress. Hilda says something to the girl and she turns with a smile on her face.

Even wearing the horrendous pink hat, Daphne Fields is still the most beautiful girl I have ever met. I openly study her as she approaches and notice the 'Happy Birthday' emblem on the front of the hat.

"Is it your birthday?" I ask the obvious question.

"What gave it away?" Daphne smarts, causing me to laugh easily.

"Happy birthday. I wish I would have known." Pulling her closer, I embrace her in a quick hug, taking a moment to inhale in her sweet scent.

Daphne pulls away, steps back and looks at me with confusion written on her face.

"Well, I mentioned it the other night when I invited you out for drinks."

Now I am the one who is confused.

"You never mentioned your birthday. Or drinks."

Was she getting me mixed up with someone else?

Wait. Was there another guy?

Maybe that was why I haven't heard from her.

Now I was beginning to sound like a girl.

Daphne lets out a frustrated sigh and shrugs. "It's not a big deal. I sent you a text message the other night. It will just be a few people getting together while my brother is in town. Katie and Paul are coming, so I thought you might like to, as well."

I pull my phone out of my back pocket and swipe to unlock the screen. "Daphne, I never received a message from you." After I find our conversation, I open the chat and the last message on the screen is the one I sent the night Vera came over. I turn the phone around and show her.

"That's odd." She examines it closer.

"Technology these days, not always reliable." We both laugh and think about what might have caused the lost message. It might also have something to do with why she has seemed so radio silent recently. "I would like to come tonight," I say, sliding the phone back into my pocket.

She smiles and nods, allowing the hat to slide forward, covering her eyes. Without a thought, I reach out and adjust it, setting it back in the proper spot. My right hand slides down her cheek and lightly grazes her soft skin.

Her eyes close at my touch and she swallows slowly before answering. "Yes, I would love that."

The jingle of the door distracts me from Daphne, and I glance back to see the box I brought in.

Picking up the box, I turn back to her, "Oh yeah, would you be interested in some local grown cucumbers for your delicious sandwiches?" I ask.

"Don't tell me you garden too?" She laughs, amused.

"While I may be good at several things, gardening is not one of them. But it happens to be one of my Ma's favorite hobbies. She practically lives outside."

"Well, please tell her thank you. I greatly appreciate it and will definitely put these to use."

"Sure." I hand her the box and feel the usual pulse when we touch. "I will let you get back to work." Leaning forward, I press my lips to her cheek and hesitate before pulling back. "Happy birthday, Daphne."

She stands frozen with a smile on her face and I wink before walking out the door.

Once I am seated in my truck, I call Paul. Now that I think about it, I haven't heard much from him recently either.

"Hey man." He answers almost immediately.

"Hey dick, thanks for letting me know about Daphne's birthday celebration." It comes out a little harsher than I had planned but Paul just laughs it off.

"I just found out from Katie when I stopped by her place after getting a new phone this morning.

"Lose another one already?" Paul is notorious for losing phones. I couldn't count the number of times he has needed to replace one.

"Nah. I met up with Rach at the bar and while we were talking, another girl called."

"Okay, and how did that lead to you needing a new phone?" I ask, unsure what the point of his story is.

"Well, you see, when the girl programmed her number into my phone, she took a picture of her boobs and assigned it as her caller-id pic. I had no idea until my phone vibrated on the bar and I looked down. Before I could do anything, the phone was submerged in my glass of beer."

He can't even finish his story before I am bent over in my truck laughing so hard that it is difficult to breathe. I am always thoroughly entertained when I hear stories of karma catching up to Paul.

"I am so happy you can find such humor in my pain. I don't know how I end up with all these crazy bitches."

Finally catching my breath, I take a long sip from my water bottle. "Here's an idea, Paul. Stop picking up girls at the bar."

"But those are the easy ones. So, are you going tonight?"

"Yeah. It was strange, Daphne kept saying she texted me telling me about the plans, yet, I have no message from her. In fact, I hadn't heard anything from her since we went to lunch."

The line is silent for a minute before Paul laughs and responds.

"I have a hunch. Find Daphne under your contacts and scroll to the bottom and let me know what it says."

Humoring Paul, I do as he says and curse out loud when I see exactly what the issue is.

"Son of a bitch. She was blocked from my phone. It had to have been Vera. How did you know?" I tap on *unblock* and feel my blood pressure rising.

"I know a thing or two about crazy women and you my friend dated their queen."

"She is insane. Thanks for the help, man. I have to go, but I will see you later on."

Hanging up, I shake my head and wait for the anger to diffuse slightly before pulling out of the parking lot. I'd love to call Vera and give her a piece of my mind, but know that is exactly the reaction she is hoping for.

I stop at the store on my way home, knowing the perfect gift I want to pick for Daphne. Before going inside, I send her a message, testing the fix.

Me: Looking forward to tonight.

Daphne: Me too. ;)

Daphne

16

Wiping the smile from my face would be a near impossible task at this point. My thirtieth birthday has been surprisingly great so far, and seeing Curtis just made it that much better. I am so relieved to know that he wasn't ignoring my texts. Still not sure why he wasn't getting them, but happy nonetheless. It would be great to see him tonight at the bar, and maybe after a few drinks I will build up the liquid courage I need to let him give me a birthday kiss.

Sweeping up the tiny mess in the lobby while fantasizing about the softest lips in the universe, the bell at the front door catches my attention. A gigantic bouquet of flowers is being carried through the door and I instantly notice the teal vase, my favorite color. Lilies and tulips spill over every edge in the most elaborate floral display I have even seen.

Setting them down on the counter the delivery guy turns and looks right at me. "Happy Birthday, Daphne. These are for you." The florist hands me the clipboard to sign for my delivery, the confusion apparent on my face. "The hat kind of gives it away."

"Oh yeah. Thanks, I keep forgetting. They are beautiful," I reply.

"Have a great day, ma'am."

"You too, take care."

As he walks out the door, I pull off the note and read the words to myself.

Daphne,

Happy Birthday, beautiful. I miss you so much every day and hope your 30th is truly amazing, because you deserve nothing but the best. Thinking of you.

Love, Nathan

Releasing a heavy sigh, I place the note back in the plastic holder and throw away the envelope. I leave it as the guilt creeps over me. Just as I was fantasizing about kissing the sexy construction worker, a bouquet on legs walks in and drags me down memory lane.

For the last few years, I have received flowers on my birthday from Nathan. The teal vase is his signature. This year's note, however, was not like the rest. There was a sadness pitted deep in his words.

"Oh dear, how beautiful." Hilda has just rounded the corner into the lobby and wraps me in a bear of a hug. For such a fragile woman, she has the firmest grip and sends warm fuzzies straight to my heart.

"Yes, they are. From Nathan." Hilda knows my backstory and squeezes a little tighter to let me know she understands.

"Sweetheart, why don't you get on out of here? This place will be just fine without the birthday girl."

"Are you sure? I have some time before Derrick gets here and we head to Papas."

"Of course I am sure. Happy birthday, sweetie. Have fun today and be careful going out tonight. I will see you next week. Tell your papa I said hello."

"Will do. I'll finish up here and head out. Have a good weekend, Hilda." I wave her off as she heads towards the back of the house.

The mess is quickly cleaned up and I grab my flowers and purse and head to my car. Checking my phone, I realize it is later than expected and still no word from Derrick. He has my address so I am sure he will just show up when he is good and ready, on his own time as usual.

Maneuvering a few things around on my floorboard, I lodge the vase between a couple bags and a random sweater hoping it will not tip over on the drive home. Closing the door to the passenger side, I notice a car approaching. As it grows closer, I recognize the black sports car and lean into my hood casually, attempting to hide my excitement.

"Hey pretty lady, just passing through town and thought I'd stop in for some sweet tea," Derrick calls from his window as he pulls into the spot next to me.

Unable to contain my excitement, I launch from the hood and nearly jump through the window, hugging around his neck.

"I am so happy to see you! Happy birthday, turd!" I kiss his cheek and step back so he can exit.

"Ah, that was quite a drive. I am ready to get out of this car and get a beer in my hand."

"Good, me too. I am all set here and on my way home. We have plans for lunch at three, so we can hang at my house until then. I only have wine though, so we can pick up some beer on the way.

"Sounds good."

"Alright, let's go." I smile wide and reach around him for one last hug. "It's really good to see you. I know it hasn't been that long, but last time was not the happiest of occasions, so I am glad we get to relax and have a fun weekend together."

He hugs me back tightly. "Me too. And it's good to be back in town. Sometimes I really miss the simplicity of this place."

"Yeah, I really like it here." I turn around and head to the driver's side. "Let's go!"

"Aye, aye," he responds and we drive off.

Back at the house, Derrick and I enjoy a few beers while catching up and I show him some of the plans for the Tea Room. He loves most of them and gives me some quick marketing advice that will definitely come in handy.

On our way to lunch, we stop at a local bakery and pick up a fresh baked apple pie. It is Papa's favorite dessert, but happens to be Derrick's as well. Southern Delights is known for their award winning pies and homemade ice cream. We have been enjoying dessert here our entire lives. I also order an assortment of her baked goods monthly to keep at the Tea Room on special.

Approaching the house, Derrick grows silent. He hasn't been here since Grams passed.

"Man, it's just not the same coming down this driveway and not seeing Grams on the porch."

"My thoughts exactly," I reply.

We pull up to the house and walk around the porch to the back, knowing Papa is more than likely already at the grill.

"Hey old man!" Papa hollers at Derrick as he approaches.

"Old man? Says this guy. Who's the one spitting dust here?" Derrick puts his arm around Papa who lets out a deep laugh.

"Spitting dust, huh? That's good. I'll let you have this one, seeing as how it's your birthday and all." He sets down the spatula in his hand and puts both arms around Derrick. "Good to see you, boy. Happy Birthday."

"Thanks. Good to see you too."

"And Happy birthday to you as well, angel." He releases Derrick and wraps me up in his arms for a tight embrace.

"Thanks, Papa. And we brought dessert." I point at the Southern Delights bag and he pats his stomach in approval.

"Maybe we just skip these burgers and go straight for the good stuff," he says.

"Speaking of good stuff, you got any beer?" Derrick asks his usual question, knowing Papa always keeps a few cold ones in the fridge.

We all sit on the porch while Papa cooks and we spend the afternoon laughing and enjoying each other's company. After we eat, I head inside to clean up the plates and put away the left over pie. Looking through the window, I see Papa take Derrick around the shoulder and walk down toward the water. He must be having the talk he mentioned to me last time I was here. Not sure what it is about, but I am sure Derrick will spill the beans later tonight when he is drunk.

We finish up the afternoon on the back porch and say our goodbyes. Katie is meeting us at our house to pre-drink before heading out and I still need to choose an outfit for the evening. Now that I know Curtis might show up, I changed my original choice and want to make sure I have enough time to get my hair curled.

Derrick is ready in fifteen minutes flat and looks sharp in a pair of dark denim jeans and striped button up with the sleeves rolled a few times. I just put the last hot curler in my hair and now have to rummage through my closet until I find the perfect outfit. The weather is nice and I am leaning towards a dress.

The doorbell rings through the apartment and I look at my phone to check the time. It is already seven thirty, so this must be Katie.

"Derrick, that should be Katie. Will you grab the door?"

I don't hear his response so I grab my robe and open my door to check.

"Heyyy, birthday girl!" Katie comes barreling around the corner and pounces into me with her arms wide open for a hug. "Ready to get silly?"

"Yeah, I just don't want to look silly. I can't decide on what to wear. Help me, please?" I point to the pile on my bed and she shakes her head and laughs. "Oh yeah, did you meet my brother?"

"Yeah, funny thing." She turns toward the bed and picks up a few dresses, almost as if she is avoiding eye contact. "I met Derrick a couple years ago, when he was in town. We have mutual friends that I went to high school with. I didn't realize it until I saw his face just now."

"Crazy, huh?" I reply and she turns and smiles her sweet, innocent smile.

"Small world I guess." There is more story behind her smile, but I decide not to dig into it tonight.

"Okay, so what do you think? I was leaning towards the navy blue lace dress."

"Duh! That is totally the one. Try it on and let me see."

I drop my robe, and throw the dress over my head. Standing up, I step into a pair of nude Mary Jane wedges and adjust the hem of the lace.

161

"Uh, yeah. Winner. You are totally wearing that."

I turn toward the mirror and check out both the front and back of my outfit. It does look amazing and I feel pretty confident this will turn heads, but one in particular that I am most interested in.

"Phew, I thought I would never choose. Thanks for the help. Let me take these curlers out and I will be all set to go."

"Great, I am grabbing a beer and calling the cab." Katie hops off my bed and heads to the kitchen.

Releasing the curlers and finishing with hair spray, I take one last look in the mirror and walk out to the living room. The music is still on, but I don't hear voices. Looking around, I notice my brother and Katie outside on the patio talking. Katie is smiling and Derrick is laughing at something she said. If I didn't know any better, I would imagine they are more acquainted than she let on. And if I know my brother, he either charmed her once before or is doing his best to charm her pants off this time around. However, from the looks of it now, maybe it is Katie who is doing the charming. They really are a lot alike, whether that is a good thing or bad, it could make for an interesting evening.

I knock on the glass door, just as the cab beeps his horn. They head inside and we all finish our drinks with a cheers and leave for what should be one hell of a night.

A couple drinks and a few shots in, the party is really taking way. So far, a few of Katie's friends and some of my friends from the Tea Room have joined us. Paul showed up a few minutes ago and has seemed to really hit it off with Derrick. As happy as I am at the turn out, I can't help but wonder if Curtis will be stopping by.

Katie and I go back and forth from the party to the dance floor and I can already sense my legs will be sore tomorrow. I don't drink, or party like this often, much less, dance like a teenager in four-inch heels. My thighs are on fire, but I just can't stop moving, it's too much fun.

"Okay, lady. I need a break, let's get some water." I motion toward our table and am shocked when Katie nods her agreement. I swear she has a hidden energy source.

I swallow down an abundance of water and finally regain feeling in my legs. Finishing my glass, I feel the breeze from the door opening behind me as a warming sensation rushes through my stomach. My senses are heightened and I feel a hand graze my shoulder and Curtis steps into my view.

His eyes rake my body as I stand from my chair to give him a hug. I easily wrap my arms over his shoulders, thankful to be wearing these shoes for the added height. His arms wrap around my middle as he slowly slides his hands down my sides as I back out of the embrace.

"Glad you could make it," I say with a smile that I am finding difficult to tame.

"I wouldn't miss it. You look absolutely incredible and I like your hair like this." He reaches up and twists one of the curls in his fingers.

I give a small curtsy and respond. "Well, thank you Mr. Dean. Would you like a drink?" I wave my hand toward the two bottles on ice at our table that Paul arranged for our group. "We have whiskey and vodka."

"Yes, please. I'll have some whiskey on ice." I grab a new glass, pour his drink and hand it to him. "Thank you."

He lifts his glass toward me and I reach for mine and bring it to his. "Happy birthday, Daphne. Hope you have an amazing night. You deserve it."

"Thank you. And I plan on it." With a wink, I tap his glass and we both keep our eyes locked as we sip our drinks.

Whether it is the alcohol or the fact that he looks sexier than I have ever seen him, either way, I am hot. Like hot and bothered, need to be touched. I wonder if anyone will notice if I drag him out the front door and hop into a cab.

"Buddy!" Paul calls out as he approaches with Derrick and slaps Curtis on the back.

Well, there goes that chance.

"Curtis, this is Derrick, my brother." I introduce them and they shake hands.

"Nice to meet you," says Curtis and Derrick responds with a friendly smile and nod.

A couple of hours have passed as we continue to drink and enjoy the night. Katie has calmed on the dance floor visits and we mostly just dance at the table so we can keep everyone company and take our turns shooting darts. Not that they would miss us if we left, neither one of us seem to be able to hit the board.

Throughout the night, Curtis and I have been stealing glances. As he finishes a game of pool, my eyes follow him, admiring his tight backside in the light blue denim as he heads to the bar. Coming back with a tray of shots, everyone grabs their glass, and we raise them up together.

"To Daphne and Derrick and smashing their twenties goodbye. Cheers!" Curtis gives me a wink.

"Cheers!" we all respond in unison and tilt the shots back.

Just as I regain composure after swallowing down the hard liquor, I hear a faint beat begin to ascend through the speakers. I close my eyes for a second and listen closer. As the last song fades out, my current favorite jam grows louder and I feel the need to have a partner for this next dance.

Thanks to the liquid courage I had been hoping for, I grab Curtis by the hand and lead him to the dance floor. He gives me a wondering look, but follows without hesitation.

I wrap my arms around his neck and sway with the beat. He moves along with me, as I turn around and place my backside to his front.

Moving my hips to Jason Derulo's words, I sing them to myself as each one rings true to my thoughts.

I continue to move and sing along, turning and dancing along as his body meets mine every step of the way. I didn't peg him for a good dancer, but his ability to move with me is impressive and keeps sending rivers of heat throughout my body.

With another spin, I wrap my arms back around his neck and he pulls me in closer to his body just as the chorus is singing through. He brushes his warm mouth against my neck, and I feel my knees weaken beneath me. Thankful his arms are around me to hold me up; I grip the shirt on his back and grind my body against his.

He pulls his head back, smirks and then leans into my ear. "You ready to get out of here?"

My body is calling and there is only one answer to his question. "Yes." I nearly whisper my response, but the widening of his smile and desire in his eyes let me know he read my lips clearly.

Curtis

17

Wrapping my fingers around her delicate hand, I lead Daphne off the dance floor and over to where her brother is sitting with Katie. I couldn't keep my eyes from roaming up and down her body the moment my gaze landed on her when I walked in the door. The dress she is wearing hugs her tight body, falling mid-thigh, and the heels only accentuate her toned legs even more. I haven't been able to keep my hands off of her since we hit the dance floor. The way she was shamelessly rubbing against me left me hard and painfully pressed against my zipper. We needed to get out of here, fast.

"Hey guys, we are going to head out," Daphne says, when we approach Derrick and Katie.

Katie looks to Daphne, wiggling her brows before wrapping her arms around me at the same time Derrick embraces his sister.

"Take care of her. I think you two are good for each other," Katie whispers in my ear before pulling away.

I nod and wave to Paul when I catch his eye from across the bar, where he is occupied with a redhead. Turning towards Derrick, I reach my hand out and he reciprocates, shaking it.

"It's good to meet you, man. I hope to see you again you before you take off."

We stand back watching as the girls whisper and giggle, like a couple of teenagers.

Derrick smiles, his eyes never leaving Katie, "Yeah, no doubt. You two get out of here. I will make sure Katie gets home safely."

"Thanks." I pat him on the shoulder, pulling his attention to me. "She's like a little sister to me." His expression turns serious, hearing the warning in my voice.

"I respect that, but you remember, Daphne *is* my sister, twin at that, and she has been through a lot recently. Be good to her."

"I wouldn't have it any other way," I respond, just as Daphne walks up and entwines her hand with mine.

"See you back at the house?" she asks her brother, who has wrapped his arm around Katie.

"Maybe around lunchtime," Katie surprises us by answering for Derrick.

Pulling her closer into his body, he smiles down at her. "The lady has spoken. See you tomorrow, sis."

With a light squeeze of my hand, I pull Daphne toward the exit and straight to my truck. The short drive from the bar to Daphne's place is rather eventful. She spends the first couple minutes searching through the radio stations, stopping at some of the most random songs, doing her own version of karaoke. I don't think I have neither laughed so hard nor been so turned on in my entire life. Part of me doesn't want the car ride to end because I could sit here and just watch her laugh and sing for hours.

She lands on an old Alanis Morissette song just as we are entering her housing community. Parking my truck in her drive, I turn in my seat and watch as she belts out the man-hating song.

As the tune fades out, Daphne reaches to turn the volume down. "Sorry," she laughs, "I love that song."

"No worries, I thoroughly enjoyed the show. Did you know, it's rumored she wrote that song after her breakup with Uncle Joey."

Her eyes go big and her mouth opens in shock. "From *Full House*?" I nod. "I don't think I even knew they dated. How do you even know that?"

"I may have had a slight Alanis crush when I was younger."

"A crush, huh? What about now? Still crushing on Alanis?" Parting her legs slightly, Daphne glides a finger up and down her thigh. "I don't know that I can compete with that."

I watch as her finger trails higher and reach my breaking point when it slips under the hem of her dress. Grasping her head in my hands, I crush my mouth against hers. Her soft lips part, allowing my tongue entrance to explore further. Running my hands down her arms, I grip her waist and lift her, depositing her on my lap, never breaking our kiss. Daphne buries her hand in my hair, giving it a squeeze, while she slowly grinds against me. Pulling my lips away, I pepper her in kisses from her jaw, down her neck, and back up again. My hands drop to her thighs and I slide them upwards, raising her dress as I go.

"Oh, Curtis," she moans, pressing her heat against my rock hardness.

I stop her movement, my hands gripping her hips. "We need to get inside before I take you right here."

Daphne gasps, nodding her head. I open my door and step out of the truck with Daphne in my arms. I lower her to the ground, her body slowly sliding down mine. Her lips are swollen and her face is flushed. I don't know that she has ever looked more beautiful.

We walk hand in hand to her door and she stops abruptly when we reach the porch.

"My keys are in my purse, which is still in your truck." She looks up at me in embarrassment and I lean forward, kissing her cheek.

"Wait here, I will go grab it."

Jogging down her short driveway, I reach into the cab and grab her purse. Yellow and silver wrapping paper catches my eye from behind the seat and I also pick up her gift I had almost forgotten.

Daphne's eyes light up when she sees the package and she reaches her hand out, trying to grab it. I laugh, snatching it away.

"No way, you can open it inside." Daphne juts her bottom lip out in a pout and I nip it gently between my teeth. "The quicker you open the door, the quicker you can open your present."

Stepping back, Daphne distances herself from me before turning around and unlocking the door. Once I am inside, she closes it and turns the deadbolt. Without further hesitation, she lays her palms out, requesting the present. I hand it over and watch as she rips the paper off like a child on Christmas morning. Her eyes light up when she sees the cooking griddle.

"It's perfect, Curtis. Thank you," she says, wrapping her arms around my neck and pressing her soft lips against mine.

"It's just something I thought you could use."

"Well, I love it. As a matter of fact, I suddenly have a craving for pancakes. I need to get out of these heels, so I will be right back and we can whip some up."

I watch Daphne walk away, my eyes glued to the sway of her hips, until she disappears to her room. She has me completely under her spell and I have never met anyone quite like her.

Bending down, I pick up the ripped scraps of paper from the present and ball them together. When I stand back up, I notice the enormous flower arrangement sitting on display. My curiosity gets the best of me and I take a glance at the card sticking out of the flowers. Dread and jealousy hit me hard as I read the card for a third time. Here this guy dropped hundreds of dollars on this ridiculous arrangement and all I got Daphne was a lousy griddle. The intimacy of the note gets to me the most and I can't help but to wonder where Daphne's head is with all this. It is obvious Nathan still has feelings for her. *Miss you. Thinking of you. Love.* Not that I can blame him, but he did let her leave. He doesn't get to send some flowers and expect to walk back into her life, right? It's just a birthday gesture from an ex-lover. *Ex-fiancé.*

I am immediately pulled from my dark thoughts when I see Daphne emerge from her room. All blood rushes below my belt as I take in her beauty. Wearing nothing but a simple pajama set of blue shorts and top, she takes my breath away.

I follow behind her, dropping the wadded ball of paper in the trash, and take a seat at the counter. Daphne flutters around the kitchen, pulling her needed ingredients from various cabinets, talking aimlessly about her day. There is music playing faintly in the background and every so often, Daphne's hips will move and sway to the beat. I don't think she even realizes that she is doing it.

She is standing with her back to me, pouring the mixture onto the hot griddle, when a song comes on that we had danced to earlier in the night. Daphne's hips start moving at their own accord and I am brought back to when she was dancing against me. I stand up, instantly hard and walk up behind her, wrapping an arm around her middle, pulling her tight against me.

She continues dancing to the music, putting more emphasis on her moves as she grinds her ass against my hardness. I can no longer take the torture and yank the cord out of the wall, unplugging the griddle.

Turning her quickly, my lips crash against hers in a demanding kiss.

Daphne

18

O ur tongues frantically explore each other's mouths, sending waves of heat throughout my veins. I stretch my arms up around his neck and dive my hands into his dark hair, gripping it between my fingers.

He breaks our kiss and moves his mouth to my neck, painting a warm trail down to my chest. His wandering hands trail from the small of my back over the arch of my backside, cupping each cheek and lifting me effortlessly onto the counter. My legs wrap themselves around his waist, pressing his hardness directly against my heat.

His next kiss to my neck pings electricity straight between my thighs, causing me to arch my back at his tender touch. With one swift move, he lifts my cami over my head and discards it on the floor while at the same time bringing his face into my chest and covering my exposed nipple with his full lips.

Reaching further into my backbend of passion, my eyes flutter open and I notice my purse next to me on the counter. Thankfully, I just purchased condoms yesterday and never put them away. Sliding my arm toward my bag, he never breaks his lips from my breast but moves with me as I lean over to retrieve one of the foil wrappers.

The next few seconds of heat and desire become a blur as his tongue increases the strokes being flicked across my peaking nipple. Once my brain and body get back on the same page, I notice he has already placed the condom on his length and he is sliding his hands up my thighs, soon gripping the waist of my shorts. I raise my bottom up, as he slowly slides them down to my ankles and they drop to the floor.

Lifting his gaze, our eyes lock and a gasp escapes my throat as I welcome him into my body, exploding a downpour of ecstasy. Curtis eases himself into me and the electricity I once felt with a simple touch of his hand is no match for the lightning storm that is coursing through my body in this moment.

"Oh, Curtis. You feel so good," I whimper.

"You have no idea, Daphne," he responds and kisses me tenderly on the lips.

We continue a passionate pace, matching each other's rhythm while my legs remain wrapped around his waist. I remove one hand from around his shoulder and place it behind me on the counter to help steady my movements. Arching my back, leaning into my palm, the heat of my release builds quickly and my breaths quicken. Curtis increases his pace and returns his mouth to my neck, sending a final wave of ecstasy as a powerful climax pulls at my core.

As I tighten around him with the passionate release, I feel him tense and a deep moan escapes his throat. Our bodies relax into one another as our breathing begins to calm.

Rolling onto my back and looking up at the ceiling, it occurs to me that last night was not a dream and was in fact, the most real thing I have felt in quite a while. A sweet aroma sweeps through the air and with a deep inhale, I also smell a hint of freshly brewed coffee. Real indeed, and yet somewhat like a dream. After our kitchen en-counter last night, my exhaustion settled quickly once the full night of drinking, dancing and sexing came to a thrashing end. Curtis carried me to bed and the last thing I remember was being wrapped in his arms as I drifted to sleep.

Crawling from my empty bed, I head to the bathroom before making my way toward the mouth-watering fragrance.

I round the corner to be graced with the sexiest morning view of a shirtless Curtis flipping French toast on my new griddle.

"Good morning," I say shyly as I grab the coffee pot to pour myself a cup.

"Morning, beautiful," he replies and leans over to kiss my forehead. "It is a little rainy outside but I thought we could eat on the porch, what do you think?"

"Sounds good to me. I'll get us all set up. You want some coffee?" I ask while grabbing plates from the cabinet.

"Yes, please. Just black."

He finished the last piece and follows behind me with the full plate and syrup. We both keep relatively silent while getting settled and begin eating.

A few quiet moments pass but not the awkward kind of silence you would expect after quite the evening. Honestly, we hardly know each other and it was way out of character for me to sleep with someone so quickly after meeting. With Curtis, however, the rulebook went straight out the window and I allowed myself to just feel and not overthink. Until now, that is.

"So, I hope you know I don't normally do that."

"What, have sex on the counter?" he asks playfully and his smile is contagious.

"No, well yes. Never actually. That was a first. But anyways, what I mean is that I don't normally just don't move this quickly when getting to know a guy."

"No, I understand. So let me take you on a real date – dinner, tonight?" he says and casually takes a sip of his coffee.

"Yeah, I think that would be nice," I reply and casually take a sip of my own cup. "I'll have to check with Derrick to make sure he didn't want to make plans, but I am sure he will be fine."

"Great, I'll plan to pick you up at seven."

I give a nod while chewing a mouthful of toast and enjoying his breakfast making skills.

"Delicious, by the way."

"Thank you. I am glad you like them. My mom taught me a few things in the kitchen, but I am no chef. Just the basics."

"Well, sometimes the basics are the most essential."

"Agreed."

We finish eating and bring our plates into the kitchen and I notice there's not much to clean.

"Thank you for cleaning up the mess from last night and for cooking me breakfast. It was great."

"You're welcome. Anytime."

I start to walk toward my bedroom and call over my shoulder, "I'm going to jump in the shower." Turning around, I admire his toned chest and low hanging jeans as he leans up against the counter. "Well, are you coming?" I ask.

Without a word, I watch his eyes darken with desire as a smile teases the corner of his mouth and he follows behind me into the bathroom.

Curtis

19

I walk out to my truck high on life after spending the night with my arms wrapped around Daphne. The feeling of being inside of her was more than I could have ever imagined. I had no doubts that being with her would be anything short of amazing, but never could have predicted this.

Now I have a few hours to spare until I come back to pick her up for our date tonight. I would have been happy spending the entire day locked away inside her townhouse, but she needs to visit with her brother and I look forward to taking her out for a proper date. I plan to use the rest of the day to get things done around the house that I have been neglecting. But, as much as I am not looking forward to it there is not much that can bring me down today.

At least until I check my phone, which I had left inside my truck last night. I skim over the missed calls from Paul and my eyes zone in on the message from Vera. What could she possible want, especially at three in the morning? With a groan, I slide my finger across the screen, dreading what's to come.

Vera: I miss you, baby. When can we get together? ;)

I can only assume this was a drunk text given the time stamp, but it is typical Vera and her custom post-break-up routine. There will no getting together. I can't even be bothered to respond to her, which would only feed into her immature games.

Closing out of the message my phone vibrates in my hand with an incoming message from Paul and I remember the multiple missed calls.

Paul: 9-1-1!!!! Stranded!!!! Call me back!!!!

I laugh at the extreme use of exclamation points before returning his call. It barely rings twice and he is on the line.

"About damn time. Where have you been?" Paul asks, sounding frantic.

"I just found all your missed calls. What's going on?" I back out of Daphne's drive and head out toward the main road.

"I need you to come pick me up. I'll text you the address."

"Is your truck broke down?"

"I didn't drive my truck last night. It's still at the bar. I'm sending the address and will be outside waiting on you," Paul rushes out and the line goes dead before I can respond.

His message comes through, giving me his location and luckily it is only a couple miles away.

I pull into the housing development and only make it two blocks before I spot Paul walking. Not seeing any traffic behind me, I veer off to the side of the road and he yanks the passenger door open, jumping in before I can completely stop.

"Where's the fire?" I ask, laughing as I turn around and head out of the development.

I look over and Paul is rubbing his hand roughly up and down his face. "I'm getting too old for this."

Unsure of the meaning behind his statement, or his behavior this morning, I can only laugh imaging what it could be. "What the hell happened?" I ask.

"Well," he starts, sitting a little straighter in the seat, "I ended up going home with the redhead. Real wildcat by the way. She did things to me last night that I can't even describe." Paul stops, his hand rubbing his mouth in thought.

"Well, if last night was so great, why are you hightailing it out this morning?"

"That would be because her husband came home. A little piece of information she forgot to mention last night."

At that, I lose it, so bad I almost need to pull over because I am laughing so hard. Only Paul would have something like this happen. He found himself in more shit when we were growing up than anyone I know.

"Husband? How do you get yourself into these situations?" I ask, after I have calmed my fit of laughter.

"I don't know, man." He is bent down with his head resting in his hands. "She shoved me out of her bedroom window. I haven't had that happen since high school."

If I didn't know any better, looking over at Paul, he almost seems hurt.

"Maybe you need to take a break from women," I suggest, knowing he will never do it. Paul has been chasing skirts since he hit puberty.

This gets a short laugh out of him. "Yeah, you are probably right. Hey, speaking of sexy blondes, how did your night go?"

Blondes? Weren't we just talking about a redhead?

"Fine. I drove Daphne home and we hung out for a bit." I stop short, not wanting to divulge too much.

Paul turns in his seat, his back against the door, looking at me as if I've lost my marbles. "That's all you have to report?" he asks in disbelief.

"Yep. Unlike you, I know how to keep things private."

"That's okay, my friend." He laughs and points at my shirt. "The clothes from last night and your wet hair tell me all I need to know."

Busted. I shake my head and continue driving, stopping at the bar to drop Paul off to his truck.

I spend my afternoon painting Hannah's dollhouse and furniture pieces I custom built. There isn't much I wouldn't do for this little girl, and she knows it too. Which helps explain the multiple princess tea parties I've attended requiring me to wear a tiara. Paul had shown up unannounced during their last visit, right in the middle of our tea party and laughed his ass off when he got a look at my attire. Not skipping a beat, Hannah grabbed ahold of his hand and led him over to our table setting. She patted her hand on the pillow and Paul lowered himself to the floor, but didn't find it nearly as funny once she wrapped a pink feather boa around his neck and demonstrated how he should hold his teacup, pinky up. Of course, she can make any grown man fall to his knees with her baby blues.

Speaking of those eyes, Hannah's photo lights up my screen as an incoming call from Jill vibrates on the table. I answer using the speaker, so I can get ready for my date and catch up with Jill at the same time. Hannah is excited about her upcoming recital and spends a good amount of time giving me the play by play of how it will all go down. She plans to show me every one of her routines when they come for their visit. Jill somehow wrangles the phone from her and we share a laugh over how much she has grown. They are coming down sooner than originally planned and I can sense in Jill's voice there is something wrong, but when I ask about Alex, she swiftly changes the subject.

After I hang up, I think back to my conversation with Ma, when she suspected there was something bothering Jill. As usual, she was right.

My nerves hit hard on the drive over to Daphne's to pick her up. It takes me back to high school as if I'm picking up my prom date. It is not a feeling I would expect to have as a grown man, but I welcome it.

I swear I momentarily stop breathing the moment Daphne opens the door. She is literally breathtaking. Wearing a deep plum colored dress that's wrapped snug to her body, I notice the tie at her ribs. All I can think about is how much I want to pull the material and watch it slowly unwrap, allowing me to see what's underneath. Even though, it's has been mere hours since I last saw her gorgeous naked body, it doesn't do anything to kill the urges I have in this moment.

"Wow. You look amazing," I say, and watch the blush spread across her cheeks.

"Thank you. You are looking rather handsome yourself."

I reach out for her hand. "Shall we?"

Smiling, she nods and reaches her hand out, lacing her fingers with mine. I lead her to my truck, opening her door and assisting her inside. Her sweet scent invades my senses and I close the door, taking my time to walk around the truck, attempting to get myself under control.

I want tonight to be special, so I made a reservation at a nice Italian restaurant just outside of town. The half hour drive speeds by as we talk about the day. Daphne spent time with her brother after he wandered in right around noon and was very tight lipped about his evening with Katie. It is easy to see the bond between her and Derrick and I know it must be hard not getting to see him often. I can understand how she feels and Jill and Hannah have only been away a couple of years. Daphne mentioned her brother has been off doing his own thing basically since college.

When we arrive at our destination, I jump out of the truck and run to Daphne's side to open the door for her, determined to do everything right tonight. I rest my hand on the small of her back, guiding her into the restaurant.

"Good evening, welcome to Spallini's. Do you have a reservation?" the young girl asks from behind her post.

"Yes, under Dean."

She takes a moment and looks down at the electronic device in her hand. "Dean, table for two on the rooftop. Right this way." With two menus in hand, the girl turns and leads us to the stairs.

I keep my hand firmly pressed against Daphne's back until we reach our table and I pull out her chair. As I push her in closer to the table, I lean over and bring my lips to her ear. "Did I tell you how beautiful you look tonight?"

I stand and walk to my seat across from hers, noticing the blush returning to her cheeks. Menus are placed before us, and the hostess retreats after informing us that our server would be with us momentarily.

"You really outdid yourself tonight, Curtis. This view is incredible." Looking around, she takes in the sights.

Spallini's is an old Italian restaurant that has been around for ages. It sits on a hilltop overlooking the river and at night you can watch the lights of the boats coming in and out. The rooftop is always the best place to sit in the entire restaurant and at times it's impossible to reserve a table. I was extremely lucky when I called this morning just after another couple canceled.

The rooftop dining area is fully enclosed in glass, but with weather permitting, sections of the walls retract, allowing for a more open experience. Above us, running below the ceiling, are lights hung across wooden trellis. The lighting sets a romantic mood, which is just what I had hoped for.

The server greets us and I order a nice bottle of Merlot. We take a moment to look over our menus before he returns with the bottle; he pours a small portion in my glass first and waits for me to taste it. Unsure of the proper etiquette, I bring the glass to my lips and take a generous sip. I nod my head and he refills my glass, followed by Daphne's. She has a full-faced smile, as we place our orders and he leaves us in private.

"Not much of a wine connoisseur?" Laughing, she takes her first sip of the red wine.

"No. I drink it and know what I like, but I am not one to twirl my glass around swishing it and smelling it before drinking it. All I need is a simple taste."

"I am the same. My dad's family owns a vineyard in California and when I visited a couple years ago, my grandmother was constantly on my case for drinking my wine out of the wrong glass."

"Wait a second, you mean there is a certain glass for the different wines?" I ask in disbelief.

"Oh yes. I tend to stick to the larger size and also tend to fill them to the brim. Honestly, who wants to keep refilling their glass? So she completely frowned upon my style when I had a big glass filled with Chardonnay."

"Well, here's to you for teaching me something new."

We both laugh as our date continues without a hitch, and I still can't get over how easy and natural everything is with Daphne.

After dinner we take a brief walk along the river, enjoying the scenery. She keeps her arm tucked into mine and I relish her company. At the end of the night, Daphne invites me in for a nightcap, but I reluctantly decline. With a movie-worthy kiss goodnight, I wait for her to go inside and force myself to walk away. I want everything to be done right from here on out with her, even if that means going home and sleeping alone after such an awesome night.

Daphne

20

Rounding the corner to my neighborhood, a text alert interrupts my music and a smile fills my face. Since our date a few nights ago, I haven't seen Curtis but we text a few times a day and have had phone conversations every night. My goal is to not get too caught up in whatever this is and to keep things slow for the time being. Curtis agrees since he also just got out of a relationship.

The more we talk, the more I see that he is one of the most honest, down to earth people I have ever met. It is a natural chemistry and nearly seems too good to be true.

Curtis: Good morning beautiful. Hope you have a great day. Be careful on your run, it's supposed to rain this morning.

I quickly read his message and look up to the sky. It was slightly darker than usual this morning, but I wasn't aware it might rain. No sooner does the thought cross my mind, a raindrop falls right onto my face and is soon followed by a million more. Picking up my pace, I sprint toward my house and make it under the overhang of my porch just as the first lightning flashes. The boom that follows sends a shiver down my spine and I hurry into the house.

I have never been afraid of many things in my lifetime, but for whatever reason, bad weather is one of them. It is borderline irrational and every year I think I will grow out of it, but I don't. I am not sure if it is more the lightning and fear of being struck, or what usually comes with bad weather like the unpredictability of a tornado. Mother Nature is a bitch and I try my best to avoid her.

Knowing that I will need to delay my shower until it clears a bit, I sit down in the kitchen and enjoy a cup of coffee while browsing through Facebook on my phone. I really don't utilize social media like the norm, but occasionally like to skim through for important news and my all-time favorite funny cat and cuddly puppy videos.

Apparently, it had been some time since I'd been on here, because I have an abundance of notifications and few new friend requests to review. I imagine one of them is Katie, so I begin to scroll through. Seeing her name, I accept the request and do the same for a few others.

I finish my coffee as I browse through a gossip magazine. Once the lightning and thunder ease up, I grab a quick shower and get ready for the day. We have quite a list of reservations, however I am not sure how many will cancel due to the weather.

Sitting in my car, waiting for the rain to ease, I hear a ping in my purse.

Curtis: Nasty storm, hope you are okay and didn't get caught in it. Did you run today?

Dang. Forgot to text him back.

Me: Good morning. :) Had a nice run, until the very end when it hit. But I am safe and sound. Just pulled into the Tea Room.

Curtis: Same here. Well, I didn't run, but just arrived at a job. Glad you're safe. I'd like to have dinner again soon.

Me: Sounds nice. I'll text you later. Have a good day.

Curtis: Same to you.

I really like that he doesn't lather his text messages with silly sweet talk. We are still getting to know each other and it's unnecessary to over flirt. We both know that we are attracted to one another and I don't need to hear that I am beautiful every other text. Once a day is enough for me. Curtis knows the fine line between sweet and toothache and I appreciate it.

"Morning, Hilda. You're here early today. I thought for sure I would be the first one in." I place my purse behind the desk and reach for my apron.

"Oh, well, I am not a fan of driving in the rain so I left my house a little early to try and avoid it," she replies and opens the calendar. "There were two cancelations so far on the machine and hopefully there won't be any more."

"Shoot. I thought that might happen. Well, maybe we will get a few walk-ins to make up for it." Tying my apron around my waist, I check a few items at the desk and head toward the back. "Well, let me know if we get any more. I'll be in the kitchen."

"Sounds good, dear."

The morning goes by quickly and there is thankfully only one more cancellation. After finishing the prep work, I allow the kitchen staff to take over and make better use of my help up front, checking on guests. I have been meaning to get some feedback cards printed so we can keep up with customer expectations. This was actually one of Derrick's suggestions.

As Hilda leads a group of ladies to their table, we pass each other in the hall and she leans over to tell me something. "Another group just arrived and they do not have a reservation, would you mind getting them to a table?"

"Oh sure, not a problem." I straighten out my apron and brush a stray hair behind my ear.

"Thanks, dear." Then she winks at me.

Why did she wink? It's not like I have never sat a table before.

With confusion in my brow, I shake it off as I round the corner to the lobby. Taking a look at the display of teapots in the window is a young girl, probably around four or five and two women.

"Hello, welcome to The Treasured Tea Cup. You ready to be seated?"

"Oh hi, you must be Daphne. You look just like your grandmother." The older woman is obviously from Truesdale and somehow knows Grams. But there is something else so familiar about her face, and the younger woman as well.

"Yes, I'm Daphne Fields. Nice to meet you." I hold out my hand and she softly grips it in return.

"I'm Eleanor Dean and this is my daughter Jill and her daughter Hannah."

Oh shit.

"Hi, nice to meet you." Jill also holds out her hand and I softly shake it, still in shock at who is standing in front of me.

His family. I am meeting his family. Does he even know they are here?

"Oh, I love this place, it's so pretty. I'm so excited to for my first real tea party!" Hannah clasps her hands together and bounces on her toes.

"Hi, Hannah. That's a really pretty dress."

She does a polite curtsy before responding, "Thank you."

"Right this way, I have a special table that I think you ladies will love. It's my all-time favorite and it just so happens to be available this afternoon."

"Yes!" Hannah whispers and grabs my hand to lead the way.

I let out a giggle as Eleanor and Jill both just shake their heads and follow.

We enter the Fountain of Youth Room and I pull out the chair for Hannah to sit. I am not sure how much Curtis has shared with his family, so I keep the conversation light and professional.

"Melody will be taking care of you this afternoon, but please don't hesitate to grab me if you need anything. The tea menu is the small one and lunch items are on the larger one. I really hope you enjoy your time this afternoon and I'll come check on you in a few."

"Thank you, Daphne," Eleanor says and there is a gleam in her eye as if she knows all there is to know.

I feel my face begin to flush and quickly respond to make my exit, "My pleasure, enjoy."

"She's pretty, Nana," Hannah whispers as I am walking away and I try to hide my smile as I round the corner pretending I didn't hear.

He could not have a more adorable family. His mother is beyond sweet and Jill has his same quiet demeanor. That Hannah, though, what a riot. She is too much for words.

After twenty minutes, I make my rounds and check in on a few tables to make sure they are enjoying themselves. My last stop is to the Deans' table and they all have smiles from cheek to cheek. It makes my heart warm to see they are having a nice time.

"How are we doing, ladies?" I ask.

"Everything is delicious as usual. You've done very well with the place. Kay would be very proud."

"Thank you so much. Oh! And thank you for the vegetables. That was very thoughtful of you and they were delicious. I would be glad to pay you for any extras you are looking to get rid of in the future."

"Oh yes! Glad you like them. I'll be sure to send Curtis over with some more very soon. And I refuse to take payment for them. It is something I love to do and I am more than happy to give them to someone who appreciates them as much as me."

"Speaking of Curtis, he did an amazing job refinishing this." I wave my hand towards the spectacular wall fountain that he amazed me with.

"Oh, wow. He did a fantastic job. Just like his father." She pulls out her phone to take a quick picture, like any proud mom would do.

"Selfie!" Hannah shouts as soon as she sees the phone.

"Hannah, quiet." Jill giggles and we all laugh at her outburst.

"Okay, sweetie. But only one," Eleanor responds.

"I can take it if you would like?" I ask politely.

"Well then, it wouldn't be a selfie," Hannah corrects me. "Plus you have to be in it!"

"Oh, okay," I reply and we all move around to fit into the screen and Hannah reaches up to press the button.

Surprisingly, we all have our eyes open and no one got cut off. It's quite honestly the cutest picture ever, mostly because of Hannah.

We share a few more laughs and I leave them to enjoy the rest of their lunch. It's easy to see where he gets his personality.

Finishing my daily log and food order, the Dean family passes by the room I am sitting in, so I stand to see them out.

"I hope you had a great time. Please come back and see us soon."

"Thank you, Daphne. We had a really great time. Hannah already made a Christmas list of her must-have teapots from the display window." Jill squeezes Hannah to her side and I watch her tiny eyes grow ten times larger.

"They are just so pretty. I need to have them all!" Hannah exclaims.

"Oh boy, we better get her out of here." Jill laughs.

"It was a pleasure to finally meet you, Daphne. I hope to see you again soon." Eleanor puts a soft hug around me and then pulls away and winks.

What is with all the winking today?

"Thanks, it was nice to meet you all too. Take care."

We wave goodbye, just as Hilda walks up.

"Take care, Eleanor. See you at Bingo Thursday!"

Eleanor winks…again. "See you, Hilda!"

Hilda! She knew all along, which must be why she asked me to seat them I'm sure. If I didn't know any better, I would venture to guess these two old ladies planned the whole thing.

Curtis: So, guess you got to meet the Dean ladies?

Me: So, news travels fast, huh?

His next response is the picture of us girls at the table.

Curtis: Beautiful. All of you.

Me: Oh geez. Lol It was very nice to meet them. Your mom and sister are super nice and Hannah is the most adorable thing.

Curtis: I know. She melts my heart. Sorry, I couldn't warn you. I honestly had no idea they were coming up there for lunch. They just sent that to me.

Me: No worries. It was fun.

Curtis: Okay, good. Well, let me get back to work. Just wanted to say hi.

I know we should be taking it slow, but after just meeting his family, I really want to see him. I was trying to go a few more days, but a little dinner date can't hurt.

Me: Do you have plans for dinner?

Curtis: No ma'am.

Me: Great, I'm cooking. My pace at seven. Sound good?

Curtis: Sounds amazing. See you at seven. :)

Curtis

21

"**U**ncle Curtis, guess what I did today?" my four-year old niece asks me, the minute I walk in the door from work.

Coming home to Hannah's smiling face beats a quiet empty house any day. It makes me realize how much I look forward to that chapter in my life. A happy marriage and house filled with noises of children running and playing.

"What did you do today, princess?" I ask, sitting down next to her on the couch, giving her my full attention.

"Me and Mommy and Nana went to this place and had a real tea party."

I laugh, watching Hannah's dramatics as she tells me about their day at The Treasured Tea Cup. She speaks very clearly for her age and is exceptionally animated with her story telling. Right now she is flipping her hair around and her hands are flying all over the place as she describes her afternoon tea.

"It was so much fun, Uncle Curtis. I wish you could have been there. I even met a new friend today. Her name is Miss Daphne, and I am pretty sure that she is a real life princess. She is super pretty and was really, really nice. I think you would like her."

I look up and see Jill standing in the entryway to the kitchen with a giant smile on her face as she watches her daughter.

"I actually know Daphne," I say and Hannah's eyes widen in surprise. "She happens to be a very good friend of mine and you know what?" She leans closer to hear my secret. "I think she is a real life princess too."

She gasps and her mouth drops open. "I knew it! I am going to go call Nana and tell her." Jumping up from the couch she screams from the top of her lungs, "MOM!"

"I am right here." Jill pushes away from the wall and joins us in the living room.

"Uncle Curtis is friends with Miss Daphne and he said that he thinks she is a real princess too. Can you believe it?" She stops for a breath and her mom just nods her head. "I need your phone so I can call Nana and tell her I was right."

Pulling her phone from her pocket, Jill passes it over and Hannah takes off to the guest room.

"So, tell me about Daphne," Jill says, taking a seat next to me on the sofa.

"We met recently while I was doing work around the Tea Room and really seem to have hit it off. Nothing too serious. We have both just come out of relationships, so we are taking things slow."

"I have to say, she is very beautiful, and she was really sweet today with Hannah. A big step up from the last one."

"That's a definite." Jill was never a fan of Vera. There has always been a slight tension between them, even in the beginning, but Jill continuously supported me. "I don't know how to explain it, Jill. Everything comes so easy with her, and it's like we just fit. Even though it is just beginning, I can't imagine my life without her. I sound crazy, don't I?"

I can't believe I just said that out loud. It sounded worse coming out of mouth than it did in my head.

"No, Curtis, you aren't crazy. I am a firm believer in the whole when you know, you know. I think it is amazing that you have found that connection with Daphne. If you let her slip by before seeing where it goes, it may end up being your biggest regret. Trust me when I say that you don't want to live with that. Hold on and hold tight." I am thrown off, not only by the hurt and pain in Jill's eyes, but also the words she has spoken. It sounds like she has regrets of her own that she's been keeping deep inside.

I reach out my hand to comfort my sister. "Is everything okay, Jill?"

I am not accustomed to seeing her unhappy and would do anything to help.

"Yeah, it will be. Sometimes life just gets in the way." Her voice cracks at the end and I am about to press for more just as Hannah comes bouncing into the living room.

Our conversation is cut off and Jill masks her emotions quickly before her daughter can suspect something is wrong. I need to try and get Jill alone so I can find out what is going on with her and Alex. It kills me to see her like this.

Hannah hooks up her iPod to my sound system and shows me three performances from her recent dance recital. It is scary how good she is for only being four. Her love of entertaining shines bright during her routines and you can't miss the pride in her mother's eyes.

Jill found her calling when she became a mother, and I always knew she would be great at it. Growing up she was always taking care of Paul and me even though she was younger than us. Not to mention our parents have set the bar high for us in terms of marriage and parenting and I can only hope to be half the husband and father my Pop is.

Combing my hair back out of my face after my shower, my phone begins ringing from my nightstand, and I jump to answer, thinking it might be Daphne.

Taking one look at the name on the screen, I hit the red ignore icon and lay it back down. Vera doesn't seem to be taking the hint that I no longer care to speak to her. The last message I received from her went unanswered, but she isn't used to being ignored by me, and is being extra persistent this time around. But there is no going back for me, I stand firm with my decision. After spending so much time with Daphne, there is definitely no way in hell I could ever go back to Vera.

Giving both Hannah and Jill a kiss on the head, I wink and tell my sister not to wait up for me. I feel bad about leaving them at the house, but Jill assured me that they would be fine and encouraged me to go out.

On the drive to Daphne's, I stop at the closest store and pick up a small bouquet of bright colored wildflowers. It pales in comparison to the gigantic display from her birthday, but to me, Daphne comes off as a girl who thinks less is more. I could be majorly off base here, but I have gut feeling I am right.

When she opens the door I am hit with mouth-watering scents of Italian spices and she looks adorable in a simple pair of colorful leggings that make her legs look amazing, and a long black top. Her hair is hanging down passed her shoulders in loose golden waves, the way I have come to enjoy the most.

We stand for a moment taking one another in. It has only been a few days since our last date, but seeing her right now has me at a loss for words.

"Hi," she says, breaking the silence.

"Hi," I return and grin as I watch her full lips spread wide in a genuine smile. "These are for you."

Her eyes lower as I lift my hand holding the flowers. "Thank you, they are beautiful." Standing on her toes, she presses her lips to my cheek.

My hand falls to her waist and wraps around her back, pulling her tightly against my body. Leaning down, my lips meet hers and the kiss begins slow and soft, but accelerates the minute her tongue traces my lip. Grasping her waist, I lift Daphne up and she wraps her legs around me, without breaking the momentum of our dancing tongues. Two steps into the house, I kick her door shut behind me and press her against the wall. A soft moan escapes her mouth and is music to my ears.

Pulling back to catch my breath, I glide my finger over her swollen lips before pressing my mouth to them twice and lowering her to the ground.

"That was an amazing hello." Daphne laughs and reaches for my hand, leading us to the kitchen.

"Something smells delicious." The Italian aroma grows stronger.

"Thank you. I made spaghetti and meatballs with Gram's homemade sauce recipe. It was always my favorite dish and comfort food," she explains, opening the cabinet beneath the sink. First, she pulls out a teal vase, but then reaches behind it and settles on a yellow one instead. After filling it with water, she arranges the wildflowers carefully and neatly.

"There is nothing like spaghetti, and I think I like it even more the next day."

"Oh my gosh, so true. I don't like many leftovers, but spaghetti is my favorite." Daphne lifts the lid to the pot and stirs the sauce. She turns the stove burner off and looks back to me, "I have the table all set; if you want to have a seat I will bring our plates over."

"Do you want me to help with anything?"

She reaches out and grabs the flowers, bringing them over me. "If you would set these on the table that would be wonderful. They are so pretty."

I take the arrangement and give her a light peck on the nose. After setting them in the middle of her dining table, I take a quick look to see that the birthday flowers from her ex are no longer in sight.

My phone vibrates in my pocket just as I sit down in my chair. I look into the kitchen and Daphne is still fixing the plates, so I pull it out to check. Shaking my head, I regretfully open the message from Vera and drop my phone in surprise when I see the full frontal nude picture she sent. Has she become this desperate? She never sent anything like this when we were together.

"Everything okay?" Daphne asks, and I panic slightly, turning my phone off and shoving it back into my pocket.

"Yeah, just something I have to deal with later," I say, hoping she won't press for more, because while I would never want to lie to her, I also have no interest in bringing her into the drama surrounding Vera.

She doesn't ask any more questions and sets our plates down before taking her own seat. I love the fact that Daphne's plate is filled just as high as mine. It's comforting to be around a woman with a real appetite.

Twirling my fork in the noodles, I gather a heaping bite and bring it to my mouth. My eyes close and I moan, taking in the explosion of flavors inside my mouth. This is by far the best spaghetti I have ever tasted, and I can't help but think back to the night of Vera's epic spaghetti fail. I couldn't imagine Daphne popping open a jar of sauce and dumping it over noodles. She puts effort into everything that she does.

"Is there anything that you can't cook?" I ask, after wiping my mouth clean.

"Fish, but it's mostly because I don't like the smell. I'll eat it, but not cook it." She scrunches up her nose and we both laugh.

"So, I was thinking. Would you be interested in coming to my place for dinner tomorrow night?"

"I would love to. Your little niece is the cutest and I would like to get to know your sister more."

"Great. You can come over whenever you are free after work and hang out with the girls while I cook." I get a slight tingle in the pit of my stomach hoping that she and Jill hit it off. "Oh, and I should warn you, Hannah is convinced that you are a real life princess. And, I may have told her that I think so as well."

Her eyes go big as she laughs and I can pick up on her nervousness. "That is a mighty big title to live up to. Is there anything specific I need to know or say? I don't want to tarnish the princess image."

"No, just be yourself and you will be perfect."

She smiles sweetly and we continue eating our meal. By the time I have cleaned my plate, I am stuffed like a Thanksgiving turkey. Daphne's talents in the kitchen are going to lead me to a gym membership in order to keep the weight off.

After dinner we work together in the kitchen putting up the leftovers, including the bowl she prepared for me, and cleaning the dishes. We set up a system where she washed and I rinsed and dried. It's quiet as we clean, and my mind wanders around thoughts of a life in which this would be a nightly routine; dinner together, then working in unison cleaning up after. Even better are the thoughts of crawling into bed every night and wrapping my arms around her.

The last dish is dried and put away, and I walk up behind Daphne as she wipes the counters. I wrap my arm around her middle and pull her hair to one side with the other. Her skin jumps with chills the moment my lips meet her neck. I create a trail going up and down and she tilts her head, allowing me better access. My hand slips under her shirt and caresses her soft skin from her stomach to her breasts.

Daphne turns in my arms, wrapping hers around my neck; she pulls my mouth to hers. There is no slow and softness in this kiss, only need and urgency. Lifting her up, she circles her legs around my waist and I blindly find my way to her bedroom. Her fingers are threaded through my hair and she grips it tightly, at the same time grinding against my hardness. Using the friction between us, I find nothing sexier than a woman who isn't ashamed to take her own pleasure

I brace myself with one arm on the bed and the other holding her back, as I lower us down. Her hands slide up under my shirt and my muscles twitch at her soft touch. Sitting back on my knees, I reach behind my head and pull my shirt off in one quick tug, discarding it somewhere on the floor. Daphne lifts herself up and swiftly removes her top, but I catch her hands when she reaches for her bra and using my free hand, I unhook the back and slide the straps down her shoulders. After it's removed, the bra joins the growing pile of clothes on the floor.

I stare at her in awe, wondering how she could be so perfect, and if I even deserve this beautiful woman. I guess I will let her be the judge of that.

"Touch me, please." Her gentle whisper causes me to lift my gaze and crash my lips to hers, lowering us back down on the mattress.

Breaking the kiss, my mouth travels across her jaw and down her neck. I continue my path down her chest, lightly grazing her skin with my tongue as I go. The closer I get to her breasts, the heavier her breathing gets and the more she squirms beneath me. I circle my tongue around her nipple, just enough to tease her before taking it in my mouth.

Daphne's fingertips glide up my back, and she squeezes tightly when I bite down on one nipple and roll the other between my fingers. Sliding them further down my back, she reaches my pants and moves to the front, undoing the button and zipper. She hooks her fingers in the waistband of my boxer briefs and pulls them, together with my jeans, far enough down that I spring free. I continue my assault on her nipples, alternating from one side to the other. Her small hand wraps around my girth and I suck in a deep breath as she strokes me up and down with a tight grip. Feeling myself start to tighten with a building release, I sit up, pulling away from her grasp.

Reaching into my pocket, I grab a condom before removing my pants completely and tossing them off the bed. I place the gold packet on the bed and run my fingers under the waistline of Daphne's leggings. She lifts her hips, urging me to continue, and I slide the pants down her legs.

"What are you doing to me?" I barely recognize my gravelly voice as I say the words. I am completely captured in her spell, as my hands skim up and down her thighs, from her knees to her hips.

Her eyes flutter closed before opening to meet my gaze. "Hopefully the same thing you are doing to me." She picks up the condom and rips it open, and I watch as she rolls it down my length, growing harder with her touch.

Bringing my body back down to hers, I press several gentle kisses against her mouth. She gasps as I slide inside her tightness.

"You are perfect," I say, once I am seated deeply inside her.

Her lips spread into a smile against my mouth before she sweeps her tongue in search of mine. Lifting her hips, urging me to move, I slowly slide out before thrusting back. Taking her hands in one of mine, I position them over her head and hold them securely against the mattress. Her chest begins to rise and fall rapidly, as I hold her gaze and continue my steady pace. Occasionally slamming harder inside, I watch as her mouth pops opens and eyes widen.

With her legs wrapped around me, she digs her heels into my ass, pushing me to go harder. I can feel her clenching me tightly and know she is getting close. With my free hand I apply pressure against her clit and push her over the edge, exploding around me. Her face is buried in my neck as she moans my name, enjoying her release. I quicken my pace, relishing in the aftershocks of her orgasm, and she clamps down on me with my release following moments later. Her name falls from my lips before I collapse on top of her, using my arm to keep my weight off.

The room is silent aside for our heavy breaths. Daphne's fingers are lightly grazing my back and running through my hair. If it wasn't for needing to throw away the pesky condom, I would stay right here the rest of the night.

Lifting up, I sprinkle Daphne's eyes and face with kisses before landing on her lips. I reluctantly pull myself out of her warmth and stand from the bed.

"Be right back," I say, leaning over to kiss her one last time. I spot my boxer briefs on the floor and grab them on the way to the bathroom.

When I return to the room, Daphne is lying on her side looking peaceful with her eyes closed. Pressing my knee into the mattress, I lean down and drop a kiss on her forehead, causing her to stir.

"Will you stay with me tonight?" She doesn't open her eyes, but pats the bed next to her.

"Nowhere else I would rather be."

Climbing in behind her, I wrap my arm around her waist and pull her tightly against me. I kiss her head and she covers my hand with hers, lacing our fingers together. When I envision my future, this is now what I see. Ending every night with her in my arms.

Daphne

22

"Morning, Hilda," I say, walking around the front desk.

"Morning, dear, and happy Friday," she replies, as she continues dusting around the front lobby.

"Yes, ma'am, happy Friday for sure. I can't believe the rush we've had this week. I'm going to come by for just a bit tomorrow, but hopefully shouldn't need to come by on Sunday."

"Sounds good, I'll be around."

Over the past few weeks, Curtis and I have been spending more and more time together. However, this week has been brutally busy and not left me much free time. He knows that I am interested in taking our time, and I can tell he feels the same way. And yet, as much as we want to take our relationship slow, our sexual attraction keeps that side of things moving right along.

My body reacts to his touch in a way that is nearly indescribable and is something I have never experienced. A heat rushes to my cheeks as soon as I feel his gaze, and just the thought of his mouth on my skin generates a throbbing pulse between my thighs. Our intimate moments are carnal and natural, but we also have a lot of fun together and are constantly laughing.

Most nights are spent at my place, but we often have dinner at his. Jill and Hannah are amazing and I am enjoying the chance to spend time with them while they are in town. Curtis and his sister are very much alike and have a great relationship. It really makes me miss my brother, Derrick.

Katie and I made plans earlier this week for dinner, but she has been picking up a few shifts at the bar for extra cash. I should probably text to confirm we are still on for tonight.

Me: Hey bartender… you still free tonight?

Katie: Yesss! Dinner at 7pm. I'm feeling sushi, you?

Me: Perfect. I'll meet you at your place.

Katie: See you then!

Closing out of our message screen, I see a new one has arrived from Curtis.

Curtis: Got a surprise for you. Will I see you this weekend?

Me: I love surprises! And you just might. I have plans with Katie tonight, but should have some free time tomorrow and Sunday.

Curtis: I might work tomorrow for a few hours. Can I borrow you on Sunday?

Me: Sunday sounds good. I'll keep my day open. Just let me know what you want to do.

Curtis: So many things I want to do... to you ;)

*Me: *Blushing* I'm sure we can arrange that.*

Curtis: You are seriously the sexiest woman ever. *Growing* But I have to stop thinking about you naked, I am about to walk up to a customer's house.

Me: Oh lord. Okay, call me tomorrow and we can make plans for Sunday. Hope your Friday grows well. I mean 'goes' lol ;)

Curtis: Haha very funny. Miss you, looking forward to Sunday.

Me: Me too :)

Sliding my phone into my pocket, I throw my hair into a high ponytail and check my reflection in the hall mirror. Blushing pink in the cheeks, I shake my head and get to work.

On my walk to Katie's, I admire the purple and orange sky as the sun begins to settle. The smile on my face is a reminder that I'm starting to come into my own here in Truesdale, and the doubts of my decision have slowly began to fade.

"Hi, lady!" Katie greets me as she opens the door and throws her arms around me for a hug.

"Hello, you look great as always. Is that a new top?" I ask as I pull back from the hug.

"Well, yes it is. Got it on sale, of course. You know I never buy anything full price." She leads the way to the car and we both get in.

The drive to the restaurant is spent discussing how our weeks have gone. I fill her in on my adventures in Curtis-land and she spills on a random one-night stand she had with an out of town visitor. Her story telling ability is quite comedic and I can already sense this will be a fun Friday night; as is most any night spent with Katie.

Our dinner is delicious and we manage to polish off quite a bit of sake and more sushi rolls than I am willing to admit. The server drops off our bill and we both reach for our fortune cookies.

"My favorite part! You go first." Katie pops open her wrapper and waits for me to follow.

Pulling the cookie from the plastic, I crack it in half and pull out the sliver of paper. "Your one true love will enter your orbit this summer."

"Oh, dang! I think I know who that might be." She wiggles her eyebrows and cracks hers open as I roll my eyes.

It is a little early to consider Curtis the love of my life. He is absolutely wonderful and there is definitely potential, but it's still too soon to be making such strong accusations. Reading it to myself one more time, I fold it up in my lap and sneak it inside the pocket of my wallet. Who knows, it may prove itself true, so I will hang on to it, just in case.

"Okay, let's see what we have here." Katie unravels her fortune and clears her throat for the announcement. "Don't trouble trouble, unless trouble troubles you."

"Yikes. That sounds dangerous," I reply.

"Try reading it. What a tongue twister." She throws it on the table and thinks nothing of it. "Let's pay the bill and go find some trouble to trouble."

"Oh boy, what did you have in mind?" I ask, already knowing the answer.

"Drinks at the bar with my summer love." She does the eyebrow wiggle thing again and this time I start to laugh. Katie is too funny for her own good.

"Oh good. So it was you they were referring to. This whole time I thought I might fall in love with a man this summer, but I guess you'll do." Giving her wink and laying my cash on the table next to hers, I stand to leave.

"Well, there's always next summer if this doesn't work out between us," she replies, never skipping a witty moment, and we both laugh as we exit the restaurant.

The bar is full of excitement, and after ordering our first round of drinks we make our way into the crowd. There is a band playing here that I have not seen before, but Katie is familiar with their music. She attended high school with one of the members and has seen them perform quite a few times.

They play mostly cover songs, so it is easy to dance and sing along. We spend the first half hour on the dance floor before taking a break for a new drink. Katie is showing signs of an increasing buzz, and I am a bit tipsy as well. I figure

I'll give myself until ten-thirty before switching to water to sober up and drive us home.

Standing at the bar laughing at another one of Katie's stories, a snarky cackle comes from behind my stool. I turn quickly, wondering who the hell is mocking me and focus my attention on a leggy brunette surrounded by a flock of blondes. Her skin tight, shorter than necessary, red dress was barely hiding any secrets. It's a shame she feels the need to over-sex her appearance because she has real natural beauty. Nonetheless, I still don't know why she is being bitchy.

Since Katie didn't notice, and continues to flirt with Brian, her favorite bartender, I decide to think nothing of it. Hell, it could just be the way she laughs. I return my attention to Katie and attempt to drown out the girl's annoying conversation about some guy who loves the dress she is wearing. Who the hell cares? Not me.

"Well, Curtis bought it, so yeah he's taken it off of me several times." The girls all giggle at her remark, and I feel my temperature increasing.

Katie must have heard her this time, and turns in her seat to stand before I even have a chance to set my drink down.

"Vera, fucking Malone. I thought I heard a rat squeaking behind me." She crosses her arms across her chest and smiles at her own joke.

Vera?

You have got to be kidding me. Just when I was starting to enjoy my evening, Curtis' ex decides to crash the party.

"I see your humor still gets you nowhere in life. Come on girls, let's go grab a drink at the back bar." In typical mean girl fashion, they march one by one away from us.

"Is that Vera, as in Curtis' Vera?" I ask, though I am pretty sure I already know the answer.

"Yep, the one and only. She is such a nasty bitch. I swear she must have multiple personality disorder. There is no way he stayed with that woman for as long as he did if she is always like this." She shakes her head and we turn back to sit at the bar.

"I wonder if she knows who I am?"

"Seriously, of course she does. The whole town saw your photo in the paper write up. Plus, she is probably a professional Facebook stalker. Does she know you are talking to Curtis?"

"No clue. But anyways, it doesn't bother me, so let's have a good night." I raise my glass and she taps hers to mine. "Cheers!"

"Cheers!" she repeats and we finish our beers.

Enjoying our time, Katie skates right through her buzz and straight to drunk. I, on the other hand, have made the switch to water and can already feel my buzz waning. Realizing it's getting late, I order another glass and get one for Katie as well.

Vera has managed to stay on the opposite side of the bar for most of the night, but with the nasty looks she throws us from time to time, it hasn't been easy keeping Katie at bay. Sober Katie is feisty, but drunk Katie is downright trouble.

Avoiding the drama for another thirty minutes, I go ahead and close out our tab not pushing my luck. Katie is on board for leaving, thank goodness, so we say goodnight to Brian and head toward the front door.

"Leaving so soon?"

Shit.

Her voice is unmistakable as it calls from behind us. I decide it's best to ignore her, but Katie thinks otherwise and turns to confront Vera.

"Yeah and you should probably do the same. You could really use some extra beauty rest. Those bags are looking mighty heavy under your sad eyes."

"If they are heavy, it's because I was up all night with Curtis. And it was well worth the extra use of concealer."

I laugh, like really loud, but don't say a word. She is out of her mind.

"Excuse me? Is something funny?" Her eyes burn into me.

"Hi, we haven't met yet. I'm Daphne. But I am sure you already know that. Otherwise you wouldn't feel the need to make up lame lies in attempt to dig at me."

I keep my cool. It is important for me to remain professional as much as possible. This town is too small for any bad gossip to flourish about the Tea Room owner having a bar brawl. It's just bad for business.

"Oh, Daphne, yes the tea girl. Curtis has told me so much about you."

I take a deep breath and gather my composure. "Listen, honey. We both know where Curtis was last night and the sooner you move on, the better. But, I don't need to remind you of that, do I? You clearly know who I am, given your sad attempt to make me jealous. And you can fool your friends, but I'm pretty sure those bags are from you crying yourself to sleep at night, knowing that you let the most amazing, kind and fucking sexy man slip through your claws. Now, if you will excuse us, we were just leaving."

The splash hits my face before I can turn away. That bitch just threw her drink at me and my eyes are burning from alcohol. Without being able to see, I can only hear Katie yell as a push hits me from behind. Finally able to open them, I see Katie in the arms of the bouncer and Vera standing with her arms crossed.

"All of you out! Now, before I call the cops," he yells and turns to set Katie down, outside of the entrance.

Wiping my face clean, I apologize to the bouncer and leave.

"He is so lucky he grabbed me in time. I would have loved to put her teeth in her throat! Stupid Bitch. Who does she think she is throwing a drink on you? We ought to call the cops; that's considered battery! I should know. I am a bartender and have had many a drinks thrown at me."

"I'm fine. She isn't worth it. Give me the keys so we can go." I hold my hand out and see a mischievous gleam hit Katie's eyes as she notices the car next to her. "Katie? Don't get crazy. Just give me the keys."

She examines the blue sedan closely and throws her head back in wild laughter as she turns her attention to the porch. I twist around and see the flock of bimbos coming through the door.

"You mean these keys?" Katie shouts and I confusingly turn around just as she finishes swiping them across the blue paint, leaving a silver trail down the driver's side door.

"Katie! No!" I yell out, but it's too late. The damage is done.

Gasps from the porch return my attention back behind me as Vera's hand covers her mouth.

"You crazy bitch! I'm calling the cops!" Vera and the girls all begin to frantically look for their phones.

Without thinking, I grab Katie by the arm and start running toward our car. I would rather not be here when they show up. Guilty or not, I need time to figure this out.

"Katie, what the hell?" I begin to lecture her as we speed off towards my house.

She laughs and slouches down into her seat. "Whatever. I'll pay her to fix it. She deserves it. Plus the look on her face was priceless!"

"You're going to pay alright, I just hope it's only money. Not jail time."

We don't speak another word the whole drive home.

Before waking Katie to drag her inside, I pull out my phone as soon as I park in my driveway.

Me: Need your help. Friend in trouble. Call me please.

After putting Katie to bed, I lie awake panicked at the situation. I haven't talked to Nathan since my birthday, and now I have to ask him for help. Katie is a teacher and this could ruin her career, or at the very least cause major waves. What a mess.

Exhausted from the dramatic night, I barely hear the knocking at the door. With a second bang, louder than the first time, I jump from bed and throw on my robe. Glancing through the peephole, my stomach drops and my throat quickly dries up.

"Truesdale Police. Please open up."

"Oh shit. I'm an idiot." I turn to see Katie, barely alive in the hallway behind me.

"It's fine. Just don't say a word until our attorney is present. Got it?"

"Lawyer? Okay, fine, I promise. Let them in."

Opening the door, the gentleman's face softens and a slight smile lifts at the corner of his mouth.

"Good morning, ma'am. Are you Daphne Fields?" he asks.

"Yes, sir."

"And Katie Hampton?"

"Present." Her sarcasm causes the gentleman to release a low laugh.

"Rough night I suspect. Well, we need you ladies to come down to the station for a few questions regarding the vandalism of a blue Chevy Malibu."

"Not a problem. May I call my lawyer first?" I remain calm and cooperative.

"Sure. We will be right out front. You can get dressed, as well."

"Thank you, sir. Five minutes max."

He nods and walks away toward the other officer standing at the end of my driveway. I leave the door open, unsure of the protocol in this situation.

The line rings three times as my shaking hands barely manage to hold the phone to my ear.

"Please pick up," I say to myself, growing more and more nervous.

"Hello," he answers, on what seems to be the last ring.

"Nathan, thank god. We need your help."

"I'm already on my way. Got your message and tried to call, but when you didn't answer I got worried and started driving. I'll be there in an hour. Don't say anything until I get there."

"You're the best. I can't thank you enough." I choke out the words, as the seriousness of the situation begins to settle.

"Don't worry, Daphne, I'll take care of you. See you soon."

"Thank you."

Hanging up the phone, I swallow the lump in my throat and quickly get dressed.

"You ready?" I ask Katie, who is sitting on the edge of my bed with her head in her hands.

She stands and nods, then throws her arms tightly around my neck. "I'm so sorry. I never meant for it to go that far. She just made me so mad. You are the nicest, most caring person and you didn't deserve that. Please don't be mad at me. You had nothing to do with this and I will make sure they know it."

"Katie, it's fine. Nathan is on his way and will take care of both of us." I hug her back and we make our way outside.

Meeting the officers at the car, they put us into the back, thankfully without cuffs. As the doors close, I reach over and grab Katie's hand.

"Thank you."

"For what? Getting you arrested?"

"For caring and sticking up for me." I whisper. "Even if you are crazy. I still love you."

"Well, you know what they say. Don't trouble trouble, unless trouble troubles you."

We both laugh silently in the back seat of the cop car and I briefly appreciate the humor of the situation.

With the officers leading us inside, I keep my head down, watching the floor in front of me. The rush of the cold air as we enter the lobby sends a shiver down my spine. I cross my arms over my chest and get mildly warmer as I hear a familiar voice.

As if I'm not embarrassed enough, I lift my gaze from the floor and lock eyes with the center of all the drama. Curtis stares back at me, as confusion burrows his brow and sadness appears in his eyes. My bewilderment as to why he is here is masked by my own embarrassment, and I drop my gaze back to the floor, continuing ahead.

Curtis

23

Afraid my mouth is hanging open, I rub my chin in sheer confusion. Having just watched two officers escort Daphne and Katie through the police station, I seriously begin to question the reason we are all here. The girls were not handcuffed, which at least gives me the impression they aren't in too much trouble, however they didn't appear to be happy about it either.

They are seated in a nearby room and I can just barely see through the partially open blinds. The officers exit the room and head further down the hallway out of sight, leaving them alone for the time being.

In the early hours of the morning, I was awakened by incessant phone calls from Vera. After ignoring the first few, I eventually gave in and answered, knowing she wouldn't give up. I figured it would be one of her usual late night attempts to discuss the possibility of getting back together, so there wasn't an ounce of pleasantries in my greeting. I was instantly taken back when I heard the desperation in her pleas.

This was the first time I had ever heard Vera so upset and was having a difficult time making out exactly what she was saying through her non-stop cries. The only words I heard were *attacked* and *police station* and I was jumping out of bed and rushing out the door. Since my arrival, she has been in the back talking with the officers, and I have yet to be able to speak with her to find out what happened.

Though the day has barely begun it has somehow already thrown me for a loop. I have been worried about Vera, but seeing the girls just now has pulled my focus fully to them. Reaching for my cell, I call Paul, knowing he would want to be here for his sister.

"Hmmm." Paul grumbles, finally answering after my third attempt. It's obvious he isn't fully awake.

"Paul, wake up, man. You need to come down to the police station."

"What did you do?" he asks, sleep still in his voice.

"It's not me," I pause, running my hand through my hair and gripping the phone, "Katie and Daphne were just escorted through the building by two officers."

"Katie?" Paul asks, now fully alert and focused. "What happened?"

"I'm not sure. I came up here to meet Vera, something happened to her last night and she called me. And as I am still waiting to find out why, I watch the girls walk through."

"Son of a bitch. I am headed that way. See you in a few."

No sooner after I hang up, Vera is exiting one of the room across from the girls with Darryl Johnson, or rather

Sergeant Johnson. We attended high school together and played on the same football team for years, yet we never got along. He was always a prick back then and now he's just a prick with a badge. Never misses an opportunity to flash his power and is always looking for a reason to take someone down.

I watch as they stand close to each other while talking and Vera lays her hand on his arm, smiling up at him. Darryl's hand nears her waist, but before he makes contact she pulls away. Her gaze meets mine and she appears both surprised and relieved. Glancing back to Darryl, it is apparent he is not too happy to see me. Vera quickly mutters something to him before walking to where I am waiting, and wraps her arms around me.

"Thank you for coming, Curtis. I know we haven't been on the best of terms, but it means the world that you are here." She bats her lashes and gazes up to me.

Looking down, I detect a gleam of hope. I don't want to be a jerk in her time of need, but also can't lead her on. Not wanting to touch that topic yet, I try to focus on the current situation.

"What happened, Vera?"

Glancing to the window in the back, I see a flash of blonde locks. I attempt to pull away and put distance between us, but Vera's grip doesn't weaken.

"Well, I was out with a couple of the girls last night having a good time when…." Her story is cut short, just as Paul comes bursting through the doors and stalks straight to where we are standing, Vera still wrapped around me.

"Have you heard anything?" he asks and then raises a questioning brow.

"They haven't come back out, so I don't know anything yet."

"Are you wondering about your psychotic sister and her friend?" Vera sneers, and I push her away, holding her at arm's length.

"Vera," I say, my tone warning her to tread lightly.

"You probably won't be seeing them anytime soon. With any luck, they will both be locked up before long," she says, defensively crossing her arms under her chest.

"What the hell are you talking about? And watch what you say about my sister, because it's no secret who the real crazy one is." Paul is clenching his fists and I can tell that he is barely hanging on. Katie is the most important person in his life.

"Oh, you think I am crazy, Paul? Your sister has had it out for me for years." She stops and points a finger in my direction. "I told you time and time again that she had a problem with me and you just blew it off. Well, tonight she finally lost it and keyed my damn car."

"You are so full of shit." Paul huffs, taking a defensive step forward.

"Really? I saw it with my own eyes, along with multiple witnesses."

Paul's chest is heaving, and his temper nearly gets the best of him. I need to diffuse the situation before he explodes.

"Vera, you should so go. You are making the situation a hell of a lot worse," I demand, just as Paul turns to walk away.

"I don't have a car. That's why I called you, I need a ride home."

"Fine. Let's go. We have some things to discuss anyways." Her smile fades just as quickly as it appeared. "I'm going to talk to Paul and I will meet you at my truck." Handing her my keys, I approach the front desk.

"Thank you, ma'am," he says, turning to meet me.

"Anything?"

"All I learned is that they were brought in for questioning, but are currently awaiting their attorney. I didn't realize keying a car was that extreme of an offense, but who am I to say. Where did your crazy ex-girlfriend run off to?"

"I am taking her home." Paul looks at me in surprise. "She doesn't have a car and it is the fastest way to get rid of her. I will come right back, but please call me if you find out anything else."

"Will do. Thanks for calling me, man."

I nod my response and leave.

The drive to Vera's house is silent, except for the low music on the radio. There are a number of things I would like to say, but I 'm not even sure where to begin. For one, she needs to realize there is absolutely no possible chance of us getting back together. I also firmly believe that she is blowing the whole car keying way out of proportion in an attempt to get me on her side.

"So are you taking their side as well?" Vera asks, breaking the silence as I pull up to her apartment building.

"I am not looking to take sides, Vera. I still haven't heard the full story, and I just can't imagine Katie vandalizing your car."

"I am not making this up, Curtis. There were — "

"Witnesses," I finish for her, "Yes, I heard you before. But all the same, I don't see Katie doing it unprovoked, so tell me everything that happened."

"I told you, I was out with girls, looking for a fun time when those two approached us and started drama. Once we walked away, we spent the rest of the night avoiding them. When I was leaving the bar, I watched Katie get the keys from her friend and walk over to my car. With a wicked laugh, she ran the metal across my driver side door." She shrugs her shoulder and shakes her head.

"Do you think it was truly necessary to involve the police?" Vera shoots her eyes towards me and I watch them turn dark with anger.

"Yes, it was necessary. Do you expect me to just let them get away with vandalizing my car? I can't imagine what they could have done, had I not been right there to stop them." She averts her eyes and stares out the window.

I rub my forehead, hoping for a way to break in all the confusion. Vera's story is making no sense and I need to get this wrapped up so I can get back up to the station and wait with Paul. Plus, I would like to be there for Daphne when they are finished. I know she mentioned having to possibly work, but maybe we can spend the day together instead. Sunday suddenly seems too far away.

"I know who she is," Vera says, quietly, bringing me out of my thoughts.

"Who?" I ask, unclear of where her head is at.

"Daphne. I know who she is to you." Her gaze is still locked out the window and the sadness in her voice causes me to feel guilt.

"Vera," I start, unsure how to say what I need without hurting her feelings. "I told you that you should move on. I want what's best for you, and I know there is someone out there that can make you happy."

Her head whips my direction and her dark irises are shooting daggers towards me. "Just because you found little miss perfect, you think everything else can just be swept under the rug. All the feelings you once had for me, gone. Well, I am sorry Curtis, but I can't just flip my switch like you can." She pauses briefly, swiping a fallen tear from her cheek. "I heard from one of the girls at the salon that your mom was gushing over how great Daphne is, and that you two are just perfect together. Do you have any idea how embarrassing that is? I am still trying to mend a broken heart, and you moved on with the first pair of legs you found. And you know what, newsflash, she's not perfect, she is just as immature and uncontrollable as Katie."

Suddenly something becomes very clear to me after listening to Vera's rant. I want to feel bad, but at the same time, I also know she was never fully invested in our relationship.

"So is that it? Why you are blowing this whole incident out of the water? Not because of Katie, but because of Daphne and your jealousy?"

"I am not jealous of your little tea girl, Curtis. Nothing is being blown up. They ruined my car for no reason at all. Maybe your precious Daphne is the one with the jealous bone."

I laugh inside at the thought of Daphne ever being jealous of Vera. During our time together, I have given her insight on the relationship between Vera and I, and ultimately what led to our falling out. I told her about the change in Vera and how it affected my feelings towards her. There would be no reason for Daphne to ever feel jealous of her.

"No, see I am still finding it hard to believe they did everything you say for no reason. What did you do, Vera?"

"Are you kidding me?" she asks, offended. "You don't even know this girl, yet you are standing up for her, as if you believe she can do no wrong."

"You're right. Maybe I don't know Daphne all that well, but I know Katie and I sure as hell know the kind of person you are."

"Screw you, Curtis." Yanking on the handle, Vera jumps out of my truck, slamming the door with all her might.

The way her mood swings can escalate from zero to sixty in a matter of seconds never ceases to amaze me. Throwing my truck in reverse, I squeal out of the parking space and make my way back to the police station. I check my phone to make sure I haven't missed anything from Paul and there are no notifications.

The possibility of Daphne encountering Vera in public had never really crossed my mind. I'm sure hers and Katie's side will have an entirely different story to tell, but either way I hate the thought of Daphne getting involved with Vera and her issues with me. Hopefully this hasn't scared her off or ruined my chances.

Getting back to the police station, Paul is still in the waiting area where I left him. When I glance back to the room they entered earlier, I am still only able to see the back of their heads.

"Any closer to leaving?" I ask, taking a seat next to him. Scrolling through my phone, I decide to send Daphne a text, hoping she has hers.

Me: I am out here waiting with Paul. We won't let anything happen to you girls. Looks like I may need to double your surprise. ;)

Hopefully, I can bring a little humor to her terrible morning and give her something to look forward to.

"Still waiting on the lawyer to show. I don't know who in the hell they called and what is taking so long, though. How did it go with bat shit crazy?"

"As well as could be expected." I release a heavy sigh.

"Was screaming involved?"

"Of course."

Paul laughs, shaking his head. The main door opens causing a warm breeze to whip through the waiting area, and I see a fancy suit saunter up to the front desk. Paul notices the guy when he walks in and scoots to the edge of his seat, both of us hoping this is the lawyer we've been waiting on.

He is talking low with the receptionist and I am unable to make out what is being said. The elderly lady disappears for a moment and comes back with one of the earlier officers.

"Nathan Grant," he says, extending a handshake. "I'm here for my client, Daphne Fields."

"Good, we have been waiting for you," the officer responds, not seeming too impressed.

"Yes, I apologize for that. I hit a bit of traffic on my way down. Have they been charged?"

Traffic? There isn't a lick of traffic on any day in Truesdale, much less on a Saturday morning. It makes me curious as to where this guy came from and how the girls know him.

"No charges yet. They wouldn't speak to us without you present and we have quite a few questions." The officer looks back to the room, "Shall we?"

Paul and I relax back in our chairs.

"Thank god this guy finally showed," Paul says, nudging me with his elbow.

My eyes are fixated on the window and I watch the girls stand, getting my first good look at Daphne since she first walked through the door. Katie shakes hands with the lawyer and then Daphne walks straight into his waiting arms. I am dumbstruck as I watch the two embrace when the light bulb turns on in my head, illuminating all the information I let slip by me. The way he is holding her is way too intimate for strangers. Hitting traffic means he more than likely travelled quite a ways to get here, and the most obvious being his name, Nathan. This is her ex-fiancé.

Suddenly, I am feeling sick to my stomach and I stand abruptly. I need to get out of here. "I'm going to run."

"Really? This guy looks like he knows what he's doing. I bet it won't be long until the girls are free." Paul is confused by my sudden mood change and I can't blame him.

"Trust me, I am not needed here."

Paul promises to call me when they are released and without looking back at the window, I exit the police station filled with doubt. Daphne doesn't need me to rescue her. She called her own hero.

When I get back to my house, I am happy to find that Jill and Hannah aren't here. As much as I love them both, right now I just want to be alone. My body feels drained from the morning's drama. Heading straight to my room, I fall into bed and pray for sleep to come. My mind is all over the map with thoughts of Daphne and her ex-fiancé.

It then occurs to me that for him to make it to Truesdale when he did, she must have contacted him way before the cops brought her in, meaning she called him last night after everything happened. It hurts a little to think that he would be the first call she made and she never thought to call or text me.

It's much later when I wake up groggy from my nap. I have never been much of a day sleeper and I always seem to wake up feeling worse than I did before. I reach for my phone to check the time and find a voicemail from Paul, left about an hour ago.

"Hey, man. The jailbirds are free! So get this, apparently there was an altercation between the girls that ended with Vera throwing a drink in Daphne's face. Ultimately that is what led my nutty sister to think it was a good idea to key her car. Anyways, they called Vera back down and Nathan informed her that Daphne was willing to press assault charges against her is she didn't drop the charge with Katie. Vera was pissed off and tried to get Johnson to help, who by the way is still a douche with a badge. But, there was nothing he could do and she accepted defeat. Then, it was wham-bam-thank you ma'am, case closed or some shit. Lucky for us, Daphne has this attorney in her back pocket. All right, well that is all I have to say. Call me later and we can grab beers."

When the message is over, I open my texts and send one to Vera. I knew there was much more to her story. A whole different version in fact.

Me: I am sick and tired of your constant lies. Delete my number and never contact me again.

Taking a trick out of her own book, I scroll through my contacts until I land on hers and block her number.

There hadn't been a response from my earlier text to Daphne, so I push my luck and send another.

Me: Heard the good news! Are we still on for tomorrow?

Daphne

24

"So, we've learned our lesson, right girls?" Nathan asks as we exit his car at my house.

"Oh my gosh, you have no idea. I swear I'll never drink again." Katie shakes her head and covers her face with her hands.

"You can drink, just maybe avoid keys and bitches," I respond, not sure how I managed a sense of humor, when all I can think about is sleep.

"True." She takes a deep breath and opens her arms to hug me. "Well, again, I am sorrier than you will ever know. And I promise to make it up to you." She hugs me tightly then pulls back and faces Nathan. "And you my good sir, are my hero. Thank you so much for helping me and please let me know if I can repay you in any way."

"It's all good. A friend of Daphne's is a friend of mine and we always take care of our friends." He smiles and gives her a reassuring hug.

"Really, though, you saved my ass. This could have been really bad for my career. I owe you. And if you're still in town tonight, maybe you guys could come let me buy you a few drinks. I work at eight."

Nathan nods, but doesn't reply, so I am not sure what his plan is at this point.

"Thanks Katie, but I need to catch some z's before I make any plans or decisions. My brain is killing me."

"Agreed. See you guys later. Nice to meet you, Nathan."

"You too, Katie."

She waves goodbye and gets in her car to head home. Nathan and I silently make our way inside and I offer him a glass of water.

"So, I need to shower and decompress for a bit. Did you plan to head back right away?"

"Not unless you want me to. I cleared my weekend just in case, so I was hoping to stay until Monday."

"Oh, okay. Yeah, that sounds good. Make yourself at home, I'll be out in a few."

I take a quick glance around the living room to make sure there isn't anything that would reveal my relationship or friendship, or whatever the hell this is, with Curtis. Not that I am hiding it, but I would rather not dive into this weekend with Nathan; the first time I have seen him since moving.

Grabbing my phone, I leave Nathan in the living room and close my bedroom door behind me. With the water warming up, I scroll through the messages on my phone and come across an unread text from Curtis. His words are easy and almost a little too blasé.

Reading it again, it begins to annoy me that he would just assume I am okay, and not explain why he was there in the first place.

'Are we still on for Sunday?'

How can I even answer that question? I start to type my response asking him if Vera will be there, but decide it's best not to text when I am upset. There really isn't a need to take it out on him, but for some reason his easy going attitude is driving me crazy. His stupid ex is causing more drama than I like to surround myself with and I need time to clear my head.

Not to mention, how would I explain that I have to cancel our plans because my ex-fiancé is staying in town? It's really all too much.

As the warm water cascades down my body, I finally start to relax and take a deep breath, inhaling the steam. With my eyes closed, Curtis' face appears in my thoughts and I can't shake the curiosity of his appearance this morning.

Why on earth would he have been at the station if not to help out Vera? Was she really still in close contact with him like she claims to be? And why has he been lying to me about it? It's not like I would be mad. I just want honesty.

Unable to continue enjoying my shower, I quickly finish washing up and throw on a pair of yoga pants and sweatshirt. Walking into the living room, I find a shirtless Nathan sleeping peacefully on my couch.

My eyes travel his body, admiring his trim cut physique. He must be hitting his workouts harder than usual because I do not remember there being an extra two pack on his lower abs.

We haven't seen each other in a few months, nor had the chance to speak much either. I am sure there will be a heart to heart conversation at some point in the evening, but for now, I will take his lead and catch some sleep; much needed, drama free sleep.

A faint knock wakes me up, and I roll over to view Nathan standing in my doorway.

"Feeling better?" he asks.

"Much. I was hoping I would wake up and last night would have been just a nightmare," I grumble and kick my legs over the side of the bed.

"Well, as nice as that would be, it would mean that I wouldn't actually be here now," he replies.

My stomach tightens and I cover it with my hands.

"You okay? Hungry?"

"Uh, yeah. Starving," I respond. And though I know I am hungry, I don't think the back flips and twisting roller coaster in my gut is the result. A mixture of anxiety, awkwardness, and guilt continue to swirl about.

"Great, let's go eat." His bright smile is calming and some of the anxiety disappears. Who knows, maybe we can be friends without feeling awkward.

"Sounds good. Let me get dressed and we can go."

We head downtown and enjoy a rather quiet dinner at Café Blair. Nathan does most of the talking and spends our meal catching me up on his work at the firm. Stories are being shared about some of our mutual friends and we begin reminiscing on fun times from our past.

The early years were filled with lots of partying and even more laughter. Focusing on those times would leave you to believe we had a perfect relationship and that I am crazy for leaving. But it wasn't always like that, we eventually fell into routine and things didn't seem as real to me anymore.

"So, how are you? Really?" he asks, and I take a moment to think about his question.

My immediate response to anyone else would be simple. 'I'm great. Better than ever in fact.' But I can't say that to him. I chose to leave and it would break his heart to let him know that I am better off. Even it is the truth.

"I'm good, Nathan. Really good. I love it here and love being a part of Grams legacy." I decide not to sugar coat it.

He smiles weakly and I sense his hurt. "That's good. I'm glad you're happy."

Saved by the waiter bringing the check, Nathan hands him cash and we both stand to leave.

The car ride back to my house is eerily quiet and I am not sure how we went from laughing and smiling, to silent and unable to look at each other. I know it must be hard for him to hear that I am happy, but he can't possibly be mad at me.

After closing the front door behind me, I turn around to see Nathan leaning into the bar with his hands across his chest. His tight-lipped grin and burrowed brow speak volumes of his thoughts. It is a look I am all too familiar with.

After a few seconds, my patience wears thin. "Well? Are you going to tell me what those wheels are spinning up there?" I point to his head and he briefly relaxes his smile.

"I don't know." He shakes his head and runs his fingers through his hair at the same time. "You don't feel weird?"

"Of course I feel weird. Not too long ago we were picking a date to get married and now you are here bailing me out of jail and sleeping on my couch."

We both let out a light giggle and the tension eases, for a moment at least.

"What was the date?" he asks as his face returns to stone.

"Seriously? I don't know, why?" I ask, not sure where he is going with this.

"What would have been the date, if you would have stayed and wanted to marry me? What date would have been perfect?" his tone is soft but his expression remains hard.

"Nathan," I plead, not wanting to take this path and start an argument.

"Just tell me. You must have thought of one at some point, right?"

And just like that, we were treading in thick mud that would only keep us stuck in the past.

"Honestly? I never picked one. I don't know why, but I could never settle. Then when Grams passed, it was the last thing on my mind. I knew that I couldn't stay."

"Why?" Now his tone matched the expression.

"Nathan, please."

"Daphne, did you ever love me? Did you want to marry me?"

"Of course I did, why would you ask that?" My voice is now raised and irritated at his ridiculous questioning. "You will never know how much I loved you and wished things would have been different. But I can't go back and change it and neither can you. We made a choice and this is it. I belong here and you belong there, but we don't belong together. If we did, none of this would even be a question." The thoughts spew from my lips as I fight the tears threatening to fall to my cheeks.

Of course I missed Nathan, we spent many years loving each other and taking care of one another, but things change and life doesn't always hand you the perfect peach.

"That's bullshit, you chose to leave!" he yells back.

"And you chose to stay!"

He growls deeply and throws his hands up, turning to walk toward the couch. "But you didn't have to leave. You could have figured it out. I couldn't leave. I worked too hard to leave it all behind for small town life."

"Really? Like your 'big town life' is so great anyways. I love it here. The people are amazing, the nights are quiet and it's where my heart is. My grams worked her ass off for the Tea Room and you are crazy to think I would allow anyone else to care for it in the same manner as I would."

He turns back around and takes a step forward with each spewing question. "What about me? What about us? How can you leave it behind without a hitch?"

"Without a hitch? Are you crazy? I cried myself to sleep for nights on end wondering if I made the right decision. This was not easy for me, Nathan. I didn't want to leave you behind and start over, but I had to. This is where I belong."

"You keep saying that, but I don't believe you. Damn it, you make me crazy!"

As he leans down into me, I hadn't realized how close we had become. As the warmth of his breath sails across my bottom lip, my mouth pops open and I feel my heart thumping fiercely, trying to escape my chest. His tongue reaches into my mouth and cautiously searches for mine.

My shaking hands reach up around his neck and pull him closer as our mouths crash deeply together, melting away the tension. Moving his hands down to my waist he lifts my shirt and breaks our kiss to pull it over my head. Following his lead, I reach for his and do the same.

With his mouth back on mine, he slides his hands lower, grasping under my butt and lifts me with ease. Wrapping my legs around his strong core, he walks us to the couch and gently sets me down.

Flashes of heat course through my body as he begins to remove my pants all while planting furious kisses to my midsection. Squirming at his touch, my back arches as his warm kisses move further south. My hands jolt to his head and I grip his hair tightly between my fingers just as his mouth covers my sensitive flesh.

Looking down at him through hooded eyes, I grip tighter, slightly tugging at his soft blonde locks. A low growl passes his lips and rumbles between my legs, causing a loud moan to escape my throat.

After a few pleasurable minutes, Nathan stands up and hastily unbuttons his pants, dropping them to the floor. With his hands on my waist he flips me to my knees, sliding his palm over my back and slowly enters me from behind. Our moans are matched and he leans over to kiss my neck before thrusting the remainder of the way inside. Enjoying this position for a few moments longer, Nathan pulls back and sits down on the couch. Knowing it's my favorite, he smiles as I stand up and climb into his lap, reconnecting our bodies.

Riding the waves of heat and passion, it only takes a few moments before release crashes over me and Nathan soon lifts me off to shutter a release of his own.

We both sit quietly catching our breath and I excuse myself to use the restroom.

Our sexual chemistry has always been magnetic, but merely sexual. Tonight was no different. There was a lot of pent up anger and unresolved closure that led Nathan and I to the couch.

The myths of making love held no true meaning, until more recently, and thoughts of my new relationship with Curtis stir in my head, spinning webs of guilt in my gut.

Though I don't know where I stand with Curtis, I do know where I stand with Nathan, and it's in separate places. Our relationship is over and does not have a future. Grams' words ring loudly in my head day after day, and my place with Nathan remains the same.

After another quick shower, and attempt to scrub away some of the guilt, I dress for bed and meet Nathan on the couch for a movie. Not mentioning the recent activity, we quietly enjoy each other's company and call it a night rather early.

Climbing into bed alone, I open my messages and respond to Curtis. Things have been way too dramatic for one weekend, so I decide to cancel our plans tomorrow and go to the Tea Room to get ready for the week.

Me: Yeah, I'm happy things worked out. Sorry to cancel last minute, but I have had a long weekend and need to get some work done at the Tea Room since my Saturday was pretty much shot. Talk to you soon.

Curtis: Yeah, no worries. I understand. Talk to you soon. Night.

Me: Night.

Waking up a little more relaxed, I get ready for the day and greet Nathan in the kitchen. I'm not sure what his plans are, but I really do need to go into work for a bit.

"Good morning. I'll make us breakfast, but then I need to go to the Tea Room to get some work done for a couple of hours. You are more than welcome to hang here until I get back."

"Okay, sounds good. I brought my computer so I can work for a bit also. You making pancakes?"

Glancing at the griddle on the counter, my appetite suddenly drops and my thoughts flip back to Curtis.

"Nah. I eat them way too much lately. Scrambled eggs okay?"

"Sounds good to me. I'll make the coffee."

Sundays are one of my favorite days at the Tea Room. Since we are closed for service, I am able to enjoy the quiet and get ready for the week ahead. With my work orders complete, I relax on the porch with my notebook, enjoying the weather and leisurely jotting down a few thoughts and ideas.

I haven't been able to tear Curtis from my mind and hope to see him soon to clear up this mess.

Nathan's car rolls into the parking lot and I glance at my phone to make sure I didn't miss a call or text. Nothing.

Standing from the bench, I greet him as he approaches.

"Hey there. Here for lunch?" I ask.

"No, I'm actually on my way home. I got a call from a client and need to get back to work. Figured I would just stop by to see you before I left."

"Oh. Okay. Want anything to go?"

"No, I'm fine, really."

"Okay, well again, I can't thank you enough for coming to my rescue. And it was really nice to see you." I reach out and grab his hand, hoping he can sense my sincerity.

"I'm glad I could help. And I'm also happy I got to see you. I miss you, Daphne and hope we can keep in touch." He wraps his arms around me for a long hug and I embrace his warmth and friendship.

"Me too," I whisper as we pull back from one another.

"I'm proud of you, Daphne. And you're right, you do belong here and I understand why you need to stay. I'm just selfish and wish I could give you more. Do me a favor, though, stay happy because you honestly deserve it."

His tender words release the heaviness centered in my chest, and I exhale a sigh of contentment. Without a response, I reach up and wrap my arms around him. After a brief embrace, Nathan pulls back and lifts his hand to the nape of my neck, planting a soft lingering kiss to my lips. The ease of closure washes over me and from the look in his eyes, I know he feels it too.

"Goodbye, Daphne."

"Bye, Nathan."

Curtis

25

"**U**ncle Curtis! Uncle Curtis!" I hear Hannah's excited voice before she comes bouncing in the kitchen.

Bending down to her level, I laugh watching her jump up and down. "Yes, princess?"

"I want to have a tea party, but I want it to be a big girl tea party. You know, like the one I had with Mommy, Nana, and Princess Daphne. Can we go back to her Tea House? Or do you think Princess Daphne wants to come over again and play with me? I really like her."

In true form, Hannah is talking a mile a minute, barely pausing to take a breath. She has really taken to Daphne and hasn't stopped talking about her since their lunch at The Treasured Tea Cup.

"Well, sweetie, Princess Daphne has to work today, but I would love to have a tea party with you. And I bet we could get your mom to join us too."

Disappointment flashes on her precious face, but she quickly masks it with a smile. "Okay, Uncle Curtis. I'll start setting up the table." She throws her little body against me, wrapping her arms around my neck and practically knocks me over. "You're the best, Uncle Curtis. Sometimes I wish me and Mommy could stay here forever."

She gives me a wet kiss on my cheek before skipping off to gather her tea party supplies, leaving me stunned. Looking up, I spot my sister leaning against the wall, wiping her eye.

"Jilly," I stand to my full height and bring her into my arms. I rub her back as a soft sob escapes her. "How bad is it?"

Pulling out of my embrace, she grabs a paper towel off the roll and dries her tears. It physically hurts me to see my sister so upset and I feel helpless and uncertain of what to do.

"Being here has made me realize how much I miss having our family in such close proximity and knowing if I needed anything you guys would be there in an instant."

"It's more than that. What's going on with you and Alex?" I keep my voice low to shelter the little ears from hearing our conversation.

"Some days, I feel like I don't even know who he is anymore, Curtis. I couldn't even tell you when the change happened, but he is never home, unless it is to sleep. And even then, Hannah and I are typically already in bed. Our family weekend time no longer exists, and it seems to be just work, work, work for him." She stops briefly and smiles at her daughter, who peeks into the kitchen before bolting away to the living room. "I even have thoughts that it may not be work that is keeping him busy, but what if there is another woman? The night I decided to come home early was the worst it had been. I waited up for hours, wanting to confront him and let him know that what he is doing is affecting our little girl." Her sobs were starting to grow heavier and my rage was increasing.

"Jilly, has he ever put his hands on you?" The thought alone of a man touching my little sister in a violent way stimulates murderous thoughts. My fists are clenched so tight they start to lose feeling.

"No, Curtis," she reassures me, resting her hand on my arm. "But, when I confronted him that night, he was furious. I had never witnessed that side of him and you know me, I don't hold back once I reach my limit. I told him everything I was feeling and that he was tearing our family apart. I also threatened him with divorce."

I am shocked by her statement and also ashamed as a brother that I haven't sat down with Jill sooner to discuss what's been going on. I have been so wrapped up in Daphne that I missed how much my sister was suffering and this plants a deep pit in my stomach.

"What did he say?" I ask, feeling a little choked up over my failure.

"He cried, dropped to his knees and begged me not to. He said that he would change and be better. You know, all the cliché things that men tell their wives."

"Do you believe him? Or are you still considering divorce?"

"I told him I needed time away and that I was coming here to think about things. I still don't know when I will be ready to return, but I owe it to Hannah to give him a chance. We grew up in a home filled with love, and that's all I have ever wanted for my daughter. I don't want her to be a part of a broken home, but I also don't want her to have an absentee father."

With her gaze clouded with the onset of fresh tears, I pull her back into my arms and hold her tight. "You're always welcome here, Jilly. And you can stay as long as you need. I love both of you girls."

"It's tea time!" Hannah screams at the top of her lungs from the dining room.

Jill squeezes me one last time. "I'm going to splash some water on my face. Let Hannah know I will be right out."

I nod my head and go in search of the pending tea party. Turning the corner, I see my transformed dining room, which now looks as if a pink fairy threw up everywhere. Her plastic tea set is bright pink and each seat has a tiara and feather boa. She even brought in a couple of her bigger stuffed animals to fill the extra places.

Hannah sits patiently with a toothy smile spread wide on her cheeks and swinging her tiny legs to and fro. From her spot at the head of the table, fully decked out in her princess gear, she looks so happy, without a care in the world. I can't help but wonder if she has picked up on the tension between her parents.

When Jill joins us, she looks refreshed and aside from the slight redness in her eyes, you wouldn't know she had been crying. We spend the next hour having an imaginary tea party with Hannah and before we clean up the mess, Jill pulls out her cell and takes a picture of the three of us. And yes, I am wearing my pink tiara and feather boa, anything to make these two girls smile.

After cleaning the mess, Jill and Hannah took off to Ma's for the afternoon. With the house too quiet in their absence, I am now on my way to the Tea Room. Daphne messaged me last night cancelling our plans and I imagine it could have something to do with her ex being in town. She mentioned needing to get some work done, so I am hoping I can catch her there and talk for a minute. Everything was going great between us and now seems completely thrown off kilter. I'd like to clear the air and see where her thoughts are.

Coming up to the stop sign across from the Tea Room, I notice Daphne and Nathan on the porch. I pull into the convenience store and feel like a stalker as I watch them together from a distance. They hug and at first glance it seems innocent, but after pulling away, she wraps her arms back around him and they share a kiss.

A pain shoots throughout my entire body as I witness the exchange and I quickly divert my eyes. Does this mean they are getting back together? I've done it enough with Vera to know how easy it is to fall right back in to old habits and routines.

When I look back to the porch, it's now empty. I need to put my mind at ease and know one way or another where I am in Daphne's life. Shifting my truck back into drive, I cross the street and pull into the parking lot, which only holds Daphne's car. I take a few deep breaths, preparing myself for what's to come. Expect the worse and hope for the best.

I knock on the door and after a moment, Daphne is on the other side, looking as beautiful as ever and also surprised.

"Curtis, hey," she says, looking past me, scanning the parking lot. I want to tell her it's okay, he's already gone, but I don't.

"I know you said you had work to do, so I was hoping I would catch you before you went home. Do you have a minute?"

"Sure, do you want to sit down?"

I nod my head and we both take a seat on the rockers out front. I can't get a good read on what she is feeling, and it's almost as though she is avoiding eye contact.

"Daphne, I first want to apologize for all the problems Vera caused. I never wanted anything like that to happen."

She laughs, surprising me. "It's not your fault, Curtis. It didn't take long to see she has a few screws loose. Besides, what's done is done and it's all in the past now." She looks away from me again, but not before I see a hint of guilt in her features.

"Speaking of pasts," I start, but don't have a clue how to finish. I can't bring myself to just come out and ask.

Shit. Why did I even come here?

We sit in an awkward silence, and watch a few cars pass by.

"It's been quite the weekend," Daphne begins, "Definitely not how I wanted our girls' night to go, but at least something good came from it." She pauses to look over at me and I brace myself for the blow. "It forced me to realize a few truths that I had been ignoring, but also solidify some things as well. I now know, without any doubt, that I made the right decision to come here and run the Tea Room. This is one-hundred percent where I am meant to be." The warm smile on her face is contagious.

"That's good, and it's great that you no longer have doubts. You are definitely doing Miss Kay proud."

"Thank you, for saying that." She takes a deep breath before continuing. "There have been so many changes in my life within such a short time frame. One minute I am engaged, planning a wedding that honestly I wasn't sure I even wanted, and the next, Grams passes away and I am uprooting my life. I'm realizing that I never took the time to allow myself to process it all."

I nod my head, understanding her feelings.

She reaches over and links her fingers through mine, squeezing tightly. "And then, you happened. You, Curtis, were an unexpected surprise. I felt an instant connection the moment we touched. Coming here, I had only one goal in mind. Work hard and do the best I can to live up to Grams' legacy. Meeting someone was nowhere on my list, but since that first day I haven't been able to get you off my mind." She squeezes my hand again, and I know it's coming. "God, Curtis I really want it to work and I think we could be great. Maybe there will be a day for us in the future, when we can revisit this, but right now, I need to take the time to get my head on straight. It's all too much, too soon and I jumped in head first, not yet ready to swim."

"I won't say I'm not disappointed, because that would be a lie." I rub my thumb across the top of her hand and she gives me a sad smile. "But, I get it. You have to do what's best for you. Take your time, because when we do this, and I have complete confidence that we will, I want you to be sure. I want you to be all in. Next time you dive in head first, I will be there waiting in the water."

Daphne stands from her rocker and I follow suit, with her hand still in mine. "Thank you, for being so understanding." A tear escapes her eye, and reaching up with my free hand I brush it away. "You are a great guy, Curtis."

"You're not so bad yourself, Miss Fields." Pulling her into me, I wrap my arms around her and kiss the top of her head. "When you're ready, come find me." I kiss her one more time, breathing her in, before walking away.

When I reach my truck, I turn back to the porch and Daphne is still standing there watching me leave. I wave my hand in the air, climb into my truck and drive away, hoping that our day will come.

Daphne

26

or the third Sunday in a row now, I find myself
working the entire afternoon, closing up alone and
sitting here, rocking peacefully on the porch. The same
porch in which just a few weeks ago, I finished a chapter in
my life and folded down the page of the next, holding its
place until I am sure I am ready to continue.

As the rain pelts the roof, and the thunder rolls
inconsistent roars through the sky, I allow my thoughts to
drift to Curtis. Over the last couple of weeks, I pulled my
focus away from my heart and kept it here at the Tea Room.
Hilda and I have been re-arranging, trying to allow more
table space and we even drew up an idea for an outside
patio area. If this next season goes well, the work outside
could be done throughout the winter months and possibly
be ready for our spring guests.

Planning for the addition has been fun, but there are so
many questions we have and only one person to answer
them. I haven't spoken to Curtis since I asked him for space,
and as a true gentleman, he has respected my wishes. I'm

not sure when I will be ready, but each day I miss him a little more.

The buzzing of my phone jolts a shock to my heart, wishfully thinking it could be him calling now.

Nope, just Katie.

"Hello, my dear."

"Hey, lady. Geez, where the heck are you? Sounds like you're being ripped away by a hurricane."

"Not quite. Just sitting outside the Tea Room, relaxing on the porch."

"Ah, yes. It's Sunday, I forgot. When are you going to stop working all these Fun-days? I miss you."

"Not sure, it's a great day to get a lot of things done. Plus, I kind of like not coming in on Mondays, so it works for me. What are you up to?"

"I guess that makes sense, no one likes to work on Mondays. Well, I'm finishing up my house cleaning for the week and just about to start making spaghetti. Want to come over and eat?"

"Yeah, that sounds great. Once the weather clears up, I'll head home and get ready. See you in about an hour?"

"Perfect. And don't bother bringing anything, I've got plenty of wine."

"You always do. See you soon." We both laugh and hang up.

Stepping out of the shower, I wrap myself in a towel and browse through my closet. I haven't done laundry yet this week so my choices are limited. Settling on a pair of jeans that I haven't worn in a while, I realize I should probably lay off the scones. Pulling them snuggly over my backside, I zip them up and turn in the mirror. Honestly, my ass looks fantastic and I may dub these a new favorite pair. Guess the baked goods aren't so bad after all.

I pair them with a navy blue tank top and nude ballet flats, leaving my damp hair in loose wavy curls. I layer my face with light make-up and doll my eyes with a little liner and mascara. Not that I plan on going out, but with Katie it is always an option. When I woke up today, I felt strong and confident and plan to carry it on through the night.

After knocking three times, I pull out my phone to text her.

Me: Crazy! Open up, I'm outside.

After just a few seconds, Katie swings the door open. She is dressed in a similar casual outfit and her hair is parted and clipped half up.

"Oh, hey! Sorry, I was in the bathroom with my radio and didn't hear you knocking. Come inside and pour some wine, I'm just finishing my hair, give me five minutes."

"Are we going out or staying in?"

"I could ask you the same thing, who are you all dolled up for? I know you think I was your summer love, but I thought we moved past that." We both laugh and step inside the door.

"No, I've just had a really peaceful day and felt like being pretty. Even if we are just dining in."

"Same here! Plus, who knows, maybe we can go have a few after-dinner drinks?

"How did I know you would say that? Though, I'm not sure I'm ready to go out with your crazy ass again."

"Oh, come on. I'm not that bad. Everyone is allowed one crazy outburst, and trust me when I say it will be my only one. I've never been more embarrassed in all my life."

"Fair enough. Let's see how we feel after dinner."

"Well, the wine is in the cabinet and you know where the corkscrew is. Dinner is done, so I'll plate it up in just a few minutes." She walks her way back to her bathroom and I get two glasses poured before her return.

With our stomachs full of pasta, we continue to sip on our wine around the table.

"That was delicious, thanks again."

"You're welcome. Want another glass?" she asks, finishing her last sip.

"Ugh. Honestly, I'm not really in the wine mood anymore. Got any vodka?" I normally never have a problem drinking wine, but for whatever reason it's not hitting the spot tonight.

"Nope, but I know who does." Her mischievous smile grows wide across her face and she bats her lashes innocently.

"Oh lord. Fine, let's go. But just a few drinks and we are out, deal?"

"Deal." She has her phone in her hand and then sets it upside down on the table and smiles even wider. "The cab will be here in ten minutes."

"Cab? I said only a few drinks, I can drive."

"Hey, you never know, right? Better safe than sorry." She shrugs her shoulders and if I didn't know any better, I would swear she had this planned all along.

I pass the driver the cash for the ride and we make our way inside. Katie leads the way and opens the door, allowing me to step inside first. With two steps in, my eyes travel down the bar and halt upon his face. Quickly turning back around, I run right into Katie.

"Shit. Curtis is here."

"So? You'll be fine. Did he see you?"

"No."

"Okay, so let's go to the bar, order drinks and go dance."

"Okay, sounds good." I am not avoiding him, just not sure what to say to him yet. I swallow hard and turn back around to walk the few feet to the bar.

With a lump in my throat, I struggle for my words. Thankfully, Katie takes note and orders for us.

"Two double vodka sodas, please. And let's get two shots of Jack as well."

The bartender nods and I keep my back turned, hoping he hasn't spotted me and decide to come over. I'm fully aware of my childish behavior towards Curtis but I did not prepare for this.

My heart getting the better of me, I turn my head to sneak a peek down the bar. His back is now towards me, and I can see he is talking to someone. Leaning a little further forward, I catch sight of Paul and snap my head back to Katie.

"Your brother is here, too." But I'm betting she already knew that.

"Oh yeah, look at that." She waves hello and I turn around and smile at Paul who is also waving, wearing his usual devilish grin.

I lift my hand and give a subtle wave as Curtis turns around to see who Paul is acknowledging. His face lights up when he sees me, and a smile reaches the corner of his mouth. I feel the pink in my cheeks and give a return grin.

"Here you are ladies." The bartender slides us our drinks and we grab the shot glass first.

"Thank you." I glance back toward Curtis, but he is already refocused on his conversation with Paul.

"Cheers, Daphne. Let's forget about boys and have a good night." She holds up her glass and we clink them together before shooting the warm liquid down our throats.

Making our way to the dance floor, I keep my eyes forward and try to forget about the sexy guy less than fifty feet away. The music pumps through the speakers and after the first song, I start to relax and enjoy myself.

Curtis

27

"**S**o, are you going to go over and say hi?" Paul asks, wagging his eyebrows and looking like an idiot.

"No," I state, a little too forcefully. Just the sight of Daphne has put me in a tailspin.

Finishing my beer, I flag down the bartender. "Another round, sweetheart, and how about two shots of Jameson?"

"It's that kind of night, huh?" Paul asks.

"Yep."

As soon as the glass is before me, I toss it back, the hot fluid warming my insides. With two fingers in the air, I signal for another round and Paul whistles beside me.

"Alright then, but for the record, neither one of us will be driving tonight."

I don't argue and down the next shot right as it is set down. Picking up Paul tonight, we originally only planned on a few beers, but things have now changed.

I do my best to avoid looking in her direction. Of course, I am nowhere near as strong as I would like, so as I glance over to their side of the bar and see her dancing with Katie. Watching her hips move to the beat, I'm reminded of the night of her birthday.

"Hey man, see those ladies across the bar?"

I look in the direction of where Paul is gesturing and spot the two women smiling directly at us.

"You mean the Barbie twins?"

"Oh, shit they are twins aren't they?" Paul laughs, "I didn't even notice. That's always been a fantasy of mine."

Paul smiles at the ladies and gives them a nod. Shaking my head, I take a lengthy pull from my beer, enjoying the ice cold liquid.

"I'm calling dibs on the slutty one, unless they are the freaks in which I am hoping will score me both."

Glancing back towards them, I try to decipher which one would be considered the slutty one.

"Have at it. I'm not interested."

"Still holding out for your true love?" he nods his head and points his beer bottle in the direction of where his sister and Daphne are dancing, but I don't respond. "That's cute. Do you write about her in your journal at night? Doodle hearts around her name?"

"Shut the hell up, asshole." I bring my bottle to my lips and drain the rest of its contents.

"I'm just screwing with you," he laughs, slapping my back. "But, have you considered what happens if she doesn't come back? I mean, she's right there, but hasn't attempted to even come say hello. Maybe she's just not the one."

Shoving away from the bar, I stand immediately. "I need some air." And without waiting for his response, I walk out of the bar.

Outside, I take a seat on a nearby bench and think about Paul's honest words. I know he didn't mean any harm and everything he said is true. It is something I have already thought about, yet my heart refuses to believe that our story is over. Nothing has been the same without Daphne's presence in my life. Words are blurred and colors are dull, even the air is stale.

My phone vibrates from my pocket and at first I think maybe she noticed I was gone and wandered where I went. Instead, I pull the phone out and see that is not the case.

Paul: Paying the tab. Let's walk to the Doug-Out.

I look down at the screen and furrow my brow in confusion. Why would Paul want to leave and go to his least favorite place? The Doug-Out is a local sports bar owned by his ex-girlfriend's family and they are never overly excited to see us there, especially her father, Doug.

Walking back inside, I notice Paul standing at the bar, pulling out his wallet.

"What's the rush, man? Let's have another round." I sit down on the barstool I was occupying earlier and look to a quiet Paul. He's deep in thought and not looking directly at me. "What's going on?" I ask, suddenly concerned.

"Nothing, this place just doesn't have much to offer."

"And The Doug-Out will?" I laugh.

"Yeah," he pauses, looking over my shoulder, "you're right. Let's call a cab and go somewhere else, or home. I mean, I am feeling pretty good, we can call it a night."

Now I sense trouble. Paul is acting strange and is never ready to go home before me. I have a sick feeling in the pit of my stomach, because there is only one thing that would cause this behavior from Paul. He's protecting me.

I spin on my stool and Paul catches my arm, shaking his head, which further peaks my curiosity. It only takes a couple seconds for me to locate Daphne on the dance floor. Her blonde waves are bouncing around her shoulders as she moves to the music. She looks undeniably sexy, but what really gets my blood boiling is the asshole who is dancing behind her. His hands are gripping her hips, touching her skin with her shirt bunching above his wrists. The words of the song are detailing the conveniences of a booty call and my jaw tightens even more.

"Why don't you go out there and put an end to all this?" Paul passes me a fresh beer and I drain half of it. The cold temperature does nothing to cool my heated temperament.

"No, she wanted space." Daphne's eyes meet mine briefly before I turn back around to the bar. "This is me giving it to her."

I order another round of shots even though I know I should slow down. I would hate to end my night praying to the porcelain gods.

"Hold that thought," Paul says. "Things are about to get a little more interesting."

I am a little terrified by the confident smile gracing Paul's face. It's a look I know all too well and is one that tells me he is up to no good.

His arm is in the air waving someone over and my eyes follow to watch in amusement as the Barbie twins saunter over. Things are definitely about to get a hell of a lot more interesting.

Daphne

28

With a quick spin, I manage to break free of the close contact with the stranger behind me. I don't mind dancing with the guy, but he is starting to get a little more comfortable than I would like. Now in the middle of our circle, I continue to move and find myself back to back with Katie. Dancing against her is a safe way to keep the nice gentleman from wanting to grind up against my ass. I would hate to give Curtis the wrong idea.

Casually glancing over my shoulder, I look toward the bar hoping to catch his eye.

What the hell! Where did they come from?

Two perfectly primped blondes are standing between Paul and Curtis, laughing and sipping on martinis. First of all, who the hell orders a martini here? Paul wraps his arm around one of their waists and pulls her in close to whisper something in her ear. The other girl seems less promiscuous, and she and Curtis appear to be exchanging simple small talk. I keep dancing trying to conceal my stalker status, but

Katie turns around when she notices I have slowed my groove.

"What's up, need another drink?" she looks at my cup and then follows my stare over to the bar.

"You know what?" I lift my drink and empty the cup in one gulp, "I do now."

I grab Katie's hand and head straight toward the guys. Curtis has yet to get friendly with the other blonde, but I would rather not give him the chance.

"Hey guys!" Katie hollers as soon as we get close. She walks up to where the girls are leaning against the bar top and stretches a fake smile across her face. "Mind if I get in here to order a drink?" Her words are soaked with sass, but it doesn't even faze the bimbos.

They smile back, and take a step away from the bar, allowing space for Katie and me. The guys remain on their stools as we stand between them to flag down the bartender. The two girls, still not taking the hint, keep close and stand on the other side of the guys, enclosing the circle.

"We will take two more vodkas and how about two shots, bartender's choice." She orders like a champ and I am thankful for the bonus shot she ordered.

Just inches away from Curtis, I accidently lean into him as I am pulling cash out of my purse. "Oh, sorry," I say as our eyes lock for the second time.

His sexy grin sends a heat wave to my core, but it's the wink that follows that nearly buckles my knees.

Turning back around, I alert the bartender as he prepares our drinks and up the order. "Better make that four shots."

Katie and I turn back around and jump into their conversation, barely acknowledging the two blondes are even still standing with us.

The bartender places the shots on the bar and Katie passes them out to the two boys and I grab mine. The girls look at one other before giving Katie and me a nasty glare.

"Well, here's to getting what you want, and at times wanting what you can't have," Katie says with a small hint of sadness in her eyes, but quickly shakes it off and lifts her glass.

I raise my glass to follow. "Here, here," I reply.

The guys both smile and shake their heads before lifting theirs to ours. We clink our shots and empty the glasses.

I lift my other drink to my lips and take a sip, hoping to cool the heat in my throat. As the current song finishes, a familiar beat pulses through the room and my heart rate increases.

With my free hand down to my side, and my birthday song cascading through my body, I reach for Curtis. Our eyes meet and a smile fills his face as I nod towards the dance floor.

Curtis

29

Daphne is leading me out to the dance floor and I can't hide the excitement I feel from the sudden change of events. The mood of the evening lightened dramatically the moment she walked up to the bar just minutes ago. I will have to thank Paul later for his little plan. The twins worked perfectly, sparking a minor jealousy within Daphne, which brought her over.

When we hit the dance floor I keep a safe distance, leaving her in charge of setting the pace. I glance back to the bar where we left our friends and I swear I just witnessed the Hampton siblings high-five. I wouldn't put it past them to have orchestrated this entire evening.

The bass is pumping through the speakers and bodies are moving around us, but all my focus is on the beautiful woman in front of me. Unable to keep my hands to myself any longer, I wrap an arm around her waist and bring her closer. Her arms circle my neck and she buries her head into my chest.

After a moment, she pulls her head back and smiles up at me. This one smile erases my doubts and I there is no way she doesn't feel this. The lyrics to the song ring true, because I want her to want me and if she does, she's got me.

Our bodies move slowly to the beat as Daphne sings along quietly. After the song ends, it rolls into the next which has a much faster beat and her moves become more seductive. Spinning around, she closes the space between her back and my chest as she grinds her backside against me. I am sure she can feel what she is doing to me, but there is nothing I can do to hide it.

While enjoying our time together, the guy she danced with earlier makes his way back onto the floor. Not that I think he would try to cut in, but I give him an all-knowing glare to back off. Just as I prepare for confrontation, Daphne spins back around and lifts up on her toes to plant a sweet kiss to the corner of my mouth. Looking back up, I notice the guy is gone.

Still on her toes and closer to eye level, we hold our gaze as both our chests rise and fall increasingly. My heart is on the verge of beating out of my chest. I rest my forehead against hers and close my eyes in an attempt to control my breathing. She starts running her fingers through the back of my hair, lulling me to calmness. Our bodies are swaying as the beat slows and I start to pay attention to the lyrics.

The artist is singing about a girl who needs to make up her mind, needing to know what she means and how she's running out of time.

I freeze when the words hit me and Daphne pulls back slightly with realization on her face. Nothing has been said in regards to her decision and as easy as it would be to assume it's me, I can't jump to conclusions.

Daphne starts to speak, but I cut her off, needing to enjoy her company a bit more before it all fades away.

"How about a drink?" I ask, offering a small smile.

She nods her head, and my hand, having a mind of its own, laces its fingers with hers as I lead us to the bar.

No sooner do we reach the Hamptons, Katie grabs Daphne and pulls her off in the direction of the restrooms. Daphne looks to me when our hands are disconnected and winks back with a bright smile.

Taking a seat next to Paul, he turns towards me after placing our drink orders.

"So, how did it go out there? You two looked cozy." He wiggles his brows, same as he did earlier, and I want to slap the look off his face.

"I think I am making progress."

We both laugh and wait for the girls to return. I don't give Paul any further information and he is good about not pressing for more. When Daphne and Katie finish with what I am sure was a gossip session, Katie suggests a game of pool.

All the tables are full, but one group is finishing up on the eight ball. Paul walks over and talks to one of the guys before setting down his quarters on the edge of the table, calling next game.

Meeting us at a side table, Paul sets his drink down. "So what are the teams?"

I look to Daphne, but Katie opens her mouth first, "Boys against girls. And, the losers have to buy a round of drinks."

We all agree to the terms and we begin as soon as the other players finish.

The game moves along smoothly, Paul and me consistently sinking our solids. Daphne surprises me with her skill level of billiards, but since I know from experience how terrible Katie is, I'm not sweating. This will be an easy win.

By the time I drop the eight ball in the corner pocket, the girls still have three stripes on the table. Daphne and Katie pout while Paul acts the part of sore winner, rubbing our victory in their faces. The girls whisper to one another, giggling back and forth at the bar, while they wait for our drinks.

"Let's play again," Katie says, after coming back with our winning drinks, and looking overly confident.

"Little sister, why do you want to embarrass yourselves? Keep your dignity."

"Are you scared, big brother?" Katie calls him out, knowing there is no way he will be shown up by a couple of girls.

"Fine. You want to lose again, by all means." Waving his hand at the table, Paul drops more quarters into the slot. "What's the wager?"

I look at my watch and see it's near closing time and know none of us are in any shape to drive. "How about losers cover the cab fare?"

Everyone nods and we shake hands in agreement. The girls keep exchanging looks and I know they are up to something. Paul sinks two stripes in during his break, but misses on his next turn. Daphne goes first for their team and knocks the blue two-ball in the middle pocket.

After her attempt at the five-ball misses by a hair, I scope out the table, looking for the best shot. Leaning down, I get my cue in the right position and focus, making sure everything is lined up correctly. I see movement out of the corner of my eye and glance over to Daphne, who is leaning over the adjacent side.

"What are you doing?" I ask, my eyes falling to the top of her newly exposed cleavage.

"Oh, just watching, to make sure you're going in at the right angle." She is trying to play innocent, but there is nothing innocent about the way her tongue runs across her lips.

I laugh, seeing right through her little act and shake my head, returning to my position. My arm pulls back slightly and just as I am moving it forward to hit the white cue ball, Daphne's breath caresses my ear.

"Don't choke," she whispers, successfully screwing up my shot and causing me to scratch.

The girls jump up and down, giggling over their accomplishment and Paul smacks me across the back of my head. Daphne meets my glare and winks.

Well played Fields, well played.

Katie is up next and I take a sip of my beer, nearly choking when she makes a combo shot that bounces off the sidewall. I look to Paul and he is equally confused.

"Did we forget to mention that Daphne has been teaching me how to play pool?" Katie asks, right before sinking another one.

She misses her next shot, but the pleased look doesn't leave either one of their faces. Paul manages to get three more of our striped balls in before Daphne's turn. Being a true hustler, she gets their remaining balls in, leaving only ours and the black eight-ball.

She focuses intently on the table, weighing out her options of which pocket to choose. While she's deciding on the route she wants to go, I walk up behind her, forcing my body right up against hers.

"Are you sure that's the angle you want?" I ask, my lips grazing the back of her ear, causing a hitch in her breath.

"You think you know better than me?" She turns only her head, keeping her ass snug against me.

"Well, I do happen to know a thing or two about balls." She laughs at my comment and returns her focus to the table. Bringing my mouth back to her ear, I finish, "and I'm damn sure an expert on hitting at the right angle."

I don't have to see her face to know that it is filled with her customary crimson blush.

Daphne shoots and misses the angle, butchering the entire shot. When she turns around, she is pissed and I blow her a kiss. She flips me off and Paul nods his head in approval, happy with my distraction pay back.

With Daphne sitting to the side with Katie, I successfully pocket our remaining balls, evening up the score. The cue ball stops in a spot that is both positive and negative. It makes for an easy shot that a person would have to be blind not to make, but if it isn't hit with the right pressure, it's sure to follow right behind the other into the pocket. A scratch on the eight ball is an instant loss.

I line up the shot and have my stick in position. I make a quick glance over to the girls and see they are in the middle of talking. It surprises me that they are leaving me wide open on this final shot and looking to Paul, he simply shrugs his shoulders. I bend down and line up the shot as my eyes swiftly move back to Daphne. She is rubbing the back of her neck with one hand as the other pulls her hair up and off her shoulders.

Focus.

Eyes back on the task at hand, I take a deep breath, feeling as though there is more than cab fare riding on this game. Against my better judgment, my focus returns to Daphne and her hand has left her neck and is now gliding down her chest. Her finger runs back and forth over her breast and I release the breath I hadn't realized I have been holding. I exhale harder than expected as I hit the cue ball, which is now rolling too fast.

Game over. The cue ball follows right behind the eight and I scratch on the easiest shot I've had all night.

The girls are hugging and jumping, screaming over their victory while Paul is yelling profanities at me.

I want to be angry, but Daphne walks up with her full lips pulled into a smile. "So, I guess we won," she says, sweetly.

"I guess you did." I hold my hand out for a good sportsman-like shake and she places hers in mine. Instead of a friendly shake, I tug her arm, crushing her into my body. "I will make you pay for that," I whisper in her ear.

She looks up, her eyes big with surprise, but also displaying a gleam of desire. "I'm counting on it."

Katie calls her name and Daphne winks before pulling away. I watch her walk knowing she is putting an extra sway to her hips just for me.

"What the hell was that, man?" Paul asks, smacking me in the back of the head again.

"Totally worth the defeat." My eyes are still glued on her body and when she catches my stare, her smile widens.

The room brightens as the lights are turned on for last call. I finish the last sip of my beer and pull my cell out to call the cab. With a driver nearby, they should only be a few minutes.

"Since you blew that entire game, it's only fair that you take the punishment and pay for the cab."

"I got it," I say and don't bother to acknowledge anything else that Paul is saying as Daphne approaches.

The last three weeks may have been hell, but I have a feeling things are about to improve.

"Ready to get out of here?" I ask, repeating my words from another night.

MICHELLE LOUISE

She smiles and replies, "Yes."

Daphne

30

Piling into the cab, I take my seat in the back next to Katie and the boys chat with the driver outside the car, most likely giving him our addresses. After a few moments, they shake hands and Paul climbs into the front seat while Curtis gets comfortable next to me in the back.

With his hand resting on his thigh, his pinkie finger tickles at my leg. I unfold my arms and slide my hand down, interlocking my little finger with his. Through the corner of my eye, I see his smile widen.

Pulling in to a small development, we arrive at Paul's house. It is newly built, but has a vintage look and is very charming. Paul turns in his seat and puts his hand up in the air.

"Fun night, guys."

Katie reaches up and meets his high five, and I follow right after.

"Yeah, it was. We should do it again soon," Katie responds. "Later, bro."

"Curtis, thanks for the ride." Paul reaches a fist toward Curtis, who meets it with a bump.

"Yeah man, no problem. Talk to you later."

"Goodnight everyone." Paul climbs out of the cab and waves us off.

The driver pulls away and we head toward Katie's and my development. We all remain quiet as Katie hums along with the radio and Curtis keeps his finger locked with mine. It is such a small gesture, but makes me feel like I'm in seventh grade again.

"Okay, this is me. Call me tomorrow, Daphne." She reaches around my neck and gives me a hug.

I break my pinkie lock and hug her back. "Will do. Have a good night."

She climbs across my lap and gives Curtis a hug as well. "Thanks for the ride."

"My pleasure. Goodnight, Katie." He smiles and Katie climbs back over and exits the car.

Rounding the corner as we reach my condo, Curtis grabs my hand and interlocks all his fingers with mine this time.

As the car comes to a stop, he leans toward the driver and lets him know he will be right back.

Curtis gets out first and closes the door behind me.

"Well, I had a good time tonight. And thanks for the ride." I smile and look up into his eyes, which are dark with desire.

"Well, we did lose and I am a man of my word." He lifts his hand and tucks a loose piece of hair out of my face and behind my ear.

His touch awakens my core as heat flushes through my body.

Curtis lets out a low chuckle and shakes his head.

"What?" I ask.

"Nothing, you are just so damn beautiful when you blush like that. It drives me crazy."

I instantly put my hands on my cheeks to feel the warmth. Grabbing my wrists he lowers them, then lifts my chin to meet his gaze. The desire in his eyes has intensified and my breath begins to quicken.

As he slowly lowers his lips to kiss me, I whisper against them, "You better go pay that guy."

His smile spreads across his cheeks before his leaves me with a chaste kiss and runs back toward the waiting cab. I turn around to unlock the door and hear his returning footsteps approaching.

With the handle turned, I feel his hands on my waist along with his hot breath just as his mouth devours the sweet spot where my neck meets my shoulder. My knees weaken at his touch.

Spinning me around, he crashes his mouth into mine and grips my waist, lifting me up against him. I wrap my legs around his midsection and with one hand tangled in my hair, he uses the other to push the door open and carry me inside.

We frantically explore each other's mouths in a search for the words we both want to say, but can't seem to find. We continue our path and enter my bedroom.

"You. Are. So. Damn. Hot." Each word lingers on his lips as he kisses down my neck.

A small moan escapes and he gently lowers me to the bed. Taking a small step back, he lifts his shirt over his head.

"Jesus. Did I every mention how sexy you are?" I ask, as I sit up and run my hands over his strong chest and abdomen.

He smiles and shakes his head as if I am crazy.

"Seriously. You. Are. So. Damn. Hot." I mimic his earlier words, placing wet kisses across his lower stomach along the edge of his pants, and leave a final kiss atop his bulging denim.

I unbutton his jeans and slowly drop down his zipper as his hands reach into my hair. Lowering them with his briefs, I gently stroke his length before placing my lips around it.

"Daphne…" My name fades from his lips as he moans.

After a few moments, he removes his hands from my hair and lifts me from my knees. Gripping the hem of my shirt, he lifts it over my head and tosses it to the floor. He continues to remove each article of my clothing but stops when he reaches my panties.

"I want you to leave these on, they are too sexy."

"Oh, you like these?" I slowly rock my hips from side to side and do a slow turn to show off my backside. I had no idea when I put on my favorite red lace thong that it would lead me here, but I'm glad it did.

"Hell, yeah. My favorite color." Curtis runs his hands down my hips and trails his fingers along the lace in the back.

I walk to my nightstand and pull out a foil packet. Tossing it to Curtis, I do another slow spin showing off my panties and crawl onto the bed, staying on all fours. Looking over my shoulder towards him, I watch as he tosses the empty wrapper to the floor and takes a heated step toward me.

Pulling my panties to the side, he rubs his fingers across my wetness and my entire body shivers at his touch.

As Curtis slides inside of me, my breath catches in my throat and with a few gentle thrusts, our bodies melt into one another. I lift onto my knees, leaning back against his chest. Moving my hair to one side, his mouth finds my neck. We instantly find a groove and he wraps his arms around my body with his hand landing atop my peaking breasts and grasping my nipple between his fingers.

The ecstasy soars through my body and my eyes flutter closed as his other hand slides down my stomach and rubs small circles of pleasure against my heat. The building release rips through me and I drop my head back against him and let a loud moan escape my chest.

"Oh my god, Curtis." It leaves my lips in a whisper as all my energy trails with my release.

"Daphne..." The same fading sound leaves his lips and his body tenses with his own release.

As the sun peers through the blinds, I roll over to hide from it and find the spot that was once filled with a sexy, warm body is now cold and empty. I sit up in bed and search the room, stopping at the note on my nightstand.

SORRY TO LEAVE YOU SO EARLY, YOU WERE TOO BEAUTIFUL TO WAKE. HAD A LITTLE FAMILY EMERGENCY. TEXT ME WHEN YOU WAKE UP. I LEFT YOU SOME WATER AND ASPIRIN.

XOXO CURTIS

Even his handwriting in all caps was sexy and controlled. I send him a quick text and take a sip from the water bottle. Surprisingly, I don't have a headache and must not have been as drunk as I thought last night.

Lying back onto my pillow, I start to drift back to sleep as I replay the night's feature film in my head. An incoming text wakes me at the best part.

Curtis: Good Morning. Hope you slept well.

Me: I did, just a little sad to find an empty bed. I was hoping to replay the night with you this morning. ;)

Curtis: Trust me. I had every intention. Sorry to leave, but Jill needed me. She locked herself out of the house this morning while Hannah was   still sleeping.

Me: Oh no. That's terrible! Too bad you don't have a hidden key.

Curtis: Hell no. I have a psycho ex, remember?

Me: Oh, good call. Well, I'm glad everything is okay.

His next message was a video, so I turned up the volume on my phone and pressed play.

"Princess Daphne. I would like to invite you over to Nana's for a very special Tea Party this evening." Hannah was twirling around in a pink dress and silver shiny tiara.

"Hannah, it's not a tea party, remember? It's dinner," Curtis whispered in the background.

"Oh yeah. Princess Daphne. I would like to invite you over to Nana's for a very special dinner party. Please say you'll come." She batted her eyelashes like a true professional princess and the video cuts off.

How could anyone say no to that? I was doing so good holding up the wall I built; yet without even trying, Curtis Dean has broken it down.

Me: Dirty! Using a little angel to lure me over to your parents' for dinner!

Curtis: Did it work?

Me: What time should I be there? :)

Curtis: Dinner is at six.

Me: See you then. XOXO

Curtis: Looking forward to it.

Curtis

31

"Smells good, Ma," I say, entering the kitchen, where my mother and sister are preparing the food for tonight's dinner. I kiss her head and reach around her, stealing a strawberry.

"Thanks, dear. Hannah asked us to make some scones for her after-dinner tea."

We all laugh at how mature and beyond her years my little niece can act at times.

"I am almost embarrassed to serve them to Daphne because I know they won't compare to hers," Jill says, as she places the baked triangles on a cooling rack.

It's a nice change having my family want to impress the girl in my life. Both have expressed multiple times how much they like Daphne and approve of any relationship I may have with her. She fits in so well that I can already see the potential of how great our future holidays could be. With Vera, we never spent holidays with each other's families. We always tended to do our own things separately. I couldn't imagine that being the case with Daphne.

"I'm sure they will taste amazing and she will love them."

The doorbell rings, halting my mother to protest more.

"You better get that," she says with a wink.

I run my hands through my hair, pushing it away from my face and straighten out the front of my shirt. Inhaling an anxious breath, I open the front door to a smiling Daphne on the other side, holding a bottle of wine.

"Hi," I say, pulling her close to me, with an arm wrapped around her waist.

She reaches on her tiptoes and presses her soft lips against mine, too briefly. "Hi," she repeats.

"Come on inside." I lead her into the house and close the door behind us.

She is wearing a floral dress that's tight on her chest and torso, flaring out from her waist and falling right above her knees. Her hair is down in loose golden waves -the way I have come to like it most.

She eyes me nervously for a moment, "Is this okay?" she asks, pulling the skirt of the dress outwards. "I was going to go casual, but then I didn't want to be too casual. I thought this would be safe, but now you have me thinking I overdressed. This is just kind of a big deal and I wanted to look nice . . ."

I pull her into me and bring my mouth down, stopping her nervous rambling. "You look amazing. Sorry, I was so caught up in your beauty, I didn't mention it when I first opened the door."

"Are you sure?" Daphne looks up with doubt in her eyes.

"I'm positive. You are perfect, and there is that blush I am so fond of."

She laughs and I drop a kiss on her temple. The sound of little feet running against the wood floor has me pulling away slightly.

"Daphne! You're here!" Hannah shouts, as she rushes over to throw her arms around her.

"Well, I had a special video invitation that I just couldn't turn down." She passes me the bottle of wine and winks before lowering herself to Hannah's level. "You look very pretty in your dress, just like a princess."

"Thank you. My favorite part is when I twirl," she does numerous spins, causing her dress to float in the air, flying around her, "and it does that." She stops short, a little wobbly from the spinning and Daphne reaches a hand out to steady her.

"Mine does that too." Standing back up to her full height, Daphne spins — not as fast as Hannah.

During her second spin around, she loses her footing and starts to fall to the ground. I rush my arm out and manage to wrap it around her back, lifting her up before she hits the ground, luckily without dropping the bottle in my other hand. The moment reminds me of a time, not too long ago, when I rescued her from hitting the floor at the Tea

Room. This time, though, I hold onto her a little longer and my eyes stay locked on hers.

"Uncle Curtis! You saved her. You were so fast. I can't believe it. You are Daphne's hero." Hannah's sweet voice reminds me that we are not alone.

"Thank you," Daphne says, softly. "You're really good at that. I guess it's a hazard, being around me."

I gently set her back on her feet. "I will always catch you." The look on her face tells me that she understands I mean more than just when she trips over her own feet.

She nods her head and links her fingers through mine.

I look over at Hannah, who is still in awe over Daphne. "Come on, let's go check on the food."

Hannah bounces away as Daphne squeezes my hand and leaves a kiss on my cheek. She reaches out for the wine and I return it to her. With my hand on her lower back, I lead her through the house.

I can't let her slip through my fingers again. Before this night is over, I need to open up to her and let her know exactly what I am feeling. After last night, I can't help but hope she is feeling the same way.

When we enter the kitchen, Ma and Jill are fussing over the salad, but quickly turn their attention to us.

"Daphne, it's so good to see you. We're so glad you could join us on such short notice." My mother wipes her hands on a towel before encircling Daphne in a tight hug.

"Thank you for having me, Mrs. Dean. I you brought this," she hands over the bottle of wine, "it's Chardonnay, I hope you like it."

"That's lovely, dear, and please, call me Eleanor."

She nods her head and Jill walks over, also embracing Daphne. "It's so good to see you again. I wasn't sure I would before we left."

"Oh, when are you heading back?" Daphne asks, seeming disappointed in my sister leaving.

Jill meets my gaze and smiles reassuringly at me. We had a long talk this morning and she explained that it was time for her to go home and work on her relationship with Alex. She is determined they can fix whatever issues are going on.

"Tomorrow morning. We have an anxious daddy just dying to see his little girl again," Jill says, and Daphne pulls her into another hug. "Don't worry, I don't tend to stay gone for too long."

"Let's exchange numbers before the evening is over. I would love to stay in touch."

Ma looks up at me after Daphne's statement and rests her hand on my arm. My family is falling in love with her and she doesn't even realize the effect she has on people.

"I would love that," Jill says, before checking the roast in the oven.

"Can I help with anything?" Daphne asks and my mother pats my arm.

"No. Today you are our guest. Curtis, why don't you give Daphne a tour of the garden? Show her all the work you and your father have put in. Speaking of which, I need to fetch him from the garage." She turns on her heels and heads off to find my father, who I have no doubt is sitting in the garage with a beer, watching whatever sports game may be on.

"Shall we?" I ask.

Daphne nods and I lay my hand against the small of her back, leading her out the kitchen door. We follow the stepping stones down a short path before turning a corner leading to the garden. My parents have a spectacular backyard. Pop and I put in many strenuous hours building the structures and the handcrafted pond, but its Ma's green-thumb that keeps the beauty alive. Without her flowers and shrubbery, it would be nothing but a simple deck and gazebo.

I fill Daphne in on the little bit of history there is on the work we put into everything over the years and give her a tour of the flourishing gardens that are spread out in the expanse of the yard.

After circling through the roses, I guide her into the gazebo and we take a seat on the bench, looking out into the yard.

"I can't believe you built this," she says, looking around and admiring the woodwork.

"Pop did most of it and I just helped out whenever I was available."

"It's beautiful, Curtis."

"Daphne," I start, waiting for our eyes to meet, "I know you said before you needed space, and I will still give you that, if it is truly what you want. I just need you to know how I feel about you."

I rest my hand on top of her thigh and she slips hers over mine, entwining our fingers. It's the reassurance I need to carry on.

"Everything you said on the porch that day, I felt the same. I was content in the life I was leading until you came along and changed everything. I have never felt so connected to someone as I do with you and certainly have never had it happen so fast. You filled a void that I never even knew existed. How is that even possible?" I laugh and she tightens her grip on my hand, smiling at me. "I think I started falling in love with you after the first time you smiled at me. You have been a constant thought in my head ever since the day you confused me for my father. I see a future with you — with us, and I want you to know that I am serious and reassure you that I will wait for you, as long as you need."

Daphne's eyes are wet with unshed tears and it hurts to think I have upset her. The last thing I wanted to do was put more pressure on her.

"I'm sorry for laying all that on you. Please, don't cry, baby."

Her eyes close and a tear falls from each lid. I gently wipe the moisture with my thumb and kiss her cheeks.

"I'm ready."

I sit frozen, letting her words sink in before I move to my feet. "Yeah. Okay. We should probably head back inside."

I am internally berating myself, thinking that she most likely wants to run away. I just basically told her I was in love with her and we've only known each other a few short months.

"Curtis, no." Daphne jumps to her feet and grabs both of my hands, pulling me closer to her. "I'm ready to jump. With you, just like this." She squeezes my hands tighter as the meaning behind her words hit me.

"Are you sure? I wasn't trying to force an answer from you."

"I'm positive. I planned on telling you tonight before I left, but this is better," she says with a smile beaming on her face.

She releases the hold on my hands and I softly grasp her cheeks and crash my mouth against her. Our tongues tangle in a passionate dance and I lean her head back, gaining better access. A sexy moan escapes her and I pull back, knowing it's not the right time or place to be getting too worked up.

"So, are we are doing this?" I ask, needing the reassurance of knowing my mind isn't playing a terrible trick on me.

"Looks like it."

"Want to get out of here?" I wink, thinking about where that question has led us in the past.

She presses her lips to mine and lingers before pulling away. "I would love to, but it's your sister and niece's last night here. We have plenty of nights ahead of us being together, but tonight we have a dinner with your family."

Yes. There was no doubt in my mind; I was completely in love with Daphne Fields.

"You're right. We should get back in there before they come looking for us."

I grab her hand and start towards the house when she pulls me to a stop and I turn to see what's wrong.

"It was your French toast."

I stare at her for a moment, confused and unsure what she is talking about.

"What was?"

"When I started to fall. You were the first guy to ever cook me breakfast."

With a swift jerk of my arm, I pull Daphne into my body. Hearing her confessions sends a familiar tingle through my veins. The same one I get every time we touch. We may not be ready to say the exact words, but I know with certainty we are finally on the same page. This is just the beginning of our story.

"Well, just wait until you see what other culinary skills I have up my sleeve."

"Looking forward to it."

We walk inside, hand in hand and no one misses the looks shared between us. As much as I love my family and will miss my Jill and Hannah, I am counting down the minutes until this dinner is over and I can take Daphne home.

Daphne

32

Pulling up the drive, I see Papa on the front porch with a wide smile spread across his face. I have come to greatly enjoy our dinner nights and try to make them a weekly event. This time, I would be solo, but more times than none Curtis joins us as well. He already had plans with Paul for the night, so I agreed to meet him at his house later.

"Hey, good looking. Hope you're hungry," Papa calls, as I approach the house.

"Like you couldn't imagine. I was so busy today, I may have forgotten to eat lunch." I throw my arms around his neck and kiss his cheek. "How are you? Feeling any better?"

Papa had caught a slight cold last week, but managed to fight it off rather quickly. I appreciate that he takes care of himself and isn't afraid to see the doctor when needed. It allows me to not to worry as much.

"Much better. I rested as much as I could and let the medicine do the magic. Today, I woke up and was able to get back outside to work in the yard," he proudly states.

"Good to hear. But don't overdo it, and keep resting." I loop my arm in his and we make our way inside.

Papa had our burgers cooked with all the fixings lined up at the table. We each make our plate and head to the back porch to sit.

"Curtis out with Paul tonight?"

"Yeah, they are meeting up with an old friend from high school that is passing through town."

We both take bites at the same time and a few silent moments pass as we enjoy our dinner. After wiping his mouth, I see Papa's smile creep out from behind his napkin.

"What?" I ask with a half full mouth of food.

"Oh, nothing. It's just funny."

"What's funny?" I ask.

"Curtis. Well, you and Curtis." He pauses and thinks on it for a minute, still smiling.

Not sure what to say, nor why my relationship with Curtis would be funny, I sit and wait for him to continue.

"Grams would love this. You know, we have known Curtis a very long time. He used to come around and help me a few times a month. Grams would feed him and they always enjoyed a cup of iced tea together at the end of the workday. She was always very fond of him, as am I."

"He is pretty great, isn't he?" I smile and Papa nods his approval.

We continue eating in silence and my mind wanders around my new life. Just a few short months ago I was trying to sort through all my feelings of leaving my fiancé behind and doubting my decision to move here. And today, my heart is full and my thoughts look only toward the future.

"There is something else I wanted to mention." Papa clears his throat, breaking the silence. "This will be my last year at the drive-in. I think it is time for me to fully retire."

"Oh, wow. I thought I would never hear those words. You love it there."

Along with Grams, Papa also had big dreams of owning his own business and at a very young age, bought a large piece of land with a loan from his father. He worked construction for many years to pay back the loan and save up the additional funds. Then, when he and Grams were in their late twenties, he finally had enough and built a drive-in theater.

Truesdale Drive-In was the first one of its kind within a thirty-mile radius and business boomed. He and Grams spent all their time there and transformed it into a local hot spot. It has always been a very lucrative business and remains a staple in the community.

"So, you can't be selling it, right? Who is going to run it?" I start to panic thinking of not having it in our family.

"Oh, Daph, relax. I would never let this leave our family. Your brother is going to be here in a few months and will be working with me to learn the ropes. The Tea Room was always yours and the drive in will be for Derrick."

My heart is nearly beating out of my chest. Excitement and confusion race through my thoughts.

"Derrick? Did he agree? Wait, how long has he known?"

"On your birthday, I pulled your brother aside and had a serious conversation. I told him not to make a decision and not to discuss it with anyone until he had thought it through. He called me earlier this week and accepted my proposal."

"Holy crow. That is great news! We haven't lived in the same town for years. This is going to be great." I stand from the table and walk over to hug Papa.

"Yes, I am thrilled that he agreed and look forward to slowing down myself." Papa stood from his chair and hugged me back. "Well, let me clean up. Why don't you go see the new flowers I planted in the garden?"

"Oh, new flowers? I will be right back to help. Just leave them in the sink and I'll wash them up in a few." I take a sip of my tea and head toward the water.

Papa began working on this project a couple of months ago and with the help of Curtis, they have really made me a believer of heaven.

The white and gray pavers extend off the walkway and lead a breathtaking path through arches of flowers, opening up to a custom built pergola. At any given time, there are hundreds of butterflies that flutter about from plant to plant.

Approaching the cedar bench, and before sitting, I trace my fingers across the engraved letters. With my eyes closed, I can almost feel them around me.

KAY AND DEANNA

Missing you Always, Loving you Forever

My mother was taken from me far too soon and my grandmother quickly took her place and gave me the love and support that a young woman needed. Grams will always be my inspiration to be a better woman. She taught me to be strong, independent and wise. It is because of her that I am who I am today.

Looking up into the blooming flowers that surround me, I allow a few tears to tickle my cheeks. Reaching into my pocket, I retrieve a folded piece of stationery and unfold the worn sheet.

As my relationship with Curtis grows with every day, I go back to her words often and wonder how she knew. Grams was always wise, but it's almost as if she was in my head when she wrote this letter. My relationship with Nathan was never bad, but it was never the one. I was just floating through the motions not knowing that my feelings were mediocre in comparison to what I feel for Curtis.

Being with Curtis is like taking a breath; it takes no effort and feels more natural than anything else in my life. The electricity that courses through me when we touch could light a city of thousands and the first moment it happened, I knew. What I felt was real and my life will never be the same again.

Wiping a fallen tear, I focus on the paper and whisper her words aloud, letting them hang in the beautiful night air as the butterflies swim through the breeze.

"A love to cherish, kept deep in the heart

A love far away, but never apart

MICHELLE LOUISE

Moments of laughter, moments of tears

Through all life's moments, throughout all years

Love holds no value, and cannot be measured

Like a fine cup of tea, it can only be treasured."

And with these words, I mentally vow to do exactly that. Curtis is the love I never knew I was missing and one I will always treasure.

EPILOGUE
Curtis

"Hey babe, this is the last one." I carry the box into the dining room, setting it down on the table.

Daphne wraps her arms around my neck and presses her lips to mine, causing the same electric current to rush through my veins I experience with every kiss. I thought at some point it would fade or disappear, but it is just as strong today as it was the first time we touched.

"It's time for a break. The guys are out back already. Grab a beer and join them, we will finish up in here." She motions toward the living room where Katie is pulling picture frames out of a box and placing them on the mantle.

I pull Daphne tighter to my front, caressing her cheek with my thumb while staring into her beautiful hazel eyes. She still takes my breath away when I see her and I hope that feeling never goes away. According to my father, it doesn't. You can't miss the love shared between my parents, even after all these years.

"Don't be too long. We can put everything away later, after everyone leaves. Why don't you girls forget about the boxes and come enjoy this beautiful weather." My lips trail her neck and when a soft gasp escapes her lips, I have to remind myself we have company.

"We only have a few more to unpack and I promise, we will be right out." She kisses my cheek before whispering in my ear, "Besides, I have better plans as to how we should spend our evening after everyone goes home."

A smile tugs at my mouth as she backs away slowly, knowing the thought she just inserted into my mind. I am half tempted to throw everybody out right now, just so I can see exactly what she has planned.

"Have I told you how much I love you today?" I ask.

"A few times," she responds, "but I never grow tired of hearing it."

I grab an ice-cold beer out of the refrigerator and reach for the back door when she calls my name.

"I love you too." She winks and returns to work with Katie, who nudges Daphne with her elbow, putting both girls in a fit of giggles.

I too will never grow tire of hearing those words. I never understood the depth at which one's love could reach, until Daphne. Being with her has taught me a multitude of things and without her, I would only be a shell of myself. I knew the day we admitted our feelings towards one another that it would be impossible to tear us apart. I wouldn't let it happen.

With the news of her brother, Derrick, moving to Truesdale, I decided to take our relationship to the next level and invited her to move in with me. We hadn't spent a night apart since that evening in my parents' garden, so it just made sense. Her brother is going to take over the townhouse and I'll be able to have Daphne in my bed, every night. Our bed. It was a win-win.

"What are you two plotting over here?" I ask as I approach Derrick and Paul. They are sitting next to each other and look to be up to no good.

"Well, I just nominated Derrick as my new bar-buddy. It's good to have a fellow single guy and I am now in need of a new wingman." Paul shakes his head at me in sarcastic disappointment.

"I should probably apologize in advance, Derrick." Bringing the bottle to my lips, I take a long pull of my beer.

He lets out a chuckle and slaps Paul on the back. "I'm sure we will get along just fine. It will be nice to have someone to venture out with."

"I am definitely the man for the job. I can also give you a heads up on which chicks to steer clear from."

The guys jump into conversation of Paul's history with women and I sit back and laugh to myself, imagining the day when a pretty girl will knock him on his ass. He is a good guy and I know from our drunk-talks that he does have goals of marriage and children, but what I don't know is why he isn't pursuing them. Based on the way he took care of and raised Katie when we were growing up, I know he would excel at being both a husband and father. I suppose it is up to him to decide when the time is right. Sometimes the right girl just falls into your lap when you least expect it.

MICHELLE LOUISE

The back door opens and the girls walk out, both holding wine glasses filled to the brim. Katie takes the last available chair, putting her next to Derrick and I reach for Daphne's hand and pull her down into my lap, careful not to spill her drink.

"I ordered pizza a while ago figuring you boys would be hungry after all your hard work," Daphne says, placing her glass on the table and relaxing her body against mine.

"Thanks, babe." I press a kiss to her cheek.

"I think I might have developed a man-crush on your brother, Daph. After dinner we are going to hit up the bar and test out this new bro-mance." Paul pauses for a moment and directs his attention to Derrick. "Given our individual histories of picking up ladies, just imagine what we can accomplish working together."

We all laugh, but I know he is dead serious about his plan. From the tales Daphne has told me about her brother, I already know that he has almost too much in common with my best friend. The two of them together would definitely be a hazard to the females of Truesdale.

My lap is suddenly empty after Daphne jumps up announcing the arrival of the pizza and we all rise from our chairs and follow inside.

The house is filled with laughter as the five of us sit around the dining table. Daphne shakes her head and smiles listening to her brother tell stories and get to know our friends. She couldn't be happier having him around. The distance between then had been hard on her and since his arrival a few weeks ago, she hasn't been able to quit smiling.

302

Family is important to the both of us. Even her father has made a couple trips down to visit and we are going to see him next month. He has been dating someone new and is finally ready for Daphne and Derrick to meet her. Apparently, this is the first serious relationship he has been involved in, in quite some time.

After dinner, Paul convinces his new bar-buddy that tonight is the perfect opportunity to test out their new duo. It's good timing because Daphne hasn't been able to stop yawning for twenty minutes and I'm pretty tired myself.

We walk our friends to the door and give our goodbyes, making plans to have dinner later in the week. It has become routine for the group to get together a few times a month, whenever our schedules allow it.

"Come on, beautiful, let's get you to bed." I turn the deadbolt and wrap my arm around Daphne.

"I had big plans for you tonight," she says in between yawns, holding her hand against her mouth.

"How about a rain-check, you've had a long day." I guide her to our room and slowly undress her.

She stares up at me, completely naked except for her panties. She is absolutely beautiful and I fall more in love with her every single day. I lower my lips to hers and they move in sync, as they always do. Stepping back, I reach behind my head and lift my shirt off my body and pull it over Daphne. Other than being naked, her wearing my shirt is my favorite look on her.

We get settled in the bed and I pull her snug against my front, lacing my fingers with hers and resting them above her heart.

"Goodnight, sweetheart."

"Goodnight, Curtis. I love you."

"I love you too, babe."

She squeezes my hand and it isn't long before her breathing evens out and she is sound asleep.

Just like every other night, I say a silent prayer, thanking Miss Kay for bringing Daphne into my life and vow to always treasure her.

The End

Enjoy a sneak peak into book two of the
Truesdale Love Stories.

CONVINCE ME

(This version is unedited and subject to change.)

CHAPTER ONE
Derrick

The crowd erupts in laughter and a smile fills my face; the sound never gets old. Movies are such a high point of entertainment in most people's lives, so when you couple it with the nostalgic atmosphere of a drive in theater, you've got yourself one hell of a night.

Walking along the dirt path, I focus on the ground as my flash light dances on the sand. The echoing audio spills from the parked cars and floats through the night air. The aroma of popcorn invades my senses as I approach the brick building in the center of the lot.

"You guys doing okay in here?" I ask the concession crew as I enter.

"Yeah, we're good, boss. Should be finished early again tonight, want some help with pick up later?" the manager, Mason, replies.

The concession area closes at eleven-thirty every night to allow ample time for cleaning. Papa has always had a great staff, but with the new manager, things have vastly improved.

Mason is the grandson of one of Papa's long-time friends and just moved back home after going through a grueling divorce. He has a degree in business management and has been a solid asset to the team thus far. He's also only a few years older than me, so we have quite a bit in common and know a few of the same people.

"That would be great. I'll meet you back down here in about forty-five minutes. Thanks again, bud." I pat Mason on the shoulder and walk outside around to the back of the building.

It will be awesome to get some help tonight; I am brutally tired. On a normal night, when the last show ends, the headlights illuminate the dirt lot as the vehicles take turns exiting the theater. Once it's empty, a small crew, typically two guys and myself, go around and do a quick sweep of the grounds, picking up left over trash.

Depending on the night, this usually takes around thirty minutes and is my least favorite part. Getting the help of just one other person saves time and allows me take care of the other closing tasks. It's my personal goal to have the employees leave before one in the morning and for me to close up by two.

Lifting heavy feet, I slug my way up the weathered staircase and enter the dusty projector room, which also doubles as my office. The spinning reels have slowly transformed into a soothing melody, and become much less of a distraction. I have been tossing around the idea of switching to a digital system, but with this machine in great working condition, it is not a necessity.

Placing the lid on another filled bin, I set it aside with the others and glance around the small, dimly lit space. Organizing has never been my strong suit, but I am finding it to be a crucial task, which keeps me sane. The innocent neglect over the last couple of years has caused quite a clutter and has been my main focus.

With the theater only open to the public four nights a week, and only a few hours each occasion, it leaves me plenty of time to work on these projects; number one being this room. This is my ninth day in a row hard at work and I'm looking forward to sleeping in and getting some chores done around the house tomorrow.

Coincidently, my sister was moving in with her boyfriend around the same time of my arrival and I was able to take over her lease. Daphne is my twin and recently took over ownership of The Treasured Tea Cup in town earlier this year after my Grams passed.

Her boyfriend, Curtis, is a great guy and has been a huge help at the drive-in. I hired his company Dean R&R to take care of the larger renovations. Papa and I can handle the majority, but would rather leave structural upgrades to the professionals.

With an exhausted sigh, I accept defeat for the night and take a seat in the new recliner that was delivered earlier today. Staring at the projector, I observe the whirling reels and follow the light traveling across the field illuminating the large screen.

Releasing the lever on the side, I recline the chair and let my eyelids fall to rest. This has been my first week without

Papa's help and the pressure to make him proud is immense.

Truesdale Drive-In was built by my Papa and has been a staple in the community for over fifty years. When he first asked me to take over, I never imagined I would be sitting here tonight. Not being a fan of small towns and slow living, it didn't seem to be the right fit. But, after a few weeks of thinking on it, I called Papa and accepted his offer. Honestly, I can't pin point the exact moment, but it eventually just became clear what the right choice was.

We worked together for the first month as I soaked in as much knowledge as possible and we both agreed I was ready. There's not much to it, but it takes a lot of hard work and dedication to keep this place running. With a growing number of upgrades needed, I spend most of my time keeping things in working condition and reviewing the budget to see where we can start improving. There is a long road ahead, but I am confident I will get the theater back to its prime within the next year.

Taking a deep breath, I relax deeper into the chair and enjoy the nights' movie audio. Just as I begin to fade into a slumber, a faint knock raps on the door. Lifting my gaze, I watch as it creaks open and the moonlit sky peeks in. A shadowed silhouette slips in and closes the door quietly.

Approaching slowly, her sweet voice whispers, "Hi, handsome."

Gliding the hem of her cotton dress up her thighs, she climbs onto the chair and straddles my lap. Reaching a hand to her neck, I pull her mouth to mine and lift my hips to meet her body. With our tongues dancing, she grinds against the thin material of my gym shorts.

She lifts her hips as I slide the shorts to my knees and glide my hand up her inner thigh to find her bare. She moans sweetly at my touch and I ease myself inside as I guide her back down onto me.

With her small hands resting on my chest and mine on her hips, she moves her body with a steady rhythm. Lost in the increasing pleasure I lay my head back against the soft leather and allow her to take control. As her pace accelerates and her small moans become more frequent, I lift my head to watch as pure ecstasy floods her body.

Holding her waist tightly, I sit up in the chair and fold the recliner with my legs. Regaining balance, I bounce her body and increase my thrusts, quickly leading to my own pleasurable escape.

With a chaste kiss to my lips, the sexy mistress stands from my lap and leaves without a word. It may seem strange if this was the first time it's happened, however, over the last week or two, it's kind of become our thing.

CHAPTER TWO
Katie

"Hey, the hot guy in the back corner is asking for you again. This is the second time this week he's been in and looking for you. Something you need to tell me?"

I glance over at my co-worker and roll my eyes as I mix the drinks on the ticket she handed me. To keep myself busy during my summer breaks from school, I like to pick up shifts at the local tavern. Some nights, dealing with drunk customers can be just as bad as the fourth graders I teach.

"No, Mia," I laugh, placing the last drink on her tray, "After serving him last weekend he asked me out, but I politely declined."

Though his appearance is above average, I don't make a habit of picking up guys at the bar; especially, where I am currently employed. Even after my initial rejection, he came back a few days later and gave it another try, which ended in the same manner. Hopefully, he doesn't think the third time is the charm.

"He has that rich-guy attitude. Are you sure you want to let him slip by?"

"Yeah, he's not really my type." I lie, a man like that was every woman's type. "But you should go for it. My shift is ending soon anyways and I need to get out of here."

She eyes me with suspicion. "Where are you running off to? Hot date?"

"Not quite. School is starting soon and I still have so much to get done beforehand."

"Our time together is coming to an end." Mia sticks her bottom lip out and wipes away an imaginary tear from her cheek.

"Stop it. You know I will end up being a regular around here. My wine consumption tends to go up during the school year." We both laugh and I swat her butt. "Deliver these drinks before we start getting complaints."

"Yeah, yeah." With the full tray in hand, Mia returns to work.

After checking on the few customers sitting at the bar, I pull my phone from my back pocket and type out a quick text.

Me: My place in an hour.

Once my replacement arrives, I clock out, grab my things and with a swift wave goodbye, I am out the door. I enjoy my shifts at the bar, as they provide me with unlimited entertainment, and the extra cash is always nice.

My brother, Paul, is a frequent visitor as well as my bestie, Daphne, and her boyfriend, Curtis. He and my brother have been friends since they were young kids and we all grew up together. Curtis is like a second brother to me and I couldn't have been more thrilled when he and Daphne got together. They are so perfect for each other that it can be nauseating at times, but I still adore them. The way they both describe the pull they felt to each other from their first meeting, gives me hope that real love exists.

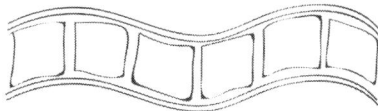

I am wrapping my satin robe around my damp body after my shower, when I hear a knock on the door. My fingers tousle my wet hair, scrunching up my natural waves. I am well aware of who is outside and I know there is no need to doll myself up.

"Hi handsome," I open the door and once he enters, he pulls it from my grip and pushes it shut. My heart rate increases as an intense heat swims through my body.

His hazel eyes are locked with mine as he stalks towards me until I am backed against the wall.

"You didn't get dressed up on my account, did you?" he asks, sliding his finger between the opening of my robe.

A soft moan leaves my lips as his hand travels farther south, causing the robe to untie and hang open. "You have impeccable timing. I just finished my shower."

"Hmmm . . . better timing would have had me here while you were still inside, wet and waiting for me." His hand slips between my parted thighs and finds my most sensitive area. "Never mind, I see you are still wet." I gasp when he inserts a finger and curls it just right, leaving me panting for more.

"Do you want a drink?" I ask, bracing myself against the wall when my legs begin to feel weak.

"That's a good idea."

He crushes his lips against mine in a demanding kiss that is over far too quickly. Instead of backing away from me, like I expected, he drops to his knees. Looking up, he winks and lifts my leg over his shoulder before his devilish mouth devours me. My fingers grasp his hair, holding him where I crave him the most. He is taking his time, bringing me to the edge and then backing off just before I am able to let go. Frustrated with his games, I yank on his short hair and his laughter vibrates against me, erupting the release I'm begging for.

Rising from the ground, he kisses his way up my body, stopping to pay extra attention to each breast. When he reaches my lips, he swipes his tongue across them and I playfully suck it hard into my mouth. I taste myself on his tongue, which further increases my arousal.

My arms find their way around his neck and as he grasps my hips, I encircle my legs around his waist. He is still dominating my mouth in a way that only he is capable of doing. I can feel his erection through the thin material of his cotton shorts. Walking blind, he finds his way to my bathroom with familiarity and sets me down, turning on the shower.

"Another shower?" I ask, my lips spread wide in a smile.

"I've had the image of you naked in the shower since the moment you opened the door. Plus, you'll need a second one after we're finished, might as well get a head start," he says, as though it makes complete sense and doesn't understand why I am even questioning his motives.

I roll my shoulders back and let the satin material fall from my body, his gaze taking in my bare skin. Stepping up to him, I pull his shirt over his head and reach my hand into the elastic of his shorts, pushing them down to the floor. My eyes fall to his erection and I lick my lips, dropping to my knees.

"Not tonight, you little minx. I'm barely holding on by a thread."

Gripping my arms, he pulls me back up and guides me into the steam filled shower. He steps in behind me, pressing his body against mine. Bracing my hands against the cool tile, I push my hips out and receive a deep growl from behind. He rubs the tip of his erection against me, using my own wetness as lubrication. A harsh breath escapes me as he swiftly enters my body. We move together in a race of pleasure, both meeting the other thrust for thrust. I feel myself getting closer and as if he could sense it, he reaches around and massages my sensitive flesh. His movements quicken and I know he is just as close to release as I am.

"I'm so close, Derrick," I confess between breaths.

"I know, me too, babe."

His hands grip my hips tighter, in a way I know will leave a mark, but I don't give a damn. I let out a scream and ride out my high as his release quickly follows.

Wrapping his hand around my chest, he pulls me close and we stand together in the stream of water, catching our breaths before he removes himself from my body.

No words are exchanged as we take turns lathering one another and rinsing off. Once the water is shut off, we towel dry and replace our clothes, and with a chaste kiss to my lips, he leaves.

Some women would be insulted if a guy showed up at their house, had his way with her and then bailed as soon as it was over. I'm not that woman. At least not when it comes to Derrick Fields.

We first met a few years back at a bar over a case of mistaken identity, which resulted with him coming home with me. He was in town for a short visit and we made the most of the few hours we spent together. After we said our goodbyes, I never imagined I would see him again. But to my surprise, he popped back into my life almost a year ago, in the form of my best friend's brother.

It became a routine that whenever he was in town visiting we would spend the nights together, in secret. Derrick is a great guy and someone who I can always be myself around, without the worry of impressing him. We have developed an amazing friendship over time, and once he made the permanent move to Truesdale, we decided it was time to set some ground rules.

Neither one of us is ready for anything serious, nor do we want to risk ruining our friendship or making a mess within our group of friends. We agreed to keep it casual between us, which meant no more sleepovers. Things have been going smoothly thus far, and when one is in need of attention, it's a quick call or text and plans are made. There are no dates or outings together and we decided it's best to keep our arrangement private.

There are times when I regret the decision, for the sole reason that I have no one to speak to about it; not that Daphne would want to hear the sordid details of my on-going fling with her twin. The only other person I am close to is Paul, and there is no way I would ever discuss my sex life with him, even though he has no problem blabbing about his.

There are no secrets between Derrick and I. At this point in time, we aren't seeing other people, but promised full disclosure when it comes to sleeping with someone else. After we underwent proper testing, we decided to forgo protection since I was on the pill. He is the only guy I have ever allowed to enter me uncovered, but it goes to show how much trust I have in him. He is my male best friend, whom I sleep with. A lot.

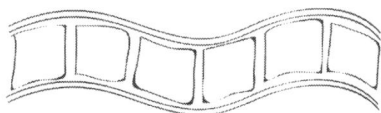

The next morning, I sleep in slightly later than planned; exhaustion brought on from the two intense orgasms Derrick delivered. Daphne and I have an early lunch date, which causes me to jump from bed and rush to get ready. Luckily, I don't have to bother showering after my double session last night.

Entering the café, I spot Daphne in the corner. She stands when I reach the table and embraces me in a tight hug.

"Hey girl, you're looking good today."

I look down at my outfit; denim shorts and a loose fitting tank. "You are crazy. I couldn't even bother with my hair." I reach up and tug on my messy bun. "Now, you, on the other hand, look cute as always."

Daphne is wearing a sundress and her hair is pulled to the side in a cute braid. She was probably up with the sun this morning and ran three miles before breakfast. When she lived around the corner from me, we would meet up in the mornings before work and make a lap around our development. Without her nearby to keep me motivated, I have severely slacked off.

"So, how are the two little lovers?" I ask, after we place our order with the server.

"We are doing well," she pauses and smiles, "Curtis' parents just purchased a house out on the lake. He and his dad want to make some renovations, but nothing too serious. It's beautiful and we'd like to get the group together for a weekend on the water."

"That sounds amazing, I am definitely in, just let me know when and my bags will be packed."

"Great. Curtis is going to talk to Paul and I need to check with Derrick on his work schedule. There is a dock on the property, so Curtis is hoping to bring his dad's boat out so the guys can fish. I am just looking forward to soaking up some Vitamin D in my bikini."

"Me too, girl. I haven't gotten nearly enough sun this summer. I think this calls for a shopping trip, one can never have too many bikinis," I laugh.

"Agreed. Let's hit up the boutique across the street after we eat."

We spend the remainder of our lunch date catching up on the latest happenings in our lives, with me obviously leaving out my adventures with her brother.

At the end of our retail therapy, I have three new bathing suits. One is a black number that I know will drive Derrick insane, and I plan on torturing him the entire weekend.

ACKNOWLEDGMENTS

Michelle...

Sarah... None of this would be possible without you. Here we are, releasing our fourth book and we don't hate each other; major success! You are, by far, the greatest business partner. We have come a long way from that Tom Petty concert. I love you!

Jon... Thank you for allowing me to borrow your wife as much as I do. Not only that, but thanks for being one of our biggest supporters!

Mom and Dad... You are always there, cheering me on throughout life, no matter what I am doing. Your love and encouragement means the world to me.

Ryan... Thank you for putting up with me when I am glued to computer and unsociable. Also, thanks for humoring me when I ask you the most random, off the wall questions. You're pretty cool, so I guess I will keep you around, even though you refuse to be our assistant. Love you!!

...Louise

First and foremost, I want to thank Brandy who inspires me daily to keep writing. Literally, she calls everyday looking for my next chapter. I love you, thanks for putting up with me.

To my husband, Jonathan, you are my everything. Thank you for your continued love and support, and for letting me spend countless weekends away from you while working on the book.

Mike and Lisa, thank you for giving me a place to relax after a long weekend of writing with your daughter.

* * *

We would also like to thank all of our friends who love what we do and share in our excitement. We appreciate you more than you know.

And last but most importantly not least, a huge thank you to Aimee and John for the inspiration of the Team Room. The Tilted Tea Cup is one of our favorite places and we treasure every visit.

ABOUT THE AUTHOR

Michelle Louise is the name used for two friends who share an obsession in reading. Both had a dream of writing, and together they planned and plotted to accomplish their goals. The experience they shared while creating, their first novel, *Picking up the Pieces,* solidified their new obsession with writing.

We would love to hear from you!

michellelouise1231@gmail.com

www.facebook.com/michellelouisebooks

www.michellelouisebooks.com

Made in the USA
Charleston, SC
27 September 2016